ATONE

BETH YARNALL

ATONE

1

BEAU

I walked out of the California Institute for Men in Chino, California two thousand, two hundred and seventy one days—nearly six years—after I walked in. I was finally free.

Free.

I don't have the same definition that most people have for that word. While I'm no longer serving a life sentence for a crime I didn't commit, I'm far from free. The repercussions of my incarceration blasted every area of my life, pitting or obliterating everything in sight. There isn't a single thing left unscarred. I don't have a home. I don't have friends. I don't have a job or any qualifications to get one. I don't have any money. I don't have the same family I had on the day of my conviction.

And I don't have Cassandra.

There's a big gaping hole in me where she once lived. Of all of the things that were taken from me she's the one thing I can never get back. I left her sleepy, naked, and sated in her bed six years ago, stealing out of her apartment with other things on my mind, unimportant things. I had an early day the next morning and needed to get home. I bent down, kissed her forehead, told her I loved her, and left.

I never saw her again.

She was brutally raped and murdered that night.

I haven't been able to take a full breath since. Not because of my subsequent arrest and conviction for her murder. That was nothing. Well, not *nothing*. It's definitely something. But it's not why I can't pull in enough air. There's a hole in my chest she used to fill. There's too much space and I can't imagine or even remember what it felt like to be whole. I've been walking around with this big, sucking chest wound since the night she died.

I'm raw yet scarred over. Little things scratch at me, reopening the wound so it never truly heals. A song. The scent of jasmine. A movie. A joke. Her name. I haven't been able to say her name out loud since I screamed it outside her apartment when her body was found and the place crawled with law enforcement personnel.

I see her everywhere. I get a glimpse of her at least once a day. Every time I turn my head I have to remind myself it's not her. It will never be her. I won't get to hold her hand, have her lay her head on my chest the way she used to or make love to her ever again. I can't call her and tell her about the stupid things that happened to me that day. She won't ever tilt her head up with the look in her eyes that was only for me. I haven't laughed in so long I'm not sure if I remember how.

My sister, Cora, thinks I should see someone, a grief councilor. I don't want to. My grief is all I have left of Cassandra. Cora doesn't understand that. No one does. I can't explain it. There are no words for what it feels like to carry it everywhere. I'm pretty sure it's the only thing holding me together. I walk around, going through the day-to-day of living, relying on those feelings to get me through. What would I have without them? Who would I be? I'm not the same man who left Cassandra's apartment that night. I'll never be him again. I shouldn't be him. I sure as shit shouldn't want to be him.

And yet...

Sometimes I wonder what it's like to be *normal*. What would happen if I took off this mantel of grief and laid it down? Would I stop seeing Cassandra everywhere? Would the smell of a common flower stop reminding me of her unique scent? Would I forget what she sounded like, her laugh, and how she felt under me? Would I lose her all over again this time forever?

The air outside of prison not only smells different, it *feels* different. I'm not used to anything resembling normal life. I'm still on prison schedule despite having been out a couple of months now. My only rebellion is letting my hair and beard grow. I don't know who that man in the mirror is. He's rougher, harder than he was six years ago. He has scars and crude tattoos jabbed into his skin by makeshift prison tattoo guns. He looks like he doesn't give a fuck about anyone or anything.

That couldn't be further from the truth.

Cora arranged for me to come to work with her. I think she's hoping it will give me something to aspire to. I'm lost. I don't recognize anyone or anything. I don't know who or what I want to be. There was a time when everything I wanted to do and be was lined up in my head just waiting for me to tick them off like a fucking checklist. Go to college. Check. Get a good paying job. Check. Marry Cassandra. Check. Buy a house. Check. Start a family. Check. Grow old with Cassandra. Check.

None of those boxes will ever be crossed off.

I have to create a new list. But where do I start? I'm twenty-four years old. I should be halfway through my checklist by now. Cora tells me I can do or be anything I want. She pushes community and technical college catalogs at me, trying to get me interested in something. At night I lay awake and attempt to imagine my life a year from now. All I see is me *still* lying on Cora's couch, *still* struggling to figure my shit out. I'm frustrating her and myself. Maybe this Take Your Brother to Work Day will give me some kind of direction even if it only helps me realize what I *don't* want to do.

I wait outside for Cora, sipping a cup of strong black coffee. I got the taste for it in prison. Before that I never touched the stuff. Cora bought me a coffee maker even though she doesn't drink it. She's been good to me. Too good. Better than I deserve. She's the reason I'm leaning against her car on a foggy San Diego morning, waiting for her instead of sitting in a prison cell wondering *why me*. She was the only person who believed in my innocence. The only one. Not even our parents—who should've stuck by me no matter what—considered for a moment that I could be innocent.

I don't know who that says more about—them or me. Cora says them, but I'm not so sure. My conviction destroyed my parents individually and as a couple. I haven't seen either one of them since shortly after being assigned a prison uniform. At first Cora made excuses for them when she visited, and then she stopped mentioning them altogether. We're supposed to have a family reunion this Sunday. Cora arranged it. She's the only reason I agreed to go. I'd do anything for her. She's more than proven she'd do anything for me. She's done *everything* for me.

Cora backs out the front door of her garage apartment,

her arms full. I jog up the walk and relieve her of the files she's carrying. She locks the door and turns to me, a big smile on her face. It gets me every time. A combination of joy and surprise like she can't believe I'm really there. I can't believe it either. I hope I never get used to this feeling or that smile. I hope she doesn't either.

I follow her down the walk to her car and put her files in the trunk. I stand just in time to see the car keys flying at my face and catch them before they smack into my nose.

"You have to practice sometime," she says. "Drive us to work."

I haven't driven in six years. My license expired while I was in prison. My parents sold my car.

"Are you sure?"

She opens the passenger door and climbs in with a wink. I let out a frosty breath in the cool morning air. This is one more thing I have to relearn in my life *outside*. I slide into the driver's seat and adjust it for my bigger body and longer legs.

"The mirrors too," Cora reminds me.

It's like I'm taking Driver's Ed all over again with my little sister as my teacher. I hope driving isn't as hard as riding a bike. That shit took me too many tries to get right. I'm wobbly like a kid riding without training wheels for the first time. Bike riding is a fucked up metaphor for my life now. Everything is an uphill struggle and scary as fuck. I suck so bad at it I wonder sometimes if I shouldn't just commit a crime for real this time so I can go back to the predictability and reliability of prison life. I won't, but the thought is scarily tempting sometimes.

You wouldn't think being free would be so hard.

I do as Cora instructs and start the car. She coaches me the whole way. I'm relieved when we arrive safely. Driving is a hell of a lot easier than riding a bike. We get out of the car and head into the offices of Nash Security and Investigation. I owe Cora and everyone in this place *everything*. If Mr. Nash and his son, Leo, hadn't agreed to help Cora find the bastard who killed Cassandra and worked to set me free, I'd still be sitting in a cell. How do you repay someone who rescued you from hell and gave you your life back?

I juggle Cora's files that I retrieved from the trunk, open the door for her, and follow her inside. The receptionist, Savannah, looks up at Cora, then does a double take when she spies me trailing behind my sister. Her first, fleeting glance is full of female appreciation that quickly morphs into avid curiosity tinged with fear. She doesn't want to be attracted to an ex-con, but I'd put money on her panties being soaked at the thought of fucking me. I'm a walking, talking good girl's bad boy dream. I'm the guy she bangs once or twice on the quiet just so she can brag about it later to her friends.

I grin at Savannah, following it with a wink and lick of the lips. She gasps and presses her hands to her chest, her cheeks bloom red. If we were alone I bet I could take her right there on top of her desk. Wouldn't even have to pull her panties all the way down, just push up her skirt and pull them aside. She'd shower after, feeling dirty, later she'd jack off reliving it. I'm not even slightest bit tempted by her or any other woman I've met since I got out. Another way my life's fucked up.

I set Cora's files down where she directs me. Her office is small with two desks in the middle facing each other. It's an odd arrangement, but Cora likes it this way I guess.

She gestures to the desk opposite hers. "Have a seat." She sifts through her pile of files until she finds what she's looking for, then pulls it out and comes around to where I'm sitting. "I thought maybe I'd start you off with some simple searches." She twitches the mouse, bringing the computer screen to life. "These are the search sites we use."

Clicking on the top three bookmarked sites, she brings them up, explaining how they use them and what info they can provide. She has me do some easy searches, then leaves me on my own. I don't suck at it. I'm actually quite good. And I like the work. I'm half way through the searches Cora wanted me to do when Savannah sticks her head in the door.

"Your ten o'clock is here," she tells Cora, her gaze darts to me then back to Cora.

"Thanks, Savannah. Want to sit in?" Cora asks me. "Take a break from the computer?"

"Sure." I stand and stretch.

Savannah jumps and squeaks, then disappears from the doorway.

Cora's mouth bends into a frown. "I don't know what's wrong with her lately."

"Don't you?"

"I'll talk to her."

"Leave it."

I follow Cora into the reception area. Savannah blocks whoever it is she's talking to so I can't see who it is, but whoever they are they're small, much smaller than Savannah's five-nine frame. Savannah shifts, revealing a pastel confection of a young woman about Cora's age.

All lace and silk, she's sweet looking in her soft colors like she just walked out of a Sunday church service. But the look in her eyes is wary...guarded...jaded, reminding me of angry, hard prison stares. This chick's seen some shit. More than that, she's experienced some shit, has maybe even done some shit. She's a survivor. This I understand. I recognize her in the same way I recognize the new man that stares back at me in the mirror.

Her costume is nearly perfect. I bet if I sniffed her she'd smell like baby powder and lemons. I edge closer to her. She catches me with a sudden flick of a glance, freezing me where I stand. Everything about her shouts *back the fuck off*. It only makes me want to draw closer. Who is she? Who or what made her this way? And why does she look at me like she knows who I am? Not the TV news segment me, but the real me, the Beau deep, down inside.

For the first time since I got out of prison I don't feel alone. There really are others out there like me. One of them is standing mere feet in front of me, regarding me with the same guarded, expectant look I'm wearing.

And she's *beautiful*.

2

VERA

The office of the private investigation agency isn't special. After all I've heard about it I was expecting something more lavish or flashy. It's understated and utilitarian like a government building. Whoever decorated it didn't care about esthetics, only functionality and, distantly second, comfort. There are a few photos on the wall and some news clippings of their most notable cases, mainly images of the two men the agency freed after serving prison sentences for crimes they didn't commit. I lean closer to get a better look.

One is of, Maurice Battle, an elderly black man who was freed after nearly four decades. The other is of Beau Hollis, a younger white man about my age. The grainy black and white newspaper photo washes out a lot of detail, but I can tell he's handsome. Other than that there's nothing remarkable about either man. You'd pass them on the street and not have a clue about what they'd been through. I'm working on that trick.

I touch a finger to the glass over the photo of Maurice

Battle. Thirty-nine years is a hell of a long time to be locked away.

The tall, blond receptionist, who greeted me when I first walked in, returns. "Cora will be with you in a moment. Can I offer you a beverage? Coffee? Tea? Water?"

"No, thank you."

She shifts, gesturing to the young woman joining us. "This is Cora Hollis." The rest of what she says fades to background noise.

It takes everything in me to stay still and not let the careful mask I've perfected slip. Behind Cora is the young man from the photographs. His gaze connects with mine and I hear an audible *snick* like the sound of a lock being engaged or the cock of a gun hammer. Danger radiates in the air around him. Instinctively I adjust my stance. He watches me like he knows me, like he knows what I'll do next before I can even think to do it. The other two women in the room seem oblivious to the force of him. No. Not the receptionist. She keeps just out of his reach.

He tilts his head to the side and looks me over like he can see through my carefully maintained appearance. It amuses him that he can do it. I raise my chin and look down my nose at him, staring right back just as bold and brazen as he does. Standing a full foot and a half taller than me, he clearly has the advantage. I've fought men his size and lost, but that wouldn't stop me from taking him on if I had to. He concedes this with a nod that tells me he means me no harm. His eyes crease at the corners in a smile that doesn't reach his mouth.

I slowly let out the breath I've been holding. He uses his size and attitude the way I use clothing and make up—to project an image the rest of world would expect and accept. His is as careful and meticulous as mine. Predictable.

Protective. Very, very protective. Inclining my head, I acknowledge him in return.

I shake Cora's offered hand. Her handshake is firm and brief. She's about my age I'd guess with striking blue eyes that match the streaks woven through her black hair. She introduces me to a man who doesn't need an introduction. Beau. Beau Hollis. Her brother. She explains that he'll be taking the meeting with her and asks if that's okay.

"Yes," I say. "That's fine."

It is. Despite my initial reaction to him I know Beau wouldn't harm me. I don't know why I know this, I just do. He responds with more eye crinkling and doesn't offer his hand. I'm glad. I don't like touching strangers. Especially men.

He gives me a wide berth as I pass, following Cora into a conference room. I can feel him behind me, but it's not an uncomfortable sensation. It's an *I've got your back* awareness unlike the *watch your back* feeling I get from most men. We move around each other like potential opponents on a battlefield, sizing up one another, gauging strengths and weaknesses. There's some admiration as well and a keen sense of attraction between us that has me struggling to maintain my cool, unaffected façade.

He mesmerizes me. I seem to hold the same fascination for him because once we make eye contact again across the conference table we're reluctant to break it. If Cora notices she doesn't let on as she asks me how the agency can help me.

"I need help finding my sister," I tell them.

Cora holds her pen suspended above a notebook. "Can you tell us about her?"

"Her name is Marie Saint Claire, but they might have her in the system as Molly Johnston. We were taken from our mother and placed in the custody of Child Protective Services when I was three and she was about six months old. We have the same mother, but different fathers. She's about to age out of the system at eighteen and I want to find her before that happens. I had a lead that she might be in a group home in Santee, but that's old information. I'm not sure where she is now."

"We'll need her birthdate, your mother's name and birthday, any information on her father you might have, and her social security number if you know it."

I pull a sheet with all of the info I have on my mother and sister from my purse and pass it Cora. "I don't know her social security number, but I do have copy of her birth certificate." I slide that over too. "There's no father listed. Our mother wasn't very...particular or careful. She liked the extra money she got to charge for going bareback."

"Your mother may be of *some* help." Cora doesn't blink at the fact that my mother was a prostitute and didn't have a clue who had fathered either one of her daughters. "Can we contact her?"

"Not unless you have a direct line to the hereafter. She was murdered about a year after we were put into the system."

Beau does a slow blink, absorbing this info as though it confirms something for him about me.

"I'm so sorry," Cora says.

I ignore her well-meaning sentiment. It's wasted on that worthless piece of shit I get to call my mother. "This is the address of the group home Marie was in. I'm concerned about her. We used to communicate through social media, but she hasn't logged into any of her accounts for months."

"Do you have a photo of your sister?"

I pull out the pictures I printed off her social media profile and give them to Cora. She glances at them and her eyebrows flinch. It's the only reaction she's had since we sat down. Marie doesn't look like me. Her father was black or half black. Who knows? But her features and coloring are nothing like mine. She's big boned. I'm petite. Her skin is dark. Mine is freckly and pale. Her black hair is in dreadlocks in some of the photos and straightened in others. I lighten my bone-straight hair to a pale blond and wear it short, cropped over my ears. It's nothing like how I used to wear it before. Back then I would've looked more like Cora's sister than Marie's.

Beau hasn't looked away from me for a second not even to check out Marie's pictures. He hasn't asked a single question even though I can see in his eyes that he has about a million of them. I don't have any for him. Not a single one. I feel like I already know too much about him and yet not enough. It doesn't matter anyway. I have a single goal here and it has nothing to do with the man sitting across from me. My sister is all I have left of whatever family I might have had and I'm terrified for her. I spent time in that group home and I know what she might have fallen into if she left it.

But I can't tell Cora and Beau anything about that.

"Please help me find her." I know I sound desperate. I am.

"We'll do our best."

I start at the sound of Beau's voice. Cora seems equally startled as she swings her gaze away from me to her brother. This time the smile reaches all the way to his lips and my own mouth tilts up at the corners in response. He's on my side. I've never had anyone take up for me. No one in any of the foster or group homes. Not even my own mother. I'm caught by the look in his eyes and what he communicates silently. He wants to champion my cause.

Cora's head swivels back and forth between Beau and me. I wonder what she sees when she looks at us. Can she feel the pull? Does she understand what's being said without words? Can she feel my barely suppressed panic? Does she know what that look on her brother's face means? Because I don't. I don't understand what's happening here except that it scares the shit out of me. And Beau too. His eyebrows draw together and he suddenly looks away. I slide my chair back from the table and stand, needing some distance.

I pull the strap of my bag over my shoulder. "Thank you."

Cora gets to her feet too, but it takes a moment for Beau to react. I head for the front door with Cora on my heels. I can't get out of there fast enough.

"Your form and the retainer," Cora reminds me.

"Oh, right." Pausing in the open doorway, I dig out the client form they wanted me to fill out and a cashier's check and hand them over.

"We'll be in touch," Cora says, accepting them.

"I look forward to hearing from you." I don't wait for her response and leave, walking to my car as quickly as possible.

Sliding behind the wheel, I glance up at the closed door of the agency. What have I done? I can't do this. I should go in and get my check back, find a different PI agency to help me. I wanted the best and Nash Security and Investigation was supposed to be the best. Anyone else I hire would just be second string. It would take time to find another agency. Time is the one thing I don't have. Marie will be eighteen in a few months. I thought I could find her by myself, but I couldn't do that without giving away who I really am. I can't ever reveal that.

I think of Marie and where she might be right now, what she might be going through. I lied when I told Cora that I was worried for her. I'm terrified. When I think of her and what she might be going through I realize that I can put up with the strangeness between Beau and me if I have to. I can handle just about anything for my sister. If I can't work around him then I'll just have to find a way to work with him. For Marie. I'd do anything to keep what happened to me from happening to her.

Anything.

Cora comes back into the conference room and closes the door quietly behind her. I'm standing exactly where I was standing when Vera freaked out and left. I stare at the stack of papers and photos Vera left behind without really seeing them. If I thought my life was complicated before it just got a shit-ton more complex.

"You want to tell me what's going on with you?" Cora asks.

"No."

She looks for a moment like she might press the issue, then takes the seat she was in before and starts flipping through the information Vera gave her. I watch her, wondering what in the hell just happened.

When I woke up this morning my life was all stop signs and red lights. I was waiting for something to happen, waiting for my turn to move forward, questioning if I'd ever get a shot. And then a pale, blond, little pixy walked into the office and quietly made me care about something other than how fucked up my life is. I try to pin down the one thing she said or did that made me actually want to give a shit about something in this world and I can't come up with it. Maybe it was a lot of little things that added up and before I knew it she'd given me a reason to get out of bed tomorrow.

I told her I'd do my best. I don't have a best. I sure as fuck don't have any experience in finding a missing person. How in the hell am I going to live up to that promise? I'm a total and complete idiot. I meet the first chick to make me look twice and I fall on my face trying to impress her. Impress her with what? I don't even have a bed or a place to live. I don't have a car. I don't have a job or the hope of one. What was I doing telling her I'd *help* her? What a fuckwit.

Cora goes through the photos of Vera's sister Marie. "What do you think of Vera's story?"

"What do you mean?"

"You have a pretty accurate bullshit detector."

"So do you."

"Yup, and I'm asking you what you think."

I drop into my chair and put a hand out for the papers and pics. She gives them to me and I leaf through them slowly, studying each one, practically memorizing them. Vera's handwriting is precise. All of the letters are the same at the bottom like she used a ruler to keep them in perfect line. If I'd ever taken a handwriting analysis course I could probably tell a lot about her from her scrawl. Control. Vera wants and needs control. I got that much from meeting her. The meticulousness of her lettering confirms it, but while she tries to keep her writing neat it swirls unexpectedly, slipping past that control. I'm going to have to Google what that means.

"Well?" Cora's impatient for my answer.

"I don't think it's bullshit, but I also think she didn't tell us everything she knows."

She nods, confirming her own suspicions. "Do you really think that's her sister?"

"Yeah. I do." Vera had a strong emotional reaction to the photos of Marie. They're connected for sure.

"Well, I guess it's time to find out if our hunches about her are correct or not."

"What do you mean?"

"We run background checks on all our potential clients. They ran one on me when I first came to them about you."

"You're kidding."

"Nope. We need to make sure she's on the up and up and that we're not putting the person she's looking for in any potential danger. Abusive husbands sometimes use PI's to find their wives. We want to make sure we're not setting this Marie up to be victimized."

"I don't think—"

"She might not be who she says she is. She might've come here helping someone else out. She *seems* harmless, but you never know. We have to be sure. I want you to run a background check on her. We need to know that Vera's legit and that we're not putting this girl in harm's way."

I glance up at my sister. She's serious. Vera didn't strike me as someone who would purposefully hurt someone else, not when she's been so badly damaged. Taking on this task would give me the opportunity to learn more about Vera and that's something I definitely want to do. But it also feels like a betrayal. I know what it's like for people to know everything about me without actually *knowing* me. I'd essentially be doing the same to Vera.

"I don't know."

"It'll have to be done whether you do it or not. Please. I could really use your help."

I can't say no to Cora. She could ask me to cut off my right leg and I'd do it. She's done more for me than I could ever repay.

"Leo's coming down today," she adds. "He can help you."

She's tamping down her excitement, but I see it in the smile that won't be confined. Her boyfriend coming down to visit from UCLA means I'll be sleeping with pillows piled on my head tonight. I don't mind. Much. Leo makes my sister happy and that's pretty much all I need to know about him. If it weren't for him taking on my case and helping Cora get trained in private investigation I'd still be sitting in a cell and Cora would still be spending all of her time and money trying to get me free. I like the guy, but it's part of my job as Cora's big brother to make sure he does right by her.

"You can do this," she says, correctly reading one of the reasons for my reluctance. "It's easy."

Cora's faith in my Internet searching skills is out of proportion with the couple of hours I spent today learning how to do it. And as much as I don't want to pry into Vera's background I also don't want anyone else to do it.

"Okay." All of my reasoning doesn't make me feel less shitty about what I'm going to do.

"We could use some help around the office. I was thinking of asking Mr. Nash about hiring you on… If you're interested."

"So I can terrorize Savannah permanently instead of temporarily?"

"You don't terrorize her."

I lift my eyebrows in response.

"She might be a bit nervous around you," she concedes. "She'll get over it."

"In the meantime I'll have to learn to ignore her flinches and suppressed screams?"

"I'll get Leo to talk to her."

"Thanks for the job offer, but no thanks."

"I could really use the help."

What she doesn't say is that I need a job so I can move out of her small garage apartment and get a place of my own. She'd never kick me out, but with Leo coming for a visit her six hundred square foot studio is about to get very, very crowded. Since no one else has been interested in hiring me this potential office job could be the start of an employment record I can build on. I need a job and money. What I don't need is a reminder of my past every time Savannah squeaks like a mouse caught in a trap.

"This isn't some bullshit charity offer, is it?"

"No. I really do need the help." She's not lying. I'd know it if she was.

"You really think I'll be any good at this investigation stuff?"

"Yeah, I do. You caught on pretty quickly and the rest isn't hard. Basically all it takes is tenacity and I know you have that in spades. Start here. See where it goes. If you don't like the work you can always quit. I won't hold it against you and neither would Mr. Nash." She puts her hand on mine to stop my drumming fingers. "You have to start somewhere, Beau. It might as well be here." Her voice is quiet yet pleading.

I know my inability to figure my shit out worries her and I can't keep disappointing her. She'd tell me I'm not, but I know I am. I'm disappointing myself. She's right. I have to start somewhere. I have to find something that makes me want to get out of bed in the morning. Maybe this is it. At the very least maybe this job will help me figure out where to go next.

"Let *me* talk to Savannah before you go to Mr. Nash," I tell her.

"Okay." She does a little bounce in her chair, her lips curling inward like she's trying to suppress a grin.

I wish she wasn't so excited. If I can't get Savannah to stop looking at me like I'll jump her, this whole conversation is a waste and so is Cora's enthusiasm.

"Hey, Bluebird." Leo leans in the doorway of the conference room.

Cora leaps out of her seat and runs at Leo. He meets her half way, catching her in a spinning hug. The months she and Leo have been together are the happiest I've ever seen my sister. I scoop up Vera's papers and photos, go around the table, and slip out the door past them. Leo kissing Cora is not something I want to stick around to watch.

Savannah's on the phone so I head to Cora's office and begin my search. My mind's back on Vera. I feel like I owe her an apology for what I'm about to do. Or at the very least a heads up. I start with the genealogy site Cora showed me earlier and plug in Trudy Saint Claire, Vera's mother's name. There's a death and birth certificate for her. I dig some more and come up with two children—a son and a daughter. The daughter is Marie Anne Saint Claire. There is no third child. No other daughter.

The question becomes—Who is Vera Swain if she's not Marie's sister?

I clear the search and type in Vera's name and birthdate from the form Cora had her fill out. While the sight does its thing I open another window and pull up the address she gave. It's to one of those PO Box places. I do a reverse look up with the phone number she listed. It comes up with no information. I go back to the genealogy site and click on Vera's birth record. The birthdate matches. Her parents are listed as Karen and Michael Swain. She was born in—ironically—Agenda, Wisconsin. I click on the other document and *holy shit*. Vera Swain died when she was three years old.

If the real Vera is dead, who was the woman who came into the office and kicked my world on its ass?

4

VERA

I don't have much of value. I've left so many things behind that objects no longer have any meaning for me. I could walk out of this pay-by-the-week motel with nothing but the clothes on my back and I'd find a way to survive. It's a skill that served me well as I got tossed from group home to foster home and back again and then when I was finally spit out into the world with literally *nothing*. I left everything when I escaped...including my name. You don't know what your limits are until they're pushed past breaking. My boundaries have been stitched and re-stitched back together too many times. I no longer have a sense of what it's like to be able to set my own parameters.

I'm working on that, but it's slow-going and meticulous. Mostly I stay isolated. Interactions with other people are kept to the bare minimum, unavoidable social necessities. I speak only when forced to and avoid eye contact. I don't like what I see. You can tell a lot about a person by what lurks in the depths of their eyes. Every ugly thing they think and feel hides there. They smile, but it doesn't pretty up the person they are inside. What's that saying? Like putting lipstick on a pig. That's what smiles are for me. People will smile at you while they hurt you. I no longer trust them.

Everybody has an agenda. I learned this from my mother whose only agenda was letting anyone who would pay her shove their dick in her so she could put a needle in her arm. I learned it from the foster families who accumulated children like part time jobs, cashing in the checks they got for taking us in then barely feeding us. And I learned it from the police who failed to protect and the only serving they did was to their own self-interests.

I don't know how long I can stay in San Diego. The need to keep moving rides me hard. I'm too close to where everything started and where it ended. Marie is the reason I'm here and the only reason I'll stay for any length of time. I have to find her. Javier knows about her. I was too stupid not to mention her when I first met him. He'll remember and he'll use her to get to me, to get back at me. I can only fight him so far. I will never win against him. But I can try to outsmart him by staying ahead of him and finding Marie first.

Someone bangs on the door and I jump. No one knows I'm here. At least they shouldn't know. I've been careful. But obviously not careful enough. I pull out my gun. It's always on hand. I don't have to check it to know it's ready if I need it. At the door, I stand off center and look through the peephole to see who's there. My heart explodes in my chest and I sag in the corner between the door and the wall, breaking out into a sweat.

What the hell is he doing here?

He strikes the door again. "Vera!"

What does he want?

"I can see your shadow under the door," he says. "Open up."

I can't make myself unhook the latch or answer back.

"I'll keep your secret, but I at least need to know why I'm keeping it."

I try to work up some spit so I can speak. *How did he find me?*

"The cameras in front of the agency picked up your Colorado license plate," he says, answering my unasked question. "It wasn't easy finding you." His voice gets quiet as if his face is pressed to the door. "I want to help you. Let me help you."

I swipe the sweat off my upper lip. The gun is heavy and reassuring in my shaky hand.

"I didn't tell Cora. I didn't tell anyone. I promise. Please, open up."

My feet barely support me as I come off the wall. I don't know why I'm doing it, but I slide the lock back and open the door, staying behind it for whatever imaginary protection it can give me. Beau sidesteps through the door and into the room. He's larger than I remember, crowding his big body into the small room. With the flat of his giant hand he closes the door. I hesitate for a moment before choosing the greater of two fears and sliding the lock back into place.

His gaze goes to my gun. He shoves his hands in the front pocket of his jeans and acknowledges it with a jerk of his head. Other than that he doesn't do anything. He doesn't say anything. We stare at each other, sizing each other up. I hope I haven't made a mistake letting him in. A thousand questions sit on my tongue, but I don't ask them. He said he was here to help. I need help. I don't want to need it. But there it is. I don't want to trust him yet somehow I do. I think I should be afraid, but there's nothing about him that drives me to run.

"Why are you here?" I finally ask.

"Is she really your sister?"

"Yes."

"You're afraid for her."

"Yes."

"You're not going to tell me why."

"No."

"Okay."

He doesn't ask the question I would ask—who are you? Because there's no doubt he knows I'm not who I say I am. He could've called the burner number I put down on the agency's form. Instead he tracked me down. Was it only to show that he could do it or is there another reason? Maybe he's trying to show me I can trust him with this gesture. He could've handled it so many different ways, but he chose to maintain my need for anonymity.

"Do you mind if I sit down?" he asks.

I hitch a shoulder like I don't care what he does. That's not true. I care way too much about what he's done and what he'll do. He pulls out one of the chairs at the rickety dining set and sits. It barely accommodates him. His gaze flickers to my open laptop, then away like he doesn't want to pry even accidentally. I stay where I am more out of shock than nerves. I'm still not over his arrival. His presence is a cold dash of water to my senses. I'm blank and sputtering to make sense of it.

"Why didn't you tell Cora about me?"

It's his turn to appear nonchalant with a jerk of his shoulder. "The agency wouldn't help you if I did."

His sister might see what he did for me as a betrayal. He's stepping way outside his comfort zone for me. I don't know what to make of that. No one's ever done something like this for me. I can't help but wonder what he expects to get in return.

"What do you want?" I have to ask.

"To help you."

"Why?"

He tilts his head to the side, studying me. It's that same look he had when I first met him. I'm an enigma, something for him to puzzle out. "I have a feeling life hasn't been generous to you. It sure as shit hasn't been generous to me."

I shake my head.

"Maybe it's time it was," he says.

"And you're the one to deliver it?"

"Why not? I'm not doing anything else worthwhile with my life."

"That's a copout."

"No, it's a fact."

I can see it is. "So I'm your new what? Hobby? Charity case?"

"I'm not charitable and I don't have any hobbies."

Why is a scream in my head. I shake it off. Maybe he doesn't understand what he's doing here anymore than I do. If I question him about it too much he might just decide I'm not worth the trouble and walk away. Now that he's here I don't want him to leave I realize. I've never had a partner in anything. I'm not sure what to do with him. He's big and commanding and watching me, gauging my reaction to him.

"Okay," I say on a sigh, sliding my skirt up with my gun and slipping it into my thigh holster.

A corner of his lips tilts up as he tracks my movements. The gleam of male appreciation flashes in his eyes. Seeing it doesn't freak me out and I marvel again at the contradiction this guy brings out in me. He thinks I'm sexy and I *like* it.

"Have you eaten?" he asks.

"No."

"There's a diner a block down."

Is he asking me out? Lips parting, I blink at him, uncertain of what I should do.

"You have to eat sometime."

I bob my head. It's all I can manage. He slowly gets to his feet, his gaze on mine, and gestures to the door. I put my coat on and grab my purse, eyeing him all the while. He gives me lots of room, slipping out sideways through the door I hold open. He waits a respectable distance away as I close the door and check to make sure it's locked. We walk side-by-side down the street. He never once accidentally brushes against me or makes any effort to touch me.

He holds the door to the diner open for me and follows me in. A tired looking waitress tells us to sit anywhere we want. This time of night the place is empty and Beau lets me choose our table. He slides in across from me and reaches for the menus tucked behind the napkin holder. He hands one to me, then opens his and looks it over. I do the same. I calculate in my head how much money I have and how long it will last me. I hadn't planned on eating out so this little extravagance is going to cost me. Selecting the cheapest sandwich, I close my menu and try to reassure myself that this one time won't make that much of a difference. If I only eat half the sandwich I can save the other half for lunch tomorrow.

Beau sets his menu aside. "When was the last time you saw your sister?"

"In person? I don't remember exactly. We were in the same foster home for a while before we were separated forever. I was maybe six or seven. I'm not sure."

"She's lucky to have you. I know what it's like to have a sister who would do anything for me."

It all suddenly become clear. "Cora's the reason you were freed."

"Yeah. Her and her boyfriend and his father, Mr. Nash, who owns the agency. She somehow talked them into helping her help me."

"So I'm a pay-it-forward project?"

"Yes and no. I have my own reasons for helping you."

"Because you're not doing anything else worthwhile with your life," I toss his words back at him.

"There are other reasons besides that, but that's also part of it."

He's not going to crack so I change the subject. "How long have you worked at the agency?"

"Since this morning."

"But you have investigative experience, right?"

"Nope."

"And you're going to help me *how*?"

His laugh is quiet and deep. It has an unused edge to it that makes it slightly awkward. And sexy. "I'm not exactly sure about that."

I tilt my head in confusion.

"Cora and Leo, her boyfriend, are going to train me while he's home for spring break. They offered me a job today. You're my first case. Well, the first case I get to help out on anyway."

"Is this a blackmail thing then? You don't tell them about me and you get a new job out of it?"

He sits up and puts his palms out. "It's not at all like that. They offered me the job before I found out you're not Vera Swain. I could tell them or not tell them and it wouldn't change a thing for me other than I don't get to help you."

The waitress shows up with two glasses of water and takes our order. Beau's mouth presses down when he hears my order, but he doesn't say anything. When she leaves she takes the energy around our table with her. I can't help but be suspicious of his motives. He seems on the level and maybe he is. I don't trust easily if at all. Me sitting here with him drinking tap water and trying not to gawk at the way the muscles of his forearms bunch and flex is new for me. He doesn't stare overlong at me or make the silence that settled over us feel uncomfortable. My hands are on the table not under it resting over my gun.

That says more about how Beau makes me feel than I have words for.

"If I give you my email address will you send me the links to your sister's social media pages?" he asks. "There might be something there that can help us find her."

"I checked them tonight and there were no new posts. But sure. I'll send you the links."

He pulls a business card out of his t-shirt pocket. "My email address. And phone number. In case you need it."

His gaze shifts away as he takes a sip of his water. The phone number is a stretch for him, an uneasy overture. He's hoping I'll call. I'm half hoping I'll have a reason to. I study it, committing his phone number to memory, and tuck his card in a sown-in pocket in my bra. Everything of value and necessity stays on me in case I have to do the cut and run thing again.

"It's warm," I tell him, humming the M.

My unexpected flirtation catches him as off guard as it catches me. I clear my throat and break eye contact. What am I doing here with him? I'm not this person. I never have been and I never will be. I can tell he's not either. I try to ignore the sensations that bombarded me from the first moment I met him. He can feel them too. His struggle to understand and control them mirrors mine. I see it in the way he studies me with a little crease between his eyebrows. We're a fucked up pair for sure.

5

BEAU

Vera's flirting with me. At least I think she is. It's been a long time since a chick showed any interest in me that wasn't morbid curiosity. She's not very good at it, but I'm not either. I'm not sure why I asked her here. I'm pretty sure she doesn't know why she came. We're each making an effort in our own way. Toward what I don't know. But it feels easy. A new and rare kind of comfortable. At least for me.

I don't need to know who she was. Getting to know who she is now is enough for me. I'm not who I used to be either. I can never be him again so I can't fault her for wanting to reinvent herself. If it wasn't for Cora I might have done what Vera did and changed my name, my location, and my life. It occurred to me more than once right after I got out that I could do just that. But I couldn't do it to Cora. She worked too hard, sacrificed too much for me to disappear on her.

"Do you really think you can find my sister?"

"I'm going to try. I found you," I remind her.

She tucks her chin under and stares at her hands. "Was it easy to find me?"

"No. It was a hunch combined with shear dumb luck and tenacity. Basically I drove by almost every pay-by-the-week motel in San Diego until I found the one with your car parked out front. If it hadn't been parked out there tonight when I drove by I wouldn't have found you. That's the dumb luck part."

She nods. "Thanks for telling me my mistake."

"You're not going to disappear on me, are you?"

"No, but I need to be a lot smarter."

"Is it dangerous for you to be here?"

"It could be."

"The gun?"

"Yeah, among other...things."

My eyebrows rise as this. She's not as tough inside as she wants to or needs to be. This isn't the life she chose, it was forced on her, but by who or what? I remind myself that the answers to those questions don't matter. I've been where she is. Hell, I'm right there now. All that matters is who she is and who she's going to be. Same as me. And yet for all of my talk of the present and future the past is an anchor I can't cut loose, dragging along behind me. Her past—like mine—sits in the booth with us, an invisible presence both of us can feel. The only difference is that she knows mine, but I don't know hers.

If I could change one thing it would be for what happened to me to be as unknown to her as what happened to her is to me.

"Should *I* get a gun?"

Her eyes widen a fraction. She's surprised by how all-in I am. Oddly I'm not. When I told her I'd do my best at the agency office I wasn't being glib. It wasn't just a line. I *am* all-in here.

"Have you ever shot one?" she asks.

"No."

"I hadn't either until a couple years ago."

"Maybe you can show me how it's done."

"Yeah, maybe."

The waitress brings our meals. I frown over Vera ordering off the kids' menu. I should've told her I was going to pay, but I have a feeling if I had she still would've ordered the same thing. She's quiet while we eat, the front of her hair falling forward to conceal her eyes. It's a trick she does when she's avoiding answering or trying not to be noticed. I can openly study her when she hides like this. I don't miss any opportunity to look at her.

There's a pinprick-sized dent just below the left side of her lower lip where a piercing used to be. There's another one on her left nostril and two near her right eyebrow. She wears no earrings now, but both ears were once filled with them. I bet if she stuck her tongue out there'd be an abandoned hole in it as well. Where else has she been pierced? My dick suddenly comes to attention at the question.

It's been so damn long since I've done anything but jerk off I began to wonder if my dick even worked without self stimulation. Prison didn't exactly make me horny and living with my sister has made it almost impossible to get off. I hide my glad smirk in a bite of burger and thank god prison didn't take that away from me too.

"What's so funny?" she asks.

Shit. Busted. "I was wondering if your tongue is also pierced."

"And that's funny?"

"My mind sort of drifted downward from there." I shake my head. "Never mind. Forget I said anything. It's none of my business."

She sets her sandwich down and wipes her mouth on

her napkin, taking her time, making me feel like a total and complete asshole. Her gaze is steady and even on mine as she takes a sip of water and swallows. She pokes her tongue out between her lips and flattens it so I can see that yes, indeed, it is pierced and missing its barbell. My chest goes tight. I can't move. I can't breathe. Her tongue slips back into her mouth, curling a little at the tip just before it disappears.

"Both nipples and two on my clit," she says.

Holy. Fuck.

For a second I think she might actually show me, but then she picks up her sandwich again and takes a bite. I don't recognize the look in her eyes. They've gone sort of blank with a sheer coating of defiance and anger. That look scares the shit out of me. I'm ashamed at how I got her to share something she so clearly didn't want me to know. My dick throbs in time with the hard, fast, beat of my heart. There's a whooshing in my ears and my dinner threatens to come up.

"I'm sorry," I stammer out.

"Anything else you want to know?"

"No."

"Can I ask you something then?"

"Whatever you want."

"Do you want to fuck me?"

Her question is forced and ugly, matching her hard, cold stare. The crudity of her question is a slap in the face. How did this get so out of control? I don't know what to say. It's clear she expects me to come up with something. Is this some kind of test?

Do I want to fuck her. The answer isn't a simple yes or no. It's complicated and as fucked up as I am.

Do I want to fuck her. I want to *want* to fuck her. But how would that sound if I said it out loud?

Do I want to fuck her. *God* yes. Give me a reason. Give me *something*. *Hell* no. Take away my memories of the only woman I've ever been with, the only woman I've ever loved.

The answer should be easy. I'm a guy. Guys think about sex. Guys want sex with hot women. A hot woman is offering me sex. But all I can come up with is, "Do *you* want to fuck *me*?"

Her head jerks back, eyes widen, lips part. Tossing her bold question back at her shocks her. The air between us fizzles and sparks. All of the hair on my body stands on end and a shiver runs up my spine. She leans toward me, studying me like she's just seeing me for the first time, like she doesn't already know too much about me. It *was* a test and I somehow passed. Our meals forgotten, we take in the new boundaries of our fledgling relationship or whatever it is that's happening between us.

I'm as astounded as she is. I slide my hand across the table and take her hand. It's small in mine. Her fingers are long and slim and cold. She doesn't pull away or break eye contact almost as though she willed me to touch her and I finally obeyed.

She breaks the silence. "You're not what I expected. Not at all."

"Neither are you."

"Is that a good thing?"

I nod.

"I'm not really that brave."

"I know. Me either."

"I know." She glances at our clasped hands. "Your hand is warm."

"Are you cold?"

"Just my fingers."

I hold my other hand out palm up and she places her

hand in it. Somehow this basic touch is more intimate in this moment than if we ripped our clothes off and fucked on top of the table. She squeezes my hands, turning them back and forth, experimenting, studying. I let her. Her expression is the most open I've ever seen it. Everything about her transforms from the set of her shoulders to the curve of her lips to the feel of her hands in mine. She seems almost giddy in her discovery. Questions begin to form about what made her the way she is, but I shove them aside, reminding myself that I don't need to know.

The only thing that matters is the here and now.

Our waitress drops off the check. "Pay up front."

Vera asks her for a box to take home what's left of her child's meal. Releasing one of her hands, I reach for the check before Vera can grab it. She frowns at me and pulls her other hand away. I frown back at her. She does something under the table I can't see and then produces a five and lays it on the table. I push it back at her.

Her frown deepens and she shoves it over with more force. "I pay my own way."

"I invited you." I slide it back over.

"Knock it off, Beau."

"Invite me to dinner and then it'll be your turn to pay."

She slaps a hand on the five and it disappears under the table again. "Thank you." She's not grateful she's pissed.

The waitress returns with Vera's To-Go container and clears away my plate.

"You're welcome," I answer when the waitress leaves.

"You're assuming I'm going to want to eat with you again."

"I don't assume anything when it comes to you."

She's suppressing a smile while making a show of

putting the other half of her tiny sandwich in the box. "You have pretty good table manners for a guy."

I laugh and her smile deepens. Her compliment is ridiculous. It's been a long time since I cared about having any manners at all. I stand and hold a hand out to help her up, practicing more of my rusty social etiquette. She keeps her hand in mine as we walk to the cash register. I don't let go to pay, using my other hand to fish my wallet out and pay the cashier. Holding the door open for her, I wait for her to walk through before following.

Out on the street Vera swings our hands as we walk back to her motel. The night is cool and I fight the urge to put my arm around her and bring her in close. She seems content the way things are so I don't push. When we get to her door I shake her hand and tell her I had a good time and thank her like we just went out on a date. There's a funny quizzical twist to her lips as I back away, waving. I make sure she's safely inside before getting into Cora's car and driving off.

6

VERA

Since I texted Beau the links to Marie's social media pages he's been sending me little notes—sometimes questions about the case and sometimes funny, brief comments about his day. His are the only texts I get so every time my phone pings with a message I know it's from him. My stomach flutters at the sound and I can feel a grin forming before I even look at the screen. This guy has makes me want to believe in things I didn't think would be mine to believe in.

My phone dings with another message.

Beau: Meet me at the agency office at six o'clock.

Me: Did you find out something about Marie?

Him: Yes.

I stare at his one word answer, my heart banging against my ribs.

Me: Did you find her?

Little dots appear on the screen like he's typing his response and then they disappear without his reply. Twenty minutes tick by with nothing from him. Those minutes stretch into an hour. Just as I'm about to climb into my car to head over to the office to demand he tell me what's going on my phone dings.

Him: No. Sorry. Had to help Cora with another case. I need to show you something.

Me: What?

Him: Marie has a Tumblr account.

Me: Send me the link.

Him: I need to show you. Meet me tonight.

Me: Fine.

Him: You're pissed.

Me: Duh.

I can almost hear him laughing.

Him: Sorry. I'm tied up with Cora stuff till then. Or we can meet tomorrow...

Me: No. Tonight.

Him: (smiling emoji)

Him: Cora just put an emoji keyboard app on my phone.

Me: Is this the important work you're tied up with?

Him: No (whistling emoji)

Me: Right

Him: (angel emoji)

Me: Are you going to stop using words entirely now?

Him: (thumps up emoji)

Me: (angry emoji)

Him: (sunglasses emoji)

Me: Stop it!

Him: Sorry. Gotta go. Cora's giving me the evil eye. See you tonight?

Me: Yeah

I glance at the clock. Three whole hours until I meet him. I open a new window on my computer and try to find Marie's secret account that Beau found. It would have to be a secret for her not to friend me. What's on there? What was she hiding on there? After half an hour I give up. I clearly don't have the same skills Beau has. Or the patience.

I go back to working on the book cover I'm creating for a client. Graphics has been a passion of mine since a class I took Freshman year in high school. I've been able to make a business out of it and support myself since I scraped together the money to buy my first computer. I use a file-hosting site to store all of my projects in case I have to take off and leave my computer behind. I funnel client payments through online accounts so I don't have to rely on banks. Basically it's a way for me to earn money anywhere and I love doing it.

I finish a mock up for a client and send it off just in time to hop in the car and head over to the agency. The door's unlocked, but the receptionist isn't at her desk. I wait in the reception area for a moment, hoping someone will show up. Voices draw me down the hall. A deep, rich laugh like hot coffee on a cold morning drifts from a doorway on the right. It's Beau. Caught by the sound, I put a hand on the wall to steady my suddenly weakened knees. I can't move. He laughs again, but stops abruptly as though he's only allotted so much time and not a second more.

"Can I help you?"

My hand automatically goes to my thigh as I spin around to see the man who snuck up behind me.

He puts his palms up in an *I'm harmless* gesture. "Didn't mean to startle you."

"I'm here to see Beau."

He takes me in from the top of my head to my toes and back again. When he's done I have the urge to knee him in the nuts. His face splits into a grin that's meant to be sexy but comes off over confidant. This guy's a player, but he's not using his moves on me. Yet. He does this thing with his head that knocks the hair out of his eyes. Another come-on move meant to draw female attention.

"What's your name?" he asks, giving me the once over again this time it has a critical edge to it like he's trying to decide if I'm worthy.

"Vera Swain."

"The new client." He straightens. "Sorry."

I give him the same slow perusal he gave me. He's got the *I'm a fuck up* thing down pat from his shoulder length hair to his scuffed skater shoes. He doesn't look employable so he must be somebody's boyfriend or son.

He sticks out his hand. "I'm Leo Nash."

I was right. Cora's boyfriend *and* the owner's son. His handshake is brief and dry.

He motions toward the room where Beau's laughter came from. "Beau's in there."

No shit, I want to say, but I keep my mouth shut and follow him into the room. Cora stands behind Beau who is sitting at a desk. Beau points to something on the computer screen in front of him. She props her arm on his shoulder as she leans closer to the monitor. She mumbles something that has Beau wiping at a smile.

"Beau. Vera Swain's here to see you," Leo interrupts.

Beau glances up and releases the grin he tamped down. "Hey. Come in. I see you met Leo."

I nod.

"Beau's done some really good work on your sister's case," Cora says, giving Beau a look of pride. "He's better at pulling stuff off the Internet than Leo and me combined."

"Good," Leo says. "Does that mean I don't have to do it anymore?"

Cora shakes her head. "You're not getting off the hook."

"You know it just occurred to me that your apartment is

empty right now," Leo waggles his eyebrows. "Take me home and have your way with me, Bluebird."

Beau clamps his hands over his ears. "Ugh. Shut up. That's my sister."

"He's all talk. I'm *still* a virgin." She rolls her eyes and adds, "For *some* reason."

"You gotta marry me," Leo says. "I'm not giving the milk away for free, you know. I've got standards."

"*Shut*. Up," Beau moans.

Cora laughs as she gives Beau a kiss on the cheek. "We'll see you later." Then to me, "Goodnight, Vera."

"Goodnight."

Leo nods at me. "Nice meeting you." He throws an arm across Cora's shoulders. "Later, Beau."

"Lock the front door, will you?" Beau asks.

"You got it," Leo says.

When they're gone Beau gets up and brings the other chair around to his side of the desk. "Have a seat."

When we're settled, he works the keyboard, opening a document with saved links.

He smells good. I forgot about that. His scent comes with the memory of our conversation in the diner and the feel of his hands around mine. He's steady and strong in a way I'll never be. I try to imagine depending on that strength, leaning into it and wrapping myself in it like a blanket. I'm not good with relying on someone else. I haven't come across very many trustworthy people. Beau could change that. If he has an agenda I have yet to spot it. I've gotten pretty good at sorting out what people want and what they want from me. It's always take, take, take. But not with Beau.

I pull in a slow, deep breath, inhaling him like a druggie getting a fix. His fingers are sure and confident on the keyboard, his focus on the screen in front of him. There are a lot of things about him that draw my curiosity, but mostly I wonder what he sees when he looks at me. I know what I *want* him to see. It's what I want the rest of the world to see. But he's not like everybody else. His look is a touch that vibrates through me like ripples in a pond, moving through me in tiny waves until I can feel him *everywhere*. It's disorienting and thrilling at the same time.

He catches me staring and does that slow blink thing as though it takes him a minute to process what's happening. His gaze drifts to my mouth and lingers. He's thinking. *I'm* thinking. He shakes it off and stares at his hands hovering over the keyboard like he doesn't know what to do. I cross my arms over my chest, making the decision for us both.

"What did you find?" My voice comes out croaky.

He doesn't move for a moment and then his fingers fly over the keyboard again. He brings up a Tumblr account with the user name VacantSorrow. The profile picture is a black and white drawing of a teenage girl with hair hanging in her face, obscuring all of her features except her bright purple lips. I know that image. Marie drew it. I saw it posted on one of her other social media accounts.

Beau points to it. "I did image searches of all the photos she had on her various accounts. This is the only one that hit. She posts to it fairly regularly. The last time was this morning. You should probably start reading from the first post."

He scrolls through the recent posts until he gets to the first entry then scoots his chair over so I can work the mouse.

The first post is dated almost two months ago. She talks about a man she met at the mall. He stopped her and told her she was beautiful and that she should be a model. He doesn't pay any attention to her friend who she thinks is prettier than her. She's known him for a month and opened this account so she could write about him. She talks about how kind he is to her and about how she can tell him anything.

This is how it all started for me.

I move through the entries. Some are about school and how boring it is. Some are about the group home she's in and the crush she used to have on one of the boys until she met her dream man. She calls this man Daddy and laughs at the irony of the nickname and how much he likes it when she calls him that. She talks about what a gentleman he is and how he makes her feel special. Special. Beautiful. Smart. These are all the things he makes her feel over and over and over. He feeds it to her like a drug and she's becoming addicted. She's never met anyone like him. No one's ever made her feel the way he makes her feel.

I called him Mr. Everything. He was my everything. Everything I ever wanted but never got, everything I wanted to hear but never heard, everything I wanted to feel but never felt. He was *my* heroin and I mainlined as much of him as I could as fast as I could. I force myself to keep reading past the memories that cloud the screen in front of me, blurring Marie's words that could be mine.

She actually does a photo shoot and he promises to talk to his agent friend about her. The pictures come out great, but Marie worries that her chest is too flat and that she still has too much baby fat under her chin and on her belly. He tells her she's perfect and then takes her to a doctor for a breast augmentation consultation. During the appointment he sits in the exam room with her to make sure she's comfortable with the doctor. She was nervous about taking her top off but 'Daddy' tells her how pretty and sexy she is and how she doesn't really need the boob job, but he'll get it for her if that's what she wants.

He fondles her breasts at the doctor's invitation. His touch is brief and clinical. She doesn't feel like she did when her foster father touched her. He talks her out of the implants and tells her he loves her small breasts. To prove it he starts touching them...a lot. But he doesn't go any further. 'Daddy' calls her his good girl. He tells her he loves her. She likes his kisses and how out of control she makes him feel.

I thought he loved me too.

Theirs is a special relationship. He shares things with her that he doesn't share with anyone else. He keeps her secrets. He's the only person she can trust. She can call him any time day or night. She tests this several times. He didn't lie and they talk until she falls asleep. Sometimes he sings to her. She stops going to school to spend more time with him. Her friends complain, but they don't understand. He's her soul mate, her one true love. She talks a lot about love.

I thought I'd die without him.

He wants her first time to be with someone she loves and laments the fact that she doesn't love him. She tries to tell him that she *does* love him, more than anyone *ever*, but he doesn't believe her. He draws her in deeper with his promises and their shared secrets. He makes her feel special and wanted. He's everything. She can't live without him.

And then the last entry... He wants her to get a tattoo...

All of the air whooshes out of me like someone just punched me in the stomach. His MO hasn't changed since he was *my* everything. The flattery. The sympathetic ear. The only one I can trust. The isolation. The secrecy. The innocent touching that leads to more and more and *more*. The absolute control of my world. The mark I got for him that *still* mars my body.

I shove away from the desk, saliva pooling in my mouth. I can't breathe. Dots fill my narrowed vision. I'm too late. Beau says something but I can't hear him. My ears roar with the blood pumping too hard and fast through me.

He has her. I'm too late. Too late.

Beau shakes my shoulders. His lips move, but I can't make out what he says. The world tilts. I grip the arms of the chair to stay in it. Bile rises up the back of my throat. Beau pushes my head down between my knees. He's saying something. He rubs my back with one hand while pulling a trash can close with the other. I still can't get enough air, but the nausea lessens.

He has her. He has her. He's going to brand her.

Beau eases me upright and studies my face for what I don't know. He makes a motion for me to stay put. I can't move. I still can't pull in enough air. The more I try the less there is. He comes back and puts a paper bag over my nose and mouth. The sides of the back suck in then puff out with each of my breaths. I blink away the dots and focus on Beau's worried face.

His coaching voice comes back to me. "You're okay. You're okay. I've got you."

I take over holding the bag, keeping my eyes on his. He kneels in front of me. His gaze roams my face like he's looking for something or trying to find an answer to an unasked question. I can't tell him. I can't talk about it. I don't have the words to express how disappointed I am in myself that *He* can still get to me after all this time and how fresh the memories still are. I knew this was a possibility. I should've been better prepared. Imagining Marie going through what I lived through brings on a fresh wave of nausea. She's in the honeymoon phase and she has no idea that her world is about to be ripped apart.

7

BEAU

Thank god the color is beginning to return to Vera's face. She watches me with haunted, wounded eyes. I brush the hair back from her face. It's soft. She's soft. On the outside and the inside. She's not nearly as tough as she tries to make people think. I put my hand over hers and lower the bag. She's open in a way I imagine she hasn't been for a very long time if ever. I *see* her agony. Her pain is an ache in my chest. It strikes an answering cord within me. She lets me look. She lets me see her. The hope shining in her eyes rips and tears at me until every feeling I've ever had pours out of me and pools at her feet in a big, sloppy mess.

What's left behind is stark and cold and empty. I'm left with nothing and it's everything. She sees me too. I reach for her and she comes into my arms willingly. We hold on tight. There's nothing outside this room. There's nothing except her and me. The feel of her is an out of body experience. I bury my face in the side of her neck and inhale. I was right —lemons and something soft and feminine. She's a resting place to hide in away from the rest of the world.

I wait for the guilt to come and it doesn't disappoint. It slips in between us and pushes us apart. I find myself pulling away from her, shoved back by my memories of Cassandra and the promises I made to her...the promises I didn't keep. The image of Cassandra smiling up at me that final night overlaps Vera's confused face as I back away. Needing the edge of the desk to steady me, I stand and move to the other side of the room. Pressing the heels of my hands into my eyes, I wish I could forget. It's the first time I've ever had that thought and it brings on a fresh surge of guilt.

I welcome it. With it comes perspective, which until a moment ago I lost. Vera is a client. She's not my friend. She's not my lover. And I'm not any of those things to her. When we find her sister she'll go back to her life in Colorado and I'll go back to lying on Cora's couch, trying to figure out my shit. My fist makes a satisfying dent in the wall. The pain radiates up into my shoulder. This agony I understand. It has a start and an end. I know where it came from and I know it will go away. Flattening my palms on the table, I bow my head and take a deep breath then another. My knuckles burn. Little dots of blood begin to form and I can already feel the swelling.

Behind me Vera is quiet. I'd give anything to know what she's thinking at the same time I'm glad I don't know.

I turn, but stay where I'm safe across the room from her. "*Who* has Marie?"

"What?"

"You kept saying 'He has her' over and over."

As I watch she picks up her forgotten armor and begins to put herself back together chunk by chunk. Her mask—the final fragment—slides into place and I'm shut out. I'll never know what she was thinking.

"You know who this *Daddy* guy is, don't you?" I press.

Her gaze slinks away. She fidgets with the bag, shredding it into little pieces.

"Who is he?"

She doesn't answer. Her hands shake as she tears the bag, but her shoulders are straight. She's a contradiction of stress and determination.

And then it hits me. "Who is he to *you*?"

"He's not anything to me." She wants this to be true, but it's not.

"Who *was* he then?"

She takes a long time to decide what to answer. In the end it comes down to whether or not she wants me to help her find her sister and we both know it.

"You came here wanting our help," I remind her. "I can't help you if you withhold information from me."

"Javier Abano." Her voice is ugly and brutal like the other night when she asked me if I wanted to fuck her. "I was with him when I was fourteen until...I wasn't anymore."

Everything in me goes still as I try to process what she's saying. My brain wants to fill in the gaps with what I read on Marie's Tumblr. I picture a much younger Vera falling into this Javier's manipulation the way Marie did and the things he might have done to her. It overlaps and blends with what happened to Cassandra. I sat in that courtroom during my trial forced to listen to every vile, cruel thing that was done to her, each description flaying me open until I was a bloody, raw gaping wound.

I don't know what to do or say. Vera's bald statement tears at the old trauma and I'm left stunned motionless. My first reaction is to go to her and hold her, but the look on her face tells me I fucked that up when I pushed her away.

She puts a hand up. "Don't. Okay?"

I nod.

"I was hoping he wouldn't go after her." Looking at the mess she made with the bag in her lap, she makes a helpless gesture. It's too close to defeat and I hate it.

I make myself move to hold out the trashcan while she scoops up the pieces and throws them away. I understand a lot of things about her now and her need for a new identity. It must have taken every ounce of strength she had to come back here to find her sister. She's risking everything for Marie. Much like Cora did for me. She didn't have to come back, but she did.

"I was also hoping we'd find her before he did," she says. "But we're too late."

"Only death is too late," I tell her gently. "We'll find her and get her away from him."

"It's not going to be easy. She thinks she's in love with him. And she barely knows me. She's not going to choose me over him."

"Maybe we don't give her a choice."

She agrees with a nod. "She's going to hate me for a long time. She'll fight. She might even try to run away."

"You won't let her."

"You're not asking me questions about him."

"No, I'm not."

"You never ask questions."

"Is that what you want?"

She shakes her head.

"You'll tell me if you want to. When you want to," I add.

She doesn't respond.

"You don't ask me questions either. I like that about you."

Her lips curve into a half smile. "Maybe I only want to know what you want me to know."

"Maybe it's a way for you to avoid opening yourself up to questions."

"For you too."

I can't disagree. We both have things we want and need to avoid. I guess we'll just keep stepping around them in this dance we do toward what I don't know.

"I should ask if you know where this Javier lives and if you have any other information on him other than his name," I tell her, changing our perspectives, moving things out of the personal and into the professional. "It might help me find Marie. I might even be able to follow him to her."

"He won't be living where he was back...then."

"What kind of car does he drive? Where does he like to shop? What habits does he have? I need anything you can tell me about him."

"I told him about Marie." She twists her hands together. "About my dream for us to be a family again."

"It's not your fault what he's doing to her."

"No? Then whose fault is it? He wouldn't even know about her if I hadn't told him about her."

"You think he might be using her to get to you?"

She nods. "I know he is." She looks so small and vulnerable.

I edge closer. "What does he want?"

Her eyes are red rimmed and tired as she stares at me. She dares me with her gaze to draw my own conclusions and to not make her say it out loud. He wants *her* and he's willing to use her sister to get to her. Another man wanted Cassandra and that man took her. I couldn't save Cassandra. I couldn't prevent what happened to her and I'll regret it until the day I die, but I can save Vera.

"Go back to Colorado," I tell her. "I'll find Marie. I promise."

"No."

"You're not safe here."

"I'm not safe anywhere."

"But you're safer in Colorado."

"I'm not leaving until we find Marie."

Sitting in the chair across from to her, I put my forearms on my knees and lean toward her. "Be reasonable—"

"There's nothing he can do to me that he hasn't already done. I'm staying and I'm helping you find my sister."

"Vera—"

"I'm not changing my mind no matter what you say."

"I really don't think—"

"*I* hired *you*. I'm your boss not the other way around. I'm staying and that's the end of it."

I need to try another tack. "You don't have anything to prove here. You don't have to put yourself in danger."

"Maybe I have something to prove to myself."

I don't have an answer for that. I know about putting myself through shit just to prove I can do it. For a long time after I got out of prison just getting out of bed in the morning was an exercise in self-assurance. Sitting through the trial of Cassandra's murderer, listening all over again to what he did to her, was an act of defiance. If she needs to face this Abano guy to prove to herself she's over him and what he did to her, who am I to stand in her way?

Just because I'm giving up the protest doesn't mean I like the idea of Vera putting herself in potential danger. He can't have her. I won't let him.

8

VERA

I can see the moment Beau decides to give up fighting me on this. I appreciate his concern. It's been a long time since someone thought about my best interests ahead of their own. It might actually be the very first time. I let that sink in a moment. Since I met him Beau has backed me at every turn. Even against his sister. I don't know what he sees in me that makes him take up for me—sometimes against his better judgment—but he does. If our roles were reversed I might not do the same for him. Or maybe I would. I like to think that I would. I mean—why wouldn't I?

He's not like anyone I've ever met. He should be angry at the world or at the very least use what happened to him to his advantage. He could've written a book that might get made into a movie. He could've hit the rounds of TV morning shows and talk shows. He could've cashed in a thousand different ways. But he didn't. He didn't grant a single interview after his release. I know because right after I met him I scoured the Internet looking for one. I wasn't interested in what everybody else thought about what happened to him. I was only interested in *his* thoughts and feelings.

And there was nothing.

I tried talking about what happened to me once. It was a horrible mistake. I could've written a book and maybe done the same TV morning show and talk show rounds. I *could've*, but like Beau I didn't. I don't know if that makes Beau and me normal or abnormal. All I know is that for whatever reason he's on my side. I need him on my side to find Marie.

We don't stand any chance of drawing Marie away from Javier if I run and hide again. She'll never leave him on her own. In the beginning I would've died if someone tried to tear me away from him. I thought I was in love. I thought I knew everything. I thought I was *so* smart. I didn't know there were people like Javier in the world. I didn't know how far he took me away from everything and everyone I knew until it was too late and there was no going back. I didn't know that someone who professed to love me so totally and completely could turn on me so brutally and cruelly.

I'm not going to let Marie make the same mistake I did. I know Javier's strengths, but I also know his weaknesses. It's not going to be easy getting Marie away from Javier and we might have to resort to some things I'm not sure Beau is willing to do. *I* might have to do things I don't want to do. But I can't let Javier have Marie. I just can't.

Even if it means trading my life for hers.

"I don't like it, but you're right," Beau concedes. "You're the *client*." He says the word *client* like it's a curse, like I've used my position to hurt him in some way.

I fight the urge to apologize. I don't owe this guy anything. And yet I do. He's done more for me in the short time I've known him than anyone else in my life.

"I can be more help here than in Colorado." This is the

truth. Well. Part of it anyway. I don't live in Colorado, but I can't tell Beau that. I *can* tell him Javier's next move and his next. He used them on me and he used them on the others who came after me. And now he's using them on Marie.

"I'll be careful," I add. "I'm not fourteen anymore and I'm not helpless."

He considers me for a long moment, then takes my hands in his, stilling their nervous fidgeting. "No, you're not. But I don't know what I'd do if he hurt you again."

His words shoot deep inside me, piercing what was left of my resistance to him. I tug him closer and he comes until our breaths mingle and the only thing in my line of sight is him. I tilt my head and slowly narrow the space between us. He doesn't move away this time. Our lips brush once, then again. I glance up to gauge his reaction. The look in his eyes is intense and thrilling. His hand goes to the back of my head and then he takes over, kissing me like he never wants to stop. I wrap my arms around his neck and bring him even closer.

We're knee to knee, lips to lips. He tastes faintly of coffee. Sensation spirals through me and I want *more*. More of him and the way he makes feel. This is what it's supposed to be like. His kiss is too much and yet not enough. His lips on mine are all I want, all I need. I started this. That's shocking on its own. Add to that I don't want it to stop. He's a great kisser. His mouth and tongue are a seduction, coaxing a low moan out of me, which jolts the kiss into a whole other stratosphere. He brackets my face in his hands. That's it. He doesn't press for more. This kiss is all he wants and it's everything I need.

He eases us out of the kiss and puts his forehead to mine. We're both a little winded and I wonder if he's as shocked as I am at what we're like together. It started as an experiment on my part. I had no idea how swept away I'd be. I don't feel overpowered at all. I feel *empowered*. He has no idea what he's done granting me this gift. Maybe he never will.

"That got...out of hand," he says.

"I'm not sorry."

He closes his eyes and exhales heavily. "I'm not either."

"But you don't want it to happen again."

"It *shouldn't* happen again." He still holds my face in his hands and isn't showing any sign of letting go.

"But it will."

He opens his eyes and stares at the way our thighs are bracketed side-by-side—his, mine, his, mine. His are so much larger and taller than mine. I imagine our limbs twined together and wonder if he pictures it too. If we'd been standing instead of sitting during the kiss, what would that be like? How would it feel to be pressed fully against him?

"It shouldn't." He moves, disconnecting from me...again. He shakes his head. "I can't do this."

"It was just a kiss." No it wasn't and I can see it in his face that he doesn't believe that either.

"Vera..." It's like he doesn't know where to look. His gaze skips around like he's searching for a lifeline.

"It was just a kiss," I insist.

"I...can't."

His gaze finally lands and I follow its resting place—on a small photo of Cassandra tucked between the phone and his monitor. I wouldn't have noticed it if he hadn't drawn my eye to it. I don't know what to say. I'm in competition with a dead woman? Not that this is a competition or even the start of anything. Except that it is and we both know it. The message couldn't be any clearer than if he threw up a big, giant, blinking STOP sign.

"You're still in love with her." I can't hide the shock from my voice.

His nod is slow and filled with regret. Misery alters the lines of his face and his body just sort of *sags*. This is the part of Beau he tries so hard to hide from the rest of the world. The part of him that died the day Cassandra did. He was smart not to grant those interviews. The camera would've picked up what I'm only just now seeing when he thinks about her. How would he transform if he talked about her? His grief is a thick fog, hanging heavy in the room. Not only is he still in love with her, he's mourning her.

I don't know what to say. What *is* there to say?

"I should go." I grab my bag and start to rise.

He grips my wrist, stopping me.

"What do you want me to do?" I ask, flapping my free hand at my side in frustration. I'm not equipped to help him. I've never done this before and I don't have the energy to fight a losing battle with a ghost.

"I'm sorry."

"I don't want you to be sorry. It was just a kiss."

"You keep saying that."

"I'm trying to make it be true."

"Okay. It was just a kiss."

I sit down again. "Really?"

"Yes."

"No it wasn't."

"You're right. It wasn't."

The knuckles on his hand that hit the wall are purple and swollen. I don't like seeing him hurt physically or emotionally.

"You need ice," I tell him.

He flexes his hand. "It's fine."

"What was she like?"

He makes a fist, breathing through his nose like he's pulling in patience with each breath. "Don't go there."

"She was pretty. She looks nice."

He glares at me, nostrils flaring.

"What do you miss most about her?"

"Stop it."

I reach for the photo. He doesn't stop me. I saw tons of pictures of Cassandra when I searched for interviews Beau might have given, but this one's different. This one's personal. It was obviously taken by Beau. There's no mistaking the look in her eyes. He's it for her—the sun, the moon, the stars, and everything in between. There's a hint of sexual desire in the curve of her lips. It's the smirk of a woman who's been well and truly pleasured and looking forward to more of the same.

Sunlight makes the right side of her glow and her eyes look two different colors. She clutches her shirt closed. Or maybe she's in the process of unbuttoning it. It's hard to tell. Either is a seduction. What made him pick up the camera and capture this moment? What significance does it have for him? What was said just before and just after it was taken? Why did he choose this photo to look at everyday? What does he see when he looks at it now?

He stares down at the picture in my hand. He's unguarded. His love for her is naked and stark on his face. So is his loss. They're intertwined. No one's ever looked at me the way Beau looks at Cassandra's picture. I'm jealous—I realize—of a dead woman. It's so stupid I almost laugh out loud. What would he trade for one more day with her? Six years of loving and grieving. A quarter of his life. How much longer will he carry it around?

I hand him the photo. "You're very lucky to have loved and been loved like that."

He tears his gaze away from it to look me in the eye. "I know."

"What does it feel like?"

My question surprises him.

"Never mind."

"No. I don't know. I don't have the words for it."

"Try."

He looks for a moment like he's going to cop out again then changes his mind. "It's..." He makes a frustrated sound and tries again. "Being with Cassandra was like...like the sun shining on me *all* the time."

I close my eyes and try to imagine what that would feel like, but my imaginings are a pale wisp of the emotion in his voice and have none of what I saw in his eyes when he looked at her picture. Blinking my eyes open, I find Beau watching me. He's got a funny look on his face.

"I tried to see if I could picture it. What you described. I can't. I loved Javier and thought he loved me, but that wasn't love. There was no sunshine."

"Ah, Vera." He brushes the knuckles of his uninjured hand along my cheek. "You deserve endless days of blue skies and sunlight."

There's a note of regret in his voice. He's a tempest and I am too. There is no sunshine in either one of us. Together we'd be a perfect storm of misery, regret, and lost youth. I'm just beginning to learn all there is to Beau and I already know he'd be worth the effort if only *I* had something to offer *him*. I haven't even started unpacking my baggage. He's only seen the outside. He has no idea the horrors that lurk inside.

It's just as well he shot me down. My past is a Pandora's box I never want opened and something tells me that Beau could be the one to release it all.

9

BEAU

It's Sunday. Family reunion day. I haven't seen my parents in almost six years. I'm not even sure why we're doing this. Cora hums along with the radio to a song I know she doesn't like. She's plastered all kinds of expectations on this visit. She wants things to go back to the way they were *before*. Am I supposed to pretend I've been away at summer camp or college and came home for a visit? My parents *abandoned* me. I didn't expect my friends to stick by me, but my own flesh and blood? Yeah. I fucking depended on them. I needed them. And they weren't there.

All I had was Cora.

She has no idea how much her visits and letters meant to me. Even as I did everything I could to push her away I looked forward to hearing from her, seeing her. I guess a part of me didn't feel like I deserved her loyalty. She not only stood by me but she was the only one who believed in my innocence. I really think my parents held on to their faith in me as long as they could, but in the end it couldn't withstand a guilty verdict. It just wasn't strong enough.

When they gave up on me I gave up on myself.

Of all the things I've done I'm most sorry about that because it hurt Cora. I'm ashamed that I left her all alone believing in me. How she stuck by me so long I have no idea. She's stronger and better than me by far. The fact that she's the one pushing for this family reunion is proof of that. Without her I wouldn't attempt to reconcile with our parents and I'm pretty sure they wouldn't make the effort either.

She has to direct me to mom's house because I don't know where she lives now. I don't know where dad lives either. Cora waited until I was released from prison to tell me what happened to our family. How my parents split, the sale of the house we grew up in, and my dad's alcoholism. What's odd is that my dad never drank. I didn't even think he liked the taste of alcohol. Cora tells me it's a weakness in him and it has nothing to do with me. That's some bullshit she learned in Al-Anon. She's not only the sister of a convicted murderer she's the daughter of an alcoholic.

My conviction didn't just happen to me it happened to my whole family.

Cora buffered everything for me. When I walked out of prison it was like I was Dorothy opening the door to Oz. The landscape of my life had totally changed. I still don't know how to navigate it. Around every turn is another thing I have to adapt to and accept as my new reality. I went to a couple of Al-Anon meetings with Cora, but they had no context for me. In my memory my dad never even drank. How am I supposed to connect what Cora tells me with what I remember? They're so far apart it's ludicrous.

She talks about how much our mom has changed. The way she says it is a warning like I shouldn't expect much of anything from our mother. Cora's tried to dampen my expectations of this reunion, but I have the feeling the effort is more for her than me. She wants this to go well—for me. She doesn't know it, but the pressure that puts on me balls my hands into fists and I have to force myself to relax my jaw. I already have a headache from the pressure. What if I fuck this up? I can't let Cora down. I just can't.

I rode my bike past our old house a couple of times looking for I don't know what in the clapboard siding and tidy yard. There weren't even any ghosts there, no shadows of my former life. It was just a house. I feel so distanced from my life *before* it feels like a movie I watched and can barely remember the plot line of or the actors who played in it. I'm not sure how to behave with our parents. Do I hug them like I used to? A handshake? An awkward wave maybe or an acknowledging head nod? I just don't know. I'd ask Cora, but I'm afraid the question would disappoint her.

I pull the car up to my mom's house and cut the engine. I take my driving test tomorrow to get my license back. Both Cora and I had to take half a day off work so she could drive me down to the DMV. I hope I pass. Cora's counting on that too. I can't deal her any more disappointment.

We get out of the car and walk up to an apartment building a few pay scales down from our old neighborhood. I wonder how my mom has handled this. She was always about appearances and fitting in. I don't imagine she's still friends with my friends' moms. Not because *they* would've dropped *her* but because she wouldn't have been able to deal with their pity and rejection. The old *you can't fire me because I quit* routine.

Cora pauses at the door and looks up at me. "You okay?"

"Yeah. Let's do this."

Her laugh isn't humorous. "It's not a root canal."

It may as well be. "Of course it's not." *Let's just get this over with* I want to say. Instead I rap on the door. Cora steps forward so she's in front instead of me.

Mom answers the door. I'm glad I'm standing behind Cora because I would've knocked backwards into her. Mom did something to her hair and—what the fuck?—her eyes. I look like her. Or at least I used to. She lightened her hair so that it's almost blond and the green contacts in her eyes blot out the near identical blue as Cora's. All of the air is sucked out of me and I can't speak. I'm looking at a stranger. There's little similarity between the woman I'm looking at and the woman who raised me.

"Beau!" Mom throws her arms out and charges toward me, nearly bumping Cora off the porch.

I'm hit with a hundred and thirty pounds of unfamiliarity that wraps around me and squeezes tight. She doesn't even smell the same. I meet Cora's gaze over the top of mom's head. She mouths *I'm sorry*. I embrace Mom back and we do this awkward dance of letting go just as the other one hugs harder until I drop my hands to my side and she's forced to drop hers too.

"Look at you." Mom pats me on the chest. "You're so handsome. But this beard…" She tries to touch my face, but I lean out of reach. She recovers and wipes her hand on her hip. She gives Cora a brief hug. "Come in. Your dad's not here yet."

We follow her into the apartment. She kept some of the furniture from our old house. It looks out of place here. The context is all wrong. There are some new pieces mixed in that confuse me.

"Have a seat." She motions to the couch that used to be in our old living room.

I put my hands up Cassandra's shirt for the first time sitting on it. The memory throws me off and I'm stuck in place by it, staring at the exact spot where we sat. I couldn't work the clasp of her bra. She laughed and unhooked it for me. I can practically feel her in my hands and hear the hitch in her breath. Cora prods me, bringing me back to the here and now. When I sit it almost feels like sitting on a grave and a chill shoots through me.

"Can I get you something to drink?" Mom looks hopeful like maybe Cora isn't the only one who put expectations on this visit.

"Water," I say and Cora echoes me.

"I have soda and iced tea," Mom offers. Water won't cut it.

"A soda," Cora says. "Beau?"

"A soda for me too."

"I'll be right back." Mom hesitates, her gaze bouncing between her two children as though she can't believe we're real. And then she goes into the kitchen. "Ice?"

"Yes, please," Cora and I say together.

Cora turns away and puts a hand over her mouth to hold back her laugh.

I nudge her with my elbow. "Dork."

She bumps me in return. "*You're* a dork."

"Shut up, dork."

"Don't tell me to shut up, dork."

Laughing, we shove each other like when we were kids and the insults fly.

"Knock it off," Mom shouts from the kitchen.

We glance at each other in surprise then dissolve into silent hysterics, gripping our stomachs. It's so normal this moment. It's the most normal moment I've had in more than six years. By the time Mom returns we've got control of ourselves again and I'm feeling a lot less tense. She hands us our drinks and takes a seat in a new chair opposite us.

"Cora tells me you're working at the agency with her," Mom says.

I can tell from the tone of her voice that she doesn't approve of either one of us working there.

"They've been very good to me. To both of us," I add.

"I'm glad." She turns to Cora. "When are you going to do something with your hair? You're never going to get a boyfriend looking like that. I'm surprised people at your job take you seriously."

"I *have* a boyfriend."

Mom gets a disbelieving look on her face. "*You do*? Does he have a *job*?"

Cora's been going out with Leo for months now. I shouldn't be surprised she didn't tell Mom about him, but I am.

"He's in law school at UCLA."

Mom turns to me. "Is this true?"

"Very."

"You've met him?"

I nod. "He's a good guy."

Mom seems momentarily stunned by this. We sit in uncomfortable silence, sipping our drinks and avoiding looking at each other. I want to text Vera something stupid and random to take myself out of this moment. She's the first person I think of in the morning and the last person I think of at night before I fall asleep. That's not something I look too hard at. It's nice to have something to occupy my mind other than the fucked up state of my life.

A panda. I'd text her a panda.

There's a knock at the door. Mom gets up and smooths

down her skirt. She glances at her reflection in the mirror next to the door before she opens it. Dad leans with a hand on the doorframe. I stand and Cora does the same. When she moves in front of me again like she did at the front door it hits me. She's trying to shield me from our parents. It would be funny except for the fact that she feels it's necessary. As the big brother I should be protecting her not the other way around.

The changes in Mom were surprising, but the changes in Dad are shocking. He's a lot grayer than he was six years ago. Smaller too. The chiseled lines of his face are crags now, carved by stress and drinking. His eyes—the same light blue as mine—are red rimmed and tired looking. He doesn't see Cora or me. He doesn't take his eyes off Mom. The look in them strikes a blow deep in my gut. I recognize the combination of grief and longing.

Mom looks him over, her lip curling. "You've been drinking."

He holds up his fingers in a pinching motion. "Just a little. I'm not drunk." His slurred words make a liar out of him.

Cora stiffens and reaches back for my hand.

"You're going to see your son for the first time in how many years *drunk*?" Mom chastises him like it hasn't been years since *she's* seen me.

"I'm not drunk."

"I can smell it on you. I told you I didn't want to see you if you were drinking." He tries to make a move around her, but she steps in front of him. "Do I need to call the police?"

I don't recognize these people and the dance they're doing. I don't know how to respond. Cora squeezes my hand in reassurance.

"Aww, come on Evy. Let me in," Dad pleads.

"I don't like you when you're like this."

"You used to like me *a lot*." Dad reaches a hand toward Mom to stroke her cheek. It's an old familiar gesture. "Remember that time—"

Mom knocks his hand away. "You make me sick."

She tries to shut the door, but Dad's faster and catches it before she can close it on him.

His face morphs into a stranger's. "And you're a shriveled up old cunt. I *said* let me in."

In front of me Cora is a statue, holding onto me like I'm an anchor keeping her from floating away. I don't want to leave her, but I can't let this go on anymore.

I walk up behind Mom and grab the edge of the door. "Don't talk to her like that."

Dad finally sees me, squinting up at me as though he doesn't recognize me. "Beau?"

"Mom doesn't want you here like this."

"Go home, Reid," Mom pleads.

"I'm sorry. I didn't mean it, Evelyn. Please. Let me in."

She turns her face away. In profile I catch the sheen of tears in her eyes as she slips past me, leaving me alone with Dad.

"Beau. Son."

I stop him from trying to hug me with a hand on his shoulder. "Not like this. Not now," I tell him. I don't want to meet this man, this broken drunk. I want my father. I want the man who raised Cora and me. I want the man I tried to emulate myself after.

The look in his eyes cuts me. His lower lip shakes as he drops his hands to his sides. The boney flesh of his shoulder is unfamiliar and in startling contrast to the place where I once laid my head as a kid. Up close I can see the gray tinge to his skin and smell the stench of alcohol and cigarettes. Since when did he start smoking? I can't reconcile this man with my father. He was so full of life and passion and now... now he's just not.

He presses his lips together. His expression turns mean. "Too good for me now that you're famous?"

"Go home."

"And what about you, Cora?" he shouts over my shoulder. "Too good for me too?"

"Leave her out of this," I warn.

"Or what?" He pushes at me, trying to start a fight.

His shove is a trigger. Drawing in a ragged breath, I have to concentrate hard on not balling my hands into fists.

Cora slips under my arm and plants herself in front of me. "Don't touch him."

His focus shifts to her and his expression softens into an imitation of affection. "Corabelle, tell them it's okay." He even uses their nickname for her from when she was a little girl.

"You said you wouldn't drink today." Her reply is heavy with disappointment and sadness. "You promised."

"Just a nip to take the edge off. Nothing a cup of coffee wouldn't cure. What do you say?"

Behind me Mom cries. Her muffled sobs fill the silence. Dad looks at the door as though he can see through it to where my mom stands with her face in her hands. I don't know what to do. Like everybody else I look to Cora for some kind of direction here. She knows them better than I do. What's going to make this right? I know it's not my fault what happened to my family. I know it and yet the guilt is there, laying low in my belly. I'd take off if it didn't mean leaving Cora alone to deal with them.

Cora shakes her head. "No, Dad."

I hook an arm around her and pull her behind me. Before Dad can react or say anything else I slam the door and lock it. Cora gasps. Mom turns her tear-streaked face toward me. For a moment it looks like she'll say something, then she ducks her head and goes down the hall. A few seconds later a door crashes shut. There's nothing from the other side of the front door. No knocking, no more pleading. Just silence. Cora dives for me, wrapping her arms around me and burying her face in my shirt. It takes me some time to react and then I'm hugging her back just as hard as she hugs me.

"I'm sorry," I tell her my voice choked and hoarse. "I'm *so* sorry."

"It's my fault. I thought he'd be okay." She pulls away and makes a helpless gesture toward where Mom disappeared. "And her too. I was hoping they'd be...better."

"Let's get the fuck out of here."

"Wait." She gathers up the glasses of undrunk soda and heads for the kitchen.

"What are you doing?"

"Mom'll have a fit if I leave these out."

Fixing. Cora's always fixing and protecting and preventing. Another way in which my conviction irrevocably altered our family. I can't go back I can only go forward, but with the future so uncertain I wonder what we're moving toward. More days like this?

I hook a finger in the curtain to make sure Dad's gone. He is. I open the door for Cora, giving the hall where my mom disappeared a final glance before heading out after her. Maybe all at once was too much to ask, too forced. If our family is going to find our way back to each other we're going to have to do it in tinier, easier to manage steps.

Maybe I'll give those Al-Anon meetings another try. There's no way I can wrap my head around the changes in my parents without some kind of road map showing us how we got here. And how we can get back.

10

VERA

I spent the weekend mostly holed up in my motel room, finalizing projects for a couple of clients. I'm running low on money and could use the payday finishing them will bring. I tried not to be drawn to that house. All of Friday and most of Saturday I resisted driving over there. Saturday evening I found myself climbing in my car, then driving down that street. I didn't know what I expected to find or even why I put myself through going back to that time and place. Maybe it was just to prove to myself I could do it. That I could face the demons and walk away.

Of course I went there armed. I'm not stupid. Masochistic yes. Dumb no.

The house looked pretty much the same. It was me—I realized—who had changed. Everyone I knew back then was long gone. Javier is smart enough to have moved the operation. My escape was a huge breach in his security and as far as I know the only time anyone got the better of him. He'd want payback for that. He'd want Marie. She wasn't his usual taste, but she was young and so obviously vulnerable it would be like picking low hanging fruit. According to her Tumblr posts he has her fooled as he once fooled me.

I want to say I made him work harder than Marie did, but that's not true. I wanted what he was offering. I didn't realize what lay hidden just beneath or that I'd be trapped in a lower level of hell for nearly four years. I don't think about that first time. Or the next or the next. The last time… now that I remember. It's that last time Javier wishes he could forget.

I sat in my car across from the house for almost an hour, the memories rushing at me in crashing waves. So many times I wondered how the neighbors didn't know what was happening in the middle of their neighborhood as they walked their dogs and took their kids to soccer practice. At first I held out the hope that I'd be rescued. As the days turned to weeks then months then years those hopes faded and died. I remember the day I finally gave up and the song that was playing on the radio.

I shake myself out of those thoughts. They don't serve me. They won't get Marie back. Beau thinks he may have a lead on Javier's new residence. Or it could be another dead end like the three before it. Javier is smart. He hasn't lasted this long doing what he does without knowing exactly what moves to make and when.

I'm jittery and tired from too much caffeine and not enough food. I haven't slept a whole night since I read Marie's Tumblr. The clock is ticking. Once she gets the tattoo that will be it. No going back. I go to the crooked mirror hanging over the scared dresser and take off my robe. I make myself look at my body, turning so I can see the tattoo on my right shoulder blade. I thought Javier designed it just for me so I was proud to sit for it.

It's pretty if you don't know it's meaning. A scrollwork

heart with a keyhole at the center and a chain attached to the top of the heart with a J shaped key dangling just below. In the flourishes around the heart—if you know where to look—are three numbers. I didn't know the significance of them at the time until I *met* another girl with the same tattoo. She gloated over hers being a lower number.

I cringe at how high the numbers could be now. What number would Marie's be?

My phone dings with a message from Beau. Since we kissed and talked things have settled into something more comfortable for both of us.

Beau: (panda emoji)

I smile.

Me: (bamboo emoji)

Beau: What are you doing?

Me: nothing

Beau: Can I come in?

He's here? I look down at my plain bra and underwear.

Me: Hold on a sec

I shimmy into my robe and tie the sash tight. I check the peephole and sure enough there he is. My heart stutters and I put a hand over it, clutching the top of my robe tight as I open the door. He takes me in from my bare feet to my makeup-less face. He doesn't look good. Something happened. Something's wrong. I motion for him to come in, nervous for a whole new reason.

"Is it about Marie?"

"No." He closes and locks the door behind him, then just stands there, staring.

"Did something happen?"

He leans back against the door with a sigh. The paper bag in his hand clanks against the door.

"What's wrong?"

"What are you wearing under that?"

"Excuse me?" Tightening my grip on my robe, I wrap my arm around myself in a defensive gesture.

"I'm an asshole." He shakes his head. "Never mind. None of my business."

"I should put some clothes on."

He puts his palms up. "I'm sorry. You're fine. I'm the one who's fucked up. Can I sit down? I brought a present." He holds up the bag and I can clearly see there's a bottle inside. "Alcohol."

"I don't know."

"You're right. I should go. I'm not fit company right now anyway. I don't know why I came here. It's just that Cora's with Leo and I didn't want to be there with them…you know, together. I'm gonna go." He unlocks the door.

"Wait. Sit down. I could use a drink."

"I promise to be on my best behavior."

"You pour and I'll go throw some clothes on."

He does that slow blink thing, then nods and sits at the table, jamming his big frame into the rickety chair. By the time I get back he's refilling his glass. I take the seat across from him and stare down into the dark liquid. Closing my eyes, I shoot the whole thing down and hold my glass out for a refill. He obliges me. We drink the second glass together and he fills them again. The booze hits me in a warm wave. It's been a long time since I've had anything to drink and with how little I've eaten today I'm instantly buzzed. I sip at the third glass, floating on a gentle sea of *I don't give a fuck.*

I wait for Beau to talk, enjoying the company and the silence. I've been alone so long I forgot how comforting it can be to just hang out with someone you're comfortable with.

"I'm sorry about earlier. I wasn't expecting you to answer the door dressed like that. My head's a mess. I don't..." He finishes off his drink and sets the glass down with a thunk. "I shouldn't think those thoughts about you."

I refill his glass. "What were you thinking?"

"You don't want to know. I'm fucked up and so are my thoughts."

"You're not fucked up."

He raises his glass. "Not yet." The liquid disappears down his throat.

This time I leave his glass empty. "What happened?"

"We should order a pizza." He pulls out his phone. "What do you like?"

"I'm fine."

"Bullshit. You're already drunk. I can tell. I'm feeding you before you pass out on me."

"Order whatever you want. I don't want any."

He calls a local pizzeria and orders a large pepperoni and a large with everything and some soda. *That's too much food* I mouth. He shakes his head at me. I pour each of us another glass. Getting fucked up is suddenly sounding really, really good right now.

I hold up my glass and he clinks his to mine. "To getting fucked up." I shoot the whole thing back and set my glass down with a giggle. "I *am* drunk."

He slides the bottle out of reach. "No more for you until you eat something."

"I love pepperoni pizza. How'd you know?"

He shrugs. "Doesn't everybody?" Twisting his glass in his fingers, he stretches his legs out. "Why do *you* want to get drunk?"

Propping my chin in my hand, I lean across the table toward him. "I asked you first."

He shoves his drink away in disgust. "My dad's an alcoholic. I shouldn't be drinking."

I push it back toward him. "Fuck that. Getting drunk once doesn't make you an alcoholic. When was the last time you got drunk?"

"Never."

"*Never*?"

"Nope."

"I don't know why I'm judging. I've never been drunk before either. I guess I thought maybe you would've led a more exciting life than me."

"I was always a rule follower. No underage drinking for me. Never even stole anything. Which is pretty fucking ironic, isn't it? Me, the convicted murderer, never even jaywalked."

I clap a hand over my mouth to keep in a chuckle.

"Go ahead and laugh," he says, gesturing with his glass. "It's fucking funny."

Pressing my lips together, I shake my head. "It's really not." The giggle gets away from me and I grip my stomach, tipping over.

Beau laughs too. "No it's not. It fucking *sucked*."

We double over in hysterics. I've never seen him laugh before. He does it with his whole body, slapping the table and making our glasses jump. The more he laughs the more I laugh until I have to wave at him to stop. My stomach and face hurt. I suck in air, trying to calm down.

"You're beautiful when you laugh," he blurts out, startling us both with his compliment. "I mean, you're always beautiful just more when you laugh. Never mind." He grabs the bottle and drinks from it. "Forget I said that."

I put my hand over his on the bottle. "Thank you." I focus on the way my hand looks with his. "No one's ever said that to me before. Not the way you just did anyway." I slide the bottle out of his grasp and take a swig, setting it down between us. "Your laugh makes me want to take my clothes off." I look away, clamping my eyes shut, shocked at myself.

His hand covers mine on the bottle. "That's the greatest fucking thing anyone's ever said to me." He slips the bottle from my grip and I hear the liquid slosh as he drinks, then a thunk when he sets it back on the table. "I can't stop thinking about you."

I don't let my gaze go any higher than my hand over his hand around the bottle. "I can't stop thinking about you." It's my turn to drink. I tilt my head back and take a big, long gulp. Wiping the back of my hand over my mouth I set the bottle between us again. I still can't meet his gaze. "I wish I was enough for you."

There's a knock at the door. Beau jumps up from the table and answers it. He sets pizza and soda on the table, pays, and closes the door. When he doesn't take his seat right away, I turn to look up at him. He's studying the carpet in the corner, his hands shoved deep into the front pockets of his jeans. I went too far with a game we never should've started.

Opening the pizza, I try to change the mood and make him forget the stupid thing I said. "Mmm, this looks good. Come and eat." I busy myself with dividing up the napkins and pouring the soda.

He eases into the seat across from me. His serious face is back, the one heavy with regret. I hate that face.

"Don't say anything," I tell him. "Just eat."

He grabs a slice with everything and bites into it. The only sounds are the traffic outside and us eating. The booze is wearing off too soon. I eye the bottle and then decide *what the hell* and take a drink to keep the buzz going. Beau takes it up when I set it down and does the same. By the time we finish eating most of the bottle is gone, but the awkwardness stayed.

"You have it wrong," he finally says. "*I'm* not enough for *you*."

"That's bullshit." The alcohol makes me bold. "That's such fucking bullshit and you know it. I thought you were brave."

"What made you think that?"

"You are about everything else."

"No, I'm not. I'm just a good actor."

"And a good liar."

"I don't lie."

I shake my head at him. "And an idiot."

"What do you want me to say? That I don't see her when I look at you?"

"Do you?"

"Sometimes."

"That's because you look for her. Stop torturing yourself."

His head jerks back and his lips part. He looks at me like he doesn't know me or doesn't *want* to know me.

I hate myself for being mean to him. "I'm sorry. I shouldn't have said that. You don't owe me anything. Just forget it. This getting drunk was a bad, bad idea."

I grab the bottle and try to stand, but my legs won't hold me and before I know it everything goes sideways. I put out a hand to catch myself and hit a hard chest. The world whooshes and rolls and we land on the bed with a bounce. He ends up on top of me, his hips between my legs. His mouth comes down hard on mine, hard enough to hurt, but I don't care. Fisting his hair, I hold him to me. His tongue clashes with mine and it's an all out war. There's no softness no finesse. Only need. Hot, hungry, angry need. His hands claw at my clothes. I shove his shirt up so I can get to his zipper.

His mouth clamps down on my breast and I let out a demented moan. Everything is frenzied and hot and aching. Need rises up and overtakes me. I'm wild, pushing down his pants to free him. My first feel of him makes us both groan. He's hard and heavy in my hand as I stroke him. He shoves one finger then two inside me. My hips buck off the bed, driving his hand to the rhythm I desperately need. He picks up on my pace and before I know it I throw my head back and cry out.

He replaces his hand with his cock and pushes into me. I twist under him, my hands clamped to his backside. He's all the way inside me and it's making me crazy. He drives into me, pistoning his hips in brutal, punishing thrusts. I can't get enough. Hooking my legs around his hips is all the encouragement he needs. I'm screaming and he keeps coming at me, plunging deeper and deeper. I hold onto him as I come, digging my nails into his ass. He makes a final thrust and buries his face in my neck on a growl.

He's heavy on top of me, but I don't care. That was the single greatest thing to ever happen to me. His breath blows hot on the side of my face. I turn to look at him. His eyes are closed, clamped tight. He ducks his head so I can't see him or try to read his reaction. Maybe I don't want to know because if he regrets this I might just shoot him.

11

BEAU

I fucked up.

I fucked Vera.

I fucking fucked Vera.

I fucking loved fucking Vera.

I shouldn't fucking love it, but I do.

It was fucking intense. It was fucking *everything*.

I'm a fucking drunk ass mess. I duck my head so she can't see my face as I squeeze back the moisture in my eyes. I'm on top of her. My dick is still inside her and all I can think about is doing it again. I shouldn't want that. I shouldn't want to finish taking off her clothes to take my time to fuck her properly. I shouldn't be thinking about anything but the feel of her under me and her breasts pressing against my chest. And I definitely shouldn't feel guilty.

I can't move. I don't want to. I can't face what she might be thinking and feeling about what we just did. What if she regrets it? What if she thinks *I* regret it? I didn't mean for it to happen. This wasn't why I came over here tonight. Oh, God what if she hates me.

Oh *shit.*

Oh *fucking* shit.

No condom. Fuuuucckkk. Fuck. Fuck. Fuck.

I try to pull out of her, but she's got her hands clamped to my ass.

"Vera, let me go."

"No regrets."

I shake my head. I still can't look at her.

"I mean it, Beau. Don't you fucking regret this or feel guilty about it."

"I don't."

"Look at me when you say that."

I raise my head and blink down at her. "We didn't use a condom."

"Oh, shit. It's okay."

"No. It really isn't."

"I'm clean and I can't get pregnant if that's what all this is about."

She releases her grip on me and I slide out of her and move to the side so I'm not crushing her.

"Well, yeah," I tell her. "It's pretty much *all* it's about."

"I thought you might be wishing it didn't happen."

I can't honestly say I don't.

She sighs and pushes at me to get off of her. Rolling onto my back, I throw my arm across my eyes. I can't face her yet. I'm a fucking coward I know. I don't want to talk about it. I just want to crawl in bed and sleep off my drunk. In the morning I'll figure everything out.

She slaps my bare leg. "Get out."

It takes me a moment to get my elbows under me so I can sit up. "What?"

"You heard me." She points at the door. "Get out."

Somewhere along the way she stripped off the rest of

her clothing and she's standing in front of me totally naked. If I had any left over drunken thoughts about regret they strolled straight out of my head.

"What? Why?"

"I don't want you here."

I manage to get into a sitting position and stare down at myself. My shirt is hooked around my arms across my back and my jeans hang around my ankles. I wiggle out of my shirt and push my jeans off with my feet.

"What are you doing?" She stands over me with her hands on her hips.

I hold my arms out to her. "Come here."

"No." She's eyeing me like that *no* might turn into a *yes*.

"Come sleep with me."

"I told you to get the fuck out."

"I know you did. Please. Come here."

She moves forward until her knees hit mine. I wrap my arms around her, pressing my face against her breasts. She smells better naked. Her skin is soft. She's soft. Her breasts are full and round and they mash my nose as she holds my head against her.

"I'm sorry," I tell her. "I'm shit at this. I don't... It's been a long time for me."

She strokes my hair. "It's been a long time for me too. Pretty much never."

I don't know what she means by that.

She pulls away and grips my face so I have to look at her. "You can't do that avoidance shit with me. Got it? You don't have a single fucking clue how this was for me. Don't take it away from me with your guilt and regret. Let me have this. Okay?"

I don't know what she means by that either. I can't read the expression on her face. It's kind of like the look she got that night at the diner only not so hard and angry. Whatever she's thinking about is not in this room. It's somewhere else.

"Yeah. Okay," I agree.

Her kiss has me reaching for her and bringing her down on top of me. *God the feel of her*. She straddles my hips, her pussy pressing against my dick. I'm already getting hard again. Her breasts bounce as leverages herself over me. I take one in each hand, running my thumbs over her nipples, marveling at how they stiffen and the little sound she makes in the back of her throat.

"It's just you and me here tonight. Promise me."

I nod. "Just you and me."

"We don't have a past or a future. Only now."

"Only now."

I don't question why she needs this reassurance because I need it too. I need the absolution of living in the moment. When I walked in this room I took off my grief and left it outside along with the past. I was so lost without it until she grounded me with her honesty. Maybe that's why I came here...to see how it would feel to let it go if only for a short while. She's a safe place to hide from the world and who I couldn't be. I hope I'm the same for her.

Pushing away any other thoughts except the way she looks and feels on top of me, I concentrate on giving her what she wants. To be fully present in the here and now. A mindless fuck. I focus on *her* pleasure and what makes her gasp and grind against me. Her face is flushed, her head thrown back. I repeat the motion, strumming her clit with one hand while hitting deep inside her with the fingers of my other hand. She clamps her hands on my wrists and cries out, her whole body taut. She's so fucking beautiful I loose my breath watching her.

My dick is hard and insistent beneath her, but I don't

make a move to relieve it. I'm too mesmerized by the new look in her eyes. I move my hands around to her hips and up to her waist. She lies down on top of me with a sigh, her head tucked beneath my chin. Smoothing my hands up her back, I close my eyes and focus on the feel of her. I could lay like this with her forever and never move.

Pressing her hot, open mouth to my chest, she sucks, marking me. The sting shoots straight to my dick and I push her hips down to relieve the ache she's creating. Her mouth begins a journey south as she inches down my body, licking and biting. I groan as her breasts rub against my dick. And then she's on her knees between my legs, taking me in her mouth. My breath hitches. I lift my head to watch.

Her eyes are on mine as her lips wrap around my shaft, pistoning along with her hand up and down. I reach down and stroke the side of her face. She takes me deep, sucking hard. My vision blurs. She does something with her other hand that makes my hips jerk. Oh *fuck*. I'm gonna come. My head drops back and I can't move. She has me pinned down. Her mouth is fucking genius. My hips buck in time with her strokes. The tightening of my fingers on her scalp is the only warning she gets. I raise my head, my whole body tight. She deep throats me and that's it. My hips flex as I come in her mouth. There's a roaring in my ears and I go temporarily blind.

She holds onto me until I go lax, her gaze never leaving mine. Lifting her head, she pulls her mouth off me slowly as though she's reluctant to let go. Her lips purse at the tip and she gives my dick a kiss. The way she looks at me in that moment is unreal. I'm ripped wide open. Who is this girl and how did I get here with her?

"Come here." I tug on her wrist.

She crawls back up my body, straddles my hips, her forearms bracketing my head, and looks down at me. I take her face in my hands and kiss her open-mouthed. It's a lazy, sated kiss. We're the wrong way on the bed. My legs dangle over the side and she's heavy on top of me, but I'm more comfortable than I've been in a long damn time. Maybe it's the booze or the sex or both. I don't know. Maybe it's just her. I can't remember feeling this easy like anything could happen and I'd roll with it instead of it rolling over me.

She breaks the kiss and traces a finger around the edge of my lips as though she's trying to memorize their shape. That's a stupid thing to think, but that's how it feels. Her eyes follow the movement around and around. It's ticklish. I let her do it anyway. She could do just about anything to me right now and I'd let her. It's not just the blowjob—although it was fucking *amazing*—it's her. I'm not supposed to compare and there's no way to do it without cheating them both, but I can't do things—do this—with Vera and not make comparisons to the only other woman I've ever slept with.

Everything with Vera is new and interesting and exciting. Everything with Cassandra toward the end was frustrating and difficult and *work*. We were trying to start over when she was killed. I was trying to forget she slept with someone else during the time we broke up. We were trying to find our way back to the new and the easy and the exciting. And then she was gone. I was left with nothing but if only's and thoughts of what might have been. It was *what might have been* that I held onto.

I saw the grief for *what might have been* in my parents and how it fucked them up like it's fucking me up. Maybe that's why I came here—to not be like them. To try something I haven't been able to do—let *what might have been* go and grab onto *what might be*. Vera is what might be. My new job at the agency is what might be. Trying to forge a new relationship with my parents is what might be.

If I'm honest with myself things with Cassandra weren't all that great. Admitting that feels disloyal like spitting on her grave. I loved her. Hell, I still love her. I think I always will. I can't talk about her without talking about how angry I was with her when she died. That's why I don't talk about her.

I never got to say goodbye. There was no closure. I was sitting in a jail cell, wondering how I got there and how it could be possible she was dead when they buried her. I've never even visited her grave. I'm not exactly sure where it is. She's been in the ground for six years. I can't picture here there. In my head she's someplace else like Europe or something. Any moment she could come back. I hold onto that along with everything else that was Cassandra and me. The good, the bad, and the tragic.

Vera taps my forehead, knocking me out of my morbid thoughts. "You promised just you and me."

"I know. I'm sorry."

She climbs off me, grabs the bottle, and tips it back, taking too big a drink, then hands it to me. I finish it off in three big gulps. My head swims. It's just the thing I need to push back the thoughts I shouldn't have had. She grabs a slice of cold pizza and takes a bite, regarding me with a solemn expression. I've disappointed her. I didn't leave everything outside. I hauled it in and piled it around me, walling myself off.

"The only time you're not feeling guilty is when you're drinking or screwing. Either we need more alcohol or we need to have more sex." She regards me over the top of the half eaten slice of pizza. "I'm too sore to have sex again and I'm already feeling hung over."

"I'm sorry."

"For which part?"

"All of it. I'm sorry I fucked this up for you. I'm sorry you're sore—I should've been gentler—and I'm sorry you're not feeling good."

"Are you staying or leaving?"

"I want to sleep with you if you'll let me."

"You gotta tell me what you were just thinking."

"Why do you want to talk about it?"

She wipes her face and hands with a napkin, then balls it up and throws it at me. I let it bounce off my chest and onto the floor. She's mad. Not just angry...pissed.

"Because it will never go away if you don't," she says. "You haul it everywhere you go."

"What do you want me to say?"

"What were you just thinking?"

I shake my head. I can't say it.

"What?" she taunts. "Afraid you'll scare me off?"

"I don't want to talk about it with you. It doesn't feel right."

"I'm laying on top of you naked and you're thinking about another woman. *That's* not right."

"I wasn't thinking about her that way. *Fuck.* Just leave it." I lean over to grab my shirt, but she snatches it and my pants away from me. I'm slow from all the fucking booze. I'd have to rip them out of her hands to get them back.

"You had a look on your face." She points at me. "Like that one."

"What one? What the hell are you talking about? Give me my clothes."

I make a swipe for her, but she's faster, scooting out of reach. I stalk toward her. She's quick, running over the bed to the other side. We're both naked and drunk. This is ridiculous.

"Give me my damn clothes."

"What are you afraid of?"

"Right now I'm afraid I'm going to have to walk home naked."

"Maybe it wasn't all sunshine."

"Shut up." I grab for her again, but she's too quick.

"Maybe she's better in bed than me."

"Don't do that."

"Why not? You were comparing us, weren't you? And don't fucking lie to me."

"Not the way you're making it sound."

"Then in what way?"

She dances away again. All this over and around is making me dizzy.

"Just stop!"

My outburst freezes her on top of the bed and she looks down at me like she won. I dive for her, knocking her legs out from under her careful to aim her so she hits the bed and not the floor. Pulling her by the ankles, I drag her toward me and lean down over her, right in her face.

"I'm fucking pissed off at her!"

"I thought she was perrrrrfect."

"Perfect people don't fuck your best friend!"

"Oh, shit."

"Perfect people don't abort your baby and then act like you *made* them do it."

"Jesus."

"Perfect people don't torture you imaging what that baby would've looked like."

"Oh, my god."

"And perfect people don't get raped and murdered by

some sick fuck so you can't be mad at them for all the fucked up things they put you through before they died."

"Oh, Beau."

"Are you fucking happy now?"

She puts her hands on my face. "I'm *so* sorry."

"I love her, but I fucking hate her. You're not supposed to hate someone who died the way she did. It's not fucking right."

"None of it is right. What she did to you or what happened to her. It's okay. It's okay."

She presses her lips to my face over and over. Her kisses are wet and then I realize it's me. I'm fucking crying like a fucking baby, which pisses me off even more. God damn it. I roll off her onto my back and scrub my hands over my face. She brings my arm around her and lays her head on my chest, holding me tight. She dries my face with my t-shirt. I'm tired. I'm so fucking tired.

I've been holding it all in for six years. I couldn't tell anyone any of this. Not my lawyers, not Cora, no one. It would've been *more* evidence to pile on the mountain they already had against me. It wouldn't have helped me and it wouldn't have brought her back. So I buried it, carrying it around inside me like a parasitic twin that fed off my good memories of Cassandra until I hardly had any left and I hated myself.

12

VERA

Beau stares at the ceiling, tears flowing from the corner of his eyes into his hair. I'm not sure he realizes he's crying or if he even knows I'm here. He's somewhere else in his head. Once the damn broke he hasn't stopped talking. All of the thoughts and feelings he's kept boarded up for the past six years keep flowing like a bleeding wound that can't be staunched.

"I don't really hate her," he mumbles. "I shouldn't have said any of that shit about her."

"I know you don't," I tell him, stroking his face. "It's okay to be mad at her."

"All the shit she went through before she died. We had our problems but I never would've wanted any of that to happen to her." He presses the heels of his hands against his eyelids. "I can't get the coroner photos out of my head. The diagrams of her wounds. The description of the rape and the... He fucking turned her over and raped her that way too. Hours. He spent hours on her. He stuffed her panties in her mouth and taped it shut to keep her quiet so he could fuck her over and over and no one would hear.

"She fucking fucked my best friend, but she didn't deserve that. She didn't deserve it." He rolls over on his side, curling his big body away from me. "She didn't fucking deserve it."

"I know." I hug him from behind. "It's okay."

"I was going to break things off with her. I couldn't deal with what she did. I tried. I just couldn't."

He rolls back toward me. We're on our sides face to face. His eyes are dry and fevered. He blinks at me slowly as though he's just remembering I'm here.

"I'm sorry." He wraps his arms around me, bringing me in close. "I shouldn't drink. I'm shit at this kind of stuff sober and, apparently, worse drunk. Tell me to shut up."

"Do you feel better?"

"No."

"Lighter?"

"No. Just tired."

"Then maybe we should go to sleep."

We get out of bed and then get back in the right way, pulling the covers over us. I've never slept in a bed with a man before. The only time I ever shared a bed was with another girl out of necessity so I don't know how this is supposed to work. Beau gets comfortable and then brings me in close to his side. He's big and warm and safe feeling.

He makes a noise somewhere between a growl and a moan as I shift to find the right spot. "I like it when you rub up against me like that."

"I'm trying to get comfortable."

"Roll on your side." I do and he spoons me from behind. "Better?"

"Except for that thing poking me."

He laughs. "That's what happens when you rub against me. Ignore it. It'll go away."

In a matter of moments he's asleep, but I lie awake thinking about the things we did and what he told me. There's so much more to him than I originally thought. I don't know what happened to him today to make him come here instead of going to Cora or a friend. Did he get what he was looking for, what he needed? I got something I didn't even know I wanted or needed. A lot more. His arm is tight around me and there isn't an inch of me that doesn't feel him. He's invaded my body and my mind and completely taken over my life.

I'm so far out of my depth with him. I don't know what to do with him and I don't want to do without him. Whatever this is between us is the biggest thing that's ever happened it me. It feels inevitable like we're opposite poles of a magnet, drawn toward each other by some unseen force. If either of us tried to walk away some other circumstances would force us back together. From that first moment in the reception area of the office we connected. Maybe it's just for the time being. Maybe we'll get what we want or need from each other then move on. But right now we're exactly where we're supposed to be.

The past few years I've learned a lot about trying to live in the moment and to just *be*. It's taken me a long time to get here. When I think about all I've been through it feels as though it happened to a different person. And yet when I read Marie's Tumblr I was brought right back to where I started. Maybe I need to go back to go forward. I drift off to sleep thinking about how far I've come and how much farther I still have to go and what part Beau will play.

I WAKE up to someone pounding on my skull with a thousand little hammers. The room is dark, but daylight glows around the edges of the curtains. *What time is it?* I try to move, but I'm pinned down. Beau's arm is banded around me just under my breasts. His leg weighs down my legs. He faces away from me on his stomach, snoring loud enough to wake the whole motel. The sound is doing terrible things to the inside of my head. Next to me the clock reads six-fifteen. My mouth feels like it's been stuffed with cotton then glued shut. I need the bathroom and a glass of water in that order. I shove at Beau, but he doesn't respond. I try shouting as loud as my head will let me and push at him. I manage to get him to stop snoring for about two seconds, then he goes back to splitting my ear drums.

I raise my hand as high as I can get it and smack him hard on his bare ass. He jumps.

Groaning, he grips his head. "Fuuuuuck."

I jab him with my elbow. "Get off me so I can pee."

He moves his leg, still complaining about his head and I slip out of bed and do my business. I come back with two glasses of water and a bottle of painkillers. Beau's on his back, rubbing his eyes, making grumbling noises about all the drinking we did last night.

"Here." I give him a glass and pour four pills into his hand.

I take some too and down the whole glass of water, then climb back into bed. Closing my eyes, I wait for the painkiller to do its work, trying to move as little as possible.

"Getting drunk sucks," Beau groans. "Why do people do it?"

"It was fun *last night*."

"But not worth it this morning. My fucking head."

"Quieter please."

"Are you all right?"

"I'm trying real hard to keep the pills down."

"No, I mean about what we did."

Cracking an eye, I turn to look at him. "The sex stuff?"

"Yeah." There's a deep crease between his brows.

I throw an arm over my eyes and try to focus on not vomiting in front of him. "I'm fine. It was great. You're a god. Blah blah blah."

His chuckle turns into a moan. "God. I am never drinking again." His arm snakes around my middle. "I meant I didn't take advantage of you, did I? The drinking..."

"I think at the end there it was *me* taking advantage of *you*."

"That part *was* pretty awesome." I can hear the smile in his voice. He kisses my shoulder. "You're sure about having the birth control covered?"

"Totally covered. No worries there."

"If anything does happen I'm here for whatever you want." He lays his head on my shoulder. His hair tickles my chin. "Shit. I really suck at this. I know better than anyone not to take chances like that. I'm sorry. I didn't mean for that to happen."

"It takes two to tango, captain. I just need to know you're clean and we're all good."

"I am. One hundred percent."

"Can we go back to sleep now?"

"Just one more thing."

"*God*, you're chatty in the morning."

I can feel his face crease into a smile. "Not usually."

"What is it?"

He runs his thumb along my collarbone in light, caressing strokes. "I don't do stuff like that. I'm not... That's not me. I don't fuck around."

"Me either." He has no idea how much I *don't* fuck around.

"Okay. That's all I wanted to get straight."

"Does this mean we're going steady now?"

"Yeah, I guess so."

"Glad that's settled. Go to sleep and try not to snore."

"I don't snore." He sounds genuinely insulted.

"Oh but you do."

"Do not."

"I'll record you and prove it."

"Is it really that bad? Are you not going to want to sleep with me anymore?"

"I'll get earplugs."

"I'll buy them for you."

"Go to sleep."

"Yes, ma'am."

In two seconds he's out, snoring like a chain saw. I hate that he can drop off so fast, that he feel asleep before me, and how glad I am that last night wasn't a one off for him. Glad isn't the right word. I'm thrilled. Way more than I should be. Us starting something is not a good idea. It's probably the stupidest idea I've had in a long time. The thing is I don't see how I could've avoided it if I wanted to. I *like* him. A lot. I even like his snoring. This big grizzly bear of a man has worked his way past my defenses as if they weren't even there. I sift my hand through his hair, wondering what in the world I'm going to do with him and where I would be without him.

13

BEAU

I leave Vera sleeping in her bed with a note to meet me later at the office and go home to take a shower and change clothes for work. It was damn hard getting out of a bed with a warm, naked, sexy woman in it, but I'm too new at the agency to take a day off. Being late is going to be bad enough. I'll have to work over time to make up the time. I don't want Mr. Nash to think I'm using my relationship with Cora to take advantage of his generosity. I'm lucky to have this job and the truth is I like it. I like following cyber trails to see where they'll take me and what I'll find out.

My head pounds like a motherfucker and I had to pull over to the side of the road to hurl in the gutter half way between Cora's apartment and Vera's motel. I'm *never* drinking again. As much fun as getting drunk was it's not worth the morning after. This is the torture my dad puts himself through every day? No thank you. The worst part is how irresponsible I was with Vera. At lunch I'm going to buy some earplugs and condoms. That shit cannot happen again. I know *way* better than that. I haven't been this disappointed in myself in a long damn time.

I'm missing parts of last night. Some of it is vivid in my memory and some of it is a black hole. I can't piece together how I got from eating pizza at the table with Vera to fucking her brains out. That is a huge chunk I'd really like to get back. I have no idea what I did or said that led up to that moment or even what Vera did or said. She seemed okay with what happened, but what if her memory is as faulty as mine? Ugh. Never *ever* again.

I unlock the door to Cora's apartment and go inside. She's in the kitchen, making herself a cup of tea in a to-go mug. Leo sits on the couch with coffee in one hand and a bagel in the other, watching a morning show.

Cora takes in my appearance and makes a face. "You look like shit."

"I feel like shit." I head straight for the coffee maker to see if Leo left me any.

"You stink too." She comes closer and sniffs me. "Were you *drinking*?"

"God. Not so loud, okay?"

"After seeing dad blitzed out of his mind yesterday you went out and got *drunk*?" She reaches up and smacks me in the head. "What is *wrong* with you?"

I wince. "Owww. That fucking hurt."

"Not cool, dude," Leo tosses in.

"Good," Cora says excruciatingly louder than necessary. "I hope you feel sick all day. I hope you vomit up your guts and your head hurts so bad it feels like it's going to roll off your shoulders. Oh, my God!" She hits me in the arm. "You didn't drink and drive did you? You don't even have your license back yet."

"I drank between the driving not during it, okay?"

"No. Not okay. I don't want two alcoholics in the family. I can't do that, Beau. I just can't."

"It was just one time. Believe me, I'm *never* doing that again."

"You're a child of an alcoholic. You're four times more likely to have a problem with alcohol than someone whose parent doesn't drink. Did you know that?"

"Fuck, Cora. Do you have to be so loud?"

"If this happens again I'm kicking you out." There are tears in her voice and her lower lips shakes. "Please don't make me kick you out after everything."

I go completely still. Seeing her like this guts me. I can't move. I did this to her. After everything she did for me I hurt her the way dad hurts her.

Leo must've heard the quiver in her voice too because he comes to stand next to Cora and puts his arm across her shoulders. He glares at me in warning.

"It was just one time," I tell her. "I swear."

"I hope that's true," she tells me.

"I missed a lot of things," I say quietly. "Getting piss drunk is one of them."

Her hand goes to her mouth. "Oh," she breathes.

"I'm sorry. It was stupid. I swear it will never happen again. Okay?"

She nods, her eyes watery above her hand.

"Come on, Bluebird. Let's let Beau get his coffee," Leo says, scrunching up his nose. "And a shower."

"Yeah, okay." She lets Leo lead her out of the little kitchen area and into the bedroom area.

I hear them whispering and her sniffing. I want to bash my head against the cabinets, but I'm pretty sure it would crack open. After a few moments they leave the apartment and I'm alone with my self-loathing. I didn't even think of Cora when I bought that bottle of alcohol last night. All I thought about was *not* thinking for a little while. When I'm with Vera is the only time my brain is quiet. I wish she were here right now. She'd say something to make the scene with Cora less of a fuck-up.

I take a quick shower and head to the office. When I get there Savannah is at her desk. Since the talk I tried to have with her she's been a little better. She stopped yelping every time I come within eight feet of her and she doesn't watch me like I'm a six foot three inch rattlesnake shaking its tail. Progress.

I pull a flower from the bunch I grabbed on the way in and hand it to her. "Happy Monday."

Her eyes do a rapid blink thing and then she takes the flower, her lips curving into a smile. The first one she's ever given me. I hope this bodes well for smoothing things over with my sister.

"Thank you."

"You're welcome.

I feel her gaze on me as I walk to Cora's office. Well, I guess it's Cora's and my office now. Cora's alone. Leo must have dropped her off before heading back up to school since I had her car. Her head is bent over a report and she taps her pen on the desk to a beat only she can hear.

I hold out the bouquet to her. "I'm sorry."

She sets down her pen and takes the flowers. She doesn't say anything just stares at the colors and shapes of the petals. I'd give anything to know what she's thinking right now.

I get down on one knee so I'm eye level with her. "I fucked up. I'm sorry I hurt you."

There are no tears in her eyes when she looks at me, only worry. I hate that I put it there almost as much as the tears I put in them earlier. I'm the most normal person she has left in our family. That's a pretty fucked up thing to think about. It's also sobering in that I have a lot to live up to that I haven't been. She deserves a better brother than she has at this moment.

"You didn't call me to let me know you weren't coming home."

"Shit. I'm sorry for that. I was too busy getting fucked up. I promise to call or text next time."

"Where were you?"

She deserves an answer, but I know she's not going to like the one I have to give and I'm not ready to talk about what's happening between Vera and me. I try to wipe the guilt from my face. "I was with a friend."

She studies me, her head tilted to one side as though I'm a puzzle she's trying to work out. "Are you okay?"

"Sometimes." It's the most honest answer I can give.

"What's going on with you? Lately you've been so...I don't know...off."

"I'm just trying to figure my shit out and not doing a very good job of it."

"I think you're doing pretty good."

"You do?"

"Yeah. I do. Other than last night I think you've done well considering."

"Thanks. That means a lot."

"Mr. Nash is impressed with your work. *I'm* impressed. You're going to be okay, Beau."

I'm stunned she thinks that. *Okay* is what I aspire to and it feels a million miles away. Like I'll need a space ship and a decade to reach it. I stand and go to my desk, my head full of her confidence in me. It takes me a moment to get my bearings and remember where I left off in my work on Friday.

"Thank you for the flowers."

"You're welcome. I wish I gave them to you for a different reason."

"I'm going to put them in some water."

I watch her walk out, her head bent over the bouquet. I wish I'd thought to give her flowers when she picked me up from the prison when I got out. Or when she helped me buy the things I needed for my new life. Or when she got me this job.

My phone dings with a text message. Other than Cora, Vera is the only person who texts me.

Vera: (emoji of a monkey with its hands over its ears) Me trying to sleep next to you.

Me: (smiling emoji) Me getting to sleep next to you.

Vera: What time should I be at the office? Your note didn't say.

Me: In an hour. I need to finish a project for Cora. I have something for you.

Vera: Is that a euphemism?

I laugh out loud.

Me: No. But it could be.

Vera: It should be.

Me: Yeah?

Vera: Yeah

Me: Then it's definitely a euphemism.

Vera: See you in an hour.

I'm smiling when Cora walks in with her flowers in a vase and sets them on her desk. "You're feeling better."

"Thank God. Did I say never again?"

"Yeah, about eighty times."

"Never, *ever* again."

"I'm glad. I'd hate to see you drink away the time you just got back."

"You didn't tell me it was *that* bad with Dad."

She lets out a heavy, resigned sigh. "I told you, but it's something you really have to experience for yourself to believe. I'm sorry you had to see it. Maybe we can try again in a couple weeks."

"I think I'll go see him on my own."

"That's not a good idea. He can be hard to handle. Yesterday was nothing."

"I'd like to go to a meeting with you again. I have a lot to learn. A lot I want to learn."

"There's one tomorrow around lunch time not too far from here."

"Okay. Let's go."

"Okay." Her expression is a lot brighter than it was when I first walked in the office.

Maybe I *will* be okay. How can I not be with Cora and Vera on my side?

14

VERA

I arrive at the agency office a few minutes early. My head finally stopped pounding, but my stomach still isn't happy with me. I missed a lot of things as a teenager, but getting wasted and hung over isn't among them. I wonder how Beau is feeling. He looked worse than I felt when he slipped out of my room. He didn't think I was awake, but I was too sick to move let alone say a proper goodbye.

The receptionist is at her desk, typing on her computer. She looks up and smiles.

"Hi. I'm here to see Beau."

"Let me see if he's ready for you." She goes down the hall and then comes back with Beau trailing behind her.

"Hey." He gives the receptionist a glance as though he doesn't know what how to greet me with her around.

"Hi." I hold out my hand and we shake like we weren't naked the last time we saw each other.

A corner of his mouth tips up. "Come on back to the office."

I follow him down the hall. As soon as we're in the room he shuts the door and backs me up against it. His mouth comes down on mine. The kiss is gentle yet full of the goodbye we should've had this morning and the hello we should've had in the reception area. He lifts his head and looks down at me. There's too much in his expression and then he blinks and it's gone as if it was never there.

"I got you something." He pulls a package of earplugs out of his pocket.

No guy has ever gotten me a present before. It's not flowers, but it's thoughtful and so totally Beau the backs of my eyes sting. No guy has ever made me cry for a good reason. I'm speechless. It's stupid to get so choked up at such a simple and sort of self-serving gift. I feel ridiculous. To hide my overreaction I throw my arms around his neck and kiss him. He reacts immediately, hauling me up against him with his big hands on my ass. All of the fire and spark from last night is back only a thousand times more intense without the dulling effects of alcohol. His mouth is incredible. The things he does with his teeth and tongue. *Oh my god.*

His hands are everywhere and yet not where I want them. He grinds his growing erection against me and stars spark behind my eyelids. I moan and he does it again...and again. He palms my breast, making my nipple hard and rolls it almost painfully. The sound I make is part whimper part plea. I want more. I *need* more. I picture him hiking up my skirt, pulling down my panties, and driving into me while I wrap my legs around his waist. As soon as I have the thought his hand is up my skirt, his fingers skating across the damp crotch of my underwear.

"Jesus," he breathes against my open mouth. "You're so fucking wet."

"Are you going to finish what you're starting?"

"I can't." He slips a finger into my panties. "Not here." He strokes into me and has to wrap his other arm around me when my knees buckle. "I could get in trouble." His thumb rubs my clit and I bite down on his shoulder to keep from crying out. "Maybe even fired." His fingers are fucking magic. "If I get fired I can't help you." I open my legs wider for him. "You want me to help you, don't you?" I nod. "I *like* helping you." He does this thing between my legs that makes my head drop back. His mouth covers mine to catch my scream as I come.

I'm pinned to the door by his big body. He's got a hand in my underwear and a hand on my tit and he's kissing me like he can't get enough of me. I'm boneless.

When he lifts his head he smiles at me. "I *really* like helping you."

"I really like your help."

He fixes my skirt and straightens my blouse. "You can't say I don't finish what I start."

"No, I can't.

"Here." He retrieves the earplugs I dropped on the floor and hands them to me. "You might need these."

"Oh, yeah?"

"I might start something again later."

"I hope you do."

He gives me a quick kiss. "Let me show you what I found." He moves the other chair around to his desk like he did before so I can sit next to him at his computer.

My legs are a little wobbly as I follow him across the room. He notices and gives me a self-satisfied smile. This guy is going to be trouble for me. I can't put him in a hidden pocket and take him with me if I suddenly have to run. What he seems to want from me won't fit in my day-by-day, temporary life style. If I disappear, how would he handle it? With his skills he'd probably try to find me, and that could be just as dangerous as what I'm running from—for him and me. I'm making a mistake here, letting him in. I shouldn't have let it get this far.

"Will you promise me something," I blurt out.

He turns to me in surprise. "What?"

"If I'm suddenly...gone...you won't try to find me."

"Are you in danger? Did something happen?"

"No. But if it does I might not be able to say goodbye. Are you going to be okay with that?"

He sits back in his chair. His hands are loose in his lap, but the rest of his body tenses. He considers my question, his blue eyes laser-focused on my face. There's not a lot of room here for negotiation. I have to know he'll let me go if I run. Self-preservation is and has to be my top priority. I can't let what's happening between us change that. My life depends on my ability to make a move at a moment's notice. Especially being this close to where it all started.

"No." I can see he has questions to ask, but he doesn't voice them. "But I'll deal with it."

"And you won't try to find me?"

"No."

"You promise?"

"I promise."

He doesn't like making the promise. I've put an unknown expiration date on what we have. I wouldn't like it anymore than he does. He turns to his computer, his face set and determined. We find Marie. We move forward until we stop moving at all. That's something we both can do to take our minds off how temporary this thing between us is.

"Marie put up a new post late last night," he says, closing

the subject of us and drawing my attention to the computer screen. "A photo."

It's at an awkward angle and there's not much to see except the drawn shape of a heart with a keyhole in the middle and a chain coming off the top of it with an old fashioned key attached at the end. A extremely *familiar* image. He's making his case for her getting his tattoo. I grip the arms of the chair and close my eyes. I can hear him, his voice deep and accented and very persuasive. He would've told her that the heart symbolizes his heart and the key is her unlocking his broken heart and opening him up to love. My stomach churns for a completely different reason than last night's alcohol.

Beau is talking about the photo of the drawing. Opening my eyes, I force myself to focus on what he's saying and not get lost again in old, ugly memories. The important thing is that Marie hasn't gotten the tattoo yet. I concentrate on that and try to ignore the ticking time clock Javier has us on.

"Tumblr doesn't scrub the EXIF info off of posted pictures like some other social media sites," he says. "If she doesn't have her phone or camera settings to not store GIS information then it will be saved within the image and we can extract it."

"English please."

"We might be able to get the GPS coordinates from the picture on where it was taken, which could lead us to where Marie is. Or at least where she *was* when she took the photo."

"Are you serious? Do it."

In a few short keystrokes we're looking at the GPS stamp on the picture. Beau copies them then pastes them into another site and up pops the Google map with a pin in the spot where the photo was taken. I lean closer to the screen as Beau zooms in on the pin.

"It looks like a strip shopping center." He changes the view to street level. "She would've been in one of these shops or just outside of them when she took the photo."

There's a convenience store, a nail salon, a sandwich shop, a tobacco store, a dry cleaners, a takeout pizza place, a Starbucks, and a frozen yogurt shop. Which one was she in?

"She might come back if she's living in the area," Beau says. "She took the photo just after seven PM. We could stake it out and see if she comes back. It could take days, but so far this is the *only* lead I have on your sister."

"How much will that cost? I budgeted according to the estimate Cora gave me. I don't know how much over that I can go."

"Don't worry about it."

"I'm pretty sure your boss isn't going to like that answer."

"I'll do it off the clock after work."

"Could you get fired for that though? I don't want to get you in trouble."

"Let me worry about that."

"You've already crossed a line by keeping my secret," I tell him. "And last night. I can't ask you to do this too."

"You're not asking me to do it. I'm volunteering."

"*Beau*," I warn.

"*Vera*," he mocks.

"I'm serious."

"I did find something else. You have an older half brother. Of course that isn't what you hired the agency to find out so I should probably not tell you about him."

My mouth falls open, but no words come out. I have a half brother? Until this moment I had no idea I had another sibling. After living so long without a family the thought that I might have more than Marie is incredible.

"You don't play fair," I tell him.

He waits me out as though he has all day, tapping his fingers on the desktop pinky to index finger over and over in a wave. I don't think I've met anyone more stubborn than Beau Hollis.

"Fine. Tell me about my brother."

"Are you sure? Don't want to cross any boundaries you're not comfortable with."

"You're mad about what I said earlier. About leaving."

"Hell yes I'm mad." He lets out a heavy sigh. "But there's nothing I can do about it, is there?"

"There's nothing *I* can do about it."

"Then don't fight me when I offer to help you. Maybe finding Marie could help change your situation."

"It won't. Nothing will."

"I didn't think my situation would ever change, but Cora didn't give up. She found a way I didn't even know existed."

His belief that he could somehow change things for me touches me more than he could ever know. I've never hand anyone in my corner before. He's become my knight in rusted, dented armor, offering to slay a very, *very* dangerous dragon. He has no idea what he's up against. The thought that he could get caught between Javier and me scares the shit out of me. He's been through so much. He deserves to live the rest of his life danger free. He sure as hell doesn't deserve the threat my secrets bring.

I take his face in my hands and kiss him. "I love that after all you've been through you still have hope."

"I don't rely on hope. I rely on what I *know* and what I can *do*."

"What do you know?"

"I know what it's like to have someone who believed in me when I didn't believe in myself. Someone who fought for me and never gave up."

"You want to be that someone for me?"

"I *am* that someone for you."

15

BEAU

She's killing me. Does she really think I'll leave her to fight alone? Has no one ever stood up for her? She looks at me like she can't believe I'm for real. I'm so motherfucking for real she has no idea. I don't know what her secret is. I may never know. But I can do my best to be someone she can confide in. I can support her and work for her and help her find her sister.

Can I save her?

I don't know.

I'm not like Cora. I don't have that kind of optimism. I sure as hell don't have anything resembling hope. What I do have is a shoulder she can lean on for as long as she needs it. I have the skills she needs to help reconnect her to her family. And I have nothing but free time to invest in seeing this through. Now if she'll only let me help her.

"Okay," she says, sounding very small and defeated. "Be my someone, but please, *please* don't get hurt."

I don't know what she means and I have a feeling the mystery behind it is locked in the vault with all of her other secrets.

"I won't," I answer.

It's a meaningless promise because I have no idea what I'm up against or how I could be hurt. The words seem to calm her so I leave them out there for her. We now have an agreement that doesn't really work for either of us, but it's the best we can do for the time being.

Taking advantage, I steal another kiss. The moment is meant to be light, but there's a heaviness around her that wasn't there before. By inserting myself into her life I've complicated it. She's thrown mine into a tailspin. Half the time I'm not sure which way is up and which way is certain disaster. I guess we're just going to have to deal with it in our own ways.

I pull the file I started on her brother out of the top drawer of my desk and open it for her. On top is his birth certificate. He's five years older than Vera and seven years older than Marie. I move his birth certificate to the side to reveal a marriage license.

"Your mother, Annabelle Marie Saint Claire, married Walter David Johnston. A year later their son, Eric Walter Johnston, was born. I didn't find any record of a divorce. I did, however, find another birth record." I pull a third document from underneath the marriage license. "A David Walter Johnston apparently had a daughter with a woman named Claire Johnston. Her name is Gwendolyn Marie Johnston." I watch Vera very closely. "That's you, isn't it?"

Her face goes pale and her eyes are huge on mine. She nods.

"You are Marie's sister just as you said. Your mom used a false name on your birth record. It took me a while to chase down my hunch. I was right to trust and believe in you."

She picks up her birth certificate and studies it as though she's never seen it before. Maybe she hasn't. Her mother wasn't exactly forthcoming with information or honest for that matter. I can't imagine Vera as a Gwendolyn. She'll always be Vera to me.

"Is this...could this Walter David or David Walter be my real father?"

"It's possible. That might be why your mom mixed up your parents' names on your birth certificate. She might've tried to hide your birth from him. There's no real way to know for sure unless you ask him."

"I can't believe this."

"I have addresses for them both if you want them. They live in Kansas." I hold out a sheet of paper with their contact info on it.

She pushes it away. "I can't do anything with that. I can't be Gwen ever again."

"I'll hold onto it for you. If you change your mind let me know."

She shakes her head. "I won't, but thank you." Her gaze drifts to the file. "I have a brother. And maybe a father."

"Yeah."

"Thank you."

"You're welcome."

"Would you... Is there somewhere you can put this?" She touches a finger to the papers. "Somewhere safe so no one else can ever find it?"

"Absolutely. Are you okay?"

She forces a brave smile. "I'm fine."

Cora opens the door and comes in. "Oh." She stumbles to a stop. "Hi, Vera." She gives me a look. "No one told me you were coming in this morning. I'm sorry I wasn't here. I take it Beau filled you in on the latest developments in your sister's case?"

I close the file and slide it into the top drawer. "We may

have another lead." I fill Cora in on what we found with the photo.

"That's good work," she says clearly impressed. "*Very* good work. We can talk to the employees in the stores to see if they know Marie or can tell us anything about her."

I don't mention my idea of staking out the shopping center. If Cora knew I was going to do that she'd want to bill Vera for our time.

"We can do that this afternoon after my appointment," I tell Cora.

"Thanks for reminding me. I almost forgot. The sooner we get your license current the sooner you can stop stealing my car and buy your own."

"She's teasing," I tell Vera. "I don't steal her car I *borrow* it."

Cora waves it away. "Potayto-potahto."

Vera stands and puts her bag over her shoulder. "I should go."

I walk her to the door. "I'll call you later and let you know if we find out anything at the shopping center."

"Thanks."

"Bye, Vera." Cora says.

Vera puts up a hand in response and goes out to the reception area. I watch her until she disappears around the corner.

Cora crosses her arms and gives me her *spill it* look. "What's going on with you and Vera?"

I avoid her gaze and sit down at my desk. "What do you mean?"

She closes the door. Shit. This is going to be a serious talk.

"I see the way you look at her."

Careful to make my expression neutral, I shrug. "I can't *not* look at her."

"Noooo." Putting her palms on my desk, she leans into my personal space. "You know what I mean. Like you've seen her naked or you want to see her naked."

My gaze sticks to my computer screen, but I don't see any of the words on it.

"Oh my god. You *fucked* her, didn't you?"

I pull out my rusty big brother voice and glare. "Don't talk like that."

"You're not denying it." She presses her fingers to her temples. "Holy shit, Beau. You could get fired for sleeping with a client. I vouched for you!"

"Sshh. Keep your voice down."

"*Why*? There are a million women in San Diego and you have to fuck a *client*?

"So the rules are different for Leo than they are for me?"

"I wasn't the client. *You* were."

"You were both employees. That's allowed?"

"Well, no, but that was different."

I stand and face off with her. "How?"

"We can't take her money if you're screwing her. That's just wrong."

"So don't take her money."

"Oh no. No you don't. We're not going there. End it. Now. Or I'm pulling you off the case."

I want to hit something. Preferably myself. In the face. Instead I strike the top of the desk. "Don't you dare do that, Cora."

"Don't make me do it."

"You have no idea what you'd be fucking up if you do."

"Enlighten me."

"I can't."

"I'm your boss. Give me a reason not to fire you."

"She's... I can't tell you. I promised."

"Let me get this straight." She props her hands on her hips. "You're choosing *her* over me and your job?"

"I'm not choosing anything. You're trying to force me to make a choice I can't and won't make."

"This isn't like you. Give me something here, Beau. Make me understand."

"Remember how you fought for me when no one believed in me and my innocence? Against mom and dad. Against the system that put me in prison for life. Against *everyone*?"

She nods, her lashing fluttering like she's fighting tears. I'm hitting her soft spot. I have to be careful not to hit it too hard.

"Vera needs a Cora. *I'm* her Cora."

"Why?"

"I can't tell you why and I'm so sorry for that. Please. Trust me."

She's wavering and she doesn't want to. "But do you have to sleep with her?"

"It just sort of happened. Neither one of us expected it. I don't know how to explain that part. It's too...big."

Tipping her head to the side, she considers me for a long moment. The corners of her mouth tilt into a reluctant almost smile. "That's actually the only part of this I think I *do* understand."

"Good. Then maybe you can explain it to me."

"No. I think this is one you're going to have to figure out for yourself."

"Yeah, well. I'm not sure that's possible."

The smile flees and she's back to frowning at me. "I'm worried about you, Beau. I probably shouldn't be, but I can't help it. I don't like these secrets. Are you sure about this girl?"

"She's the only thing I am sure of in all this."

"Be careful. I don't want to see you get hurt."

"I will."

She's the second woman today to have that concern about me. I wonder if maybe I should have it too.

16

VERA

I have a brother and maybe a father. I have them, but I can't *have* them. The irony of that would be funny if it wasn't so tragic. When I told Beau I couldn't be Gwen again I wasn't being overly dramatic. I won't get a reboot on my life like Beau did. When I left Gwen behind I left behind everything Gwen had or might have had. Even if we find Marie I can't be a sister to her. I can only make sure she's safe and then go back to my carefully managed life.

Alone.

I can't even have Beau. Even if I could take him with me he won't want to go. He's not going to understand why I made the decisions I made and why I live the way I do. When you've been hiding from something as long as I have there's no going back. The decisions I made affected more than just me. I can't and won't undo them. I have to live with that and it doesn't make me fit to have relationships.

Especially with someone like Beau.

I don't want to be selfish, having him for just now, but I'm so deprived I can't help myself. Our time together will have to last me the rest of my life. I'll never find someone like him again. He's the only person I've ever met who doesn't ask questions, who just *trusts*. That's a powerful draw for someone like me. I won't be able to walk away from him until I absolutely have to. Hopefully before he finds out my secret and why I will always be on the run. Because once it's out he won't be able to get past it. I'm on stolen time and I intend to take everything I can from of it.

I'm waiting outside my new hotel for Beau to pick me up. I have to keep moving. If I stay in one place too long it makes it easier to find me. The burner phone I've been using is broken in a dumpster with it's SIM card stripped. The SIM card is in pieces floating in a baggy of salt water in a different dumpster. I have a new phone now with a new number. That's why I memorized Beau's phone number. I lost all of our text messages when I ditched the phone. I'm sadder about that than I should be.

I also shouldn't be as keyed up as I am to see Beau. You'd think it's been days not hours since we've been together. Our phone call this afternoon wasn't enough to tide me over.

He pulls up to the curb and I get in the car. He immediately draws me in for a kiss. I can't read too much into that. I just enjoy the moment and the kiss. He's so good at it I want to go back for more and more. I make myself sit back and buckle my seat belt.

"Did you pass?" I ask.

His smile flashes in the darkened car and he holds up his temporary paper driver's license. "Yup."

"Oh my gosh. Let me see." I tilt it so I can read it by the streetlights we pass. "Your middle name is Reid."

"My dad's name."

"Nice. I like it. Beau Reid Hollis. It suits you. That was the hardest part for me, picking a new name."

"You'll always be Vera to me."

"You think I look like a Vera?"

"Yeah."

"I was worried it sounded too old fashioned."

He glances over at me. "You pull it off."

"Thanks."

"We talked to the people in the shops. Showed your sister's picture around. No one recognized her as a regular. One guy thought she looked familiar, but couldn't tell us anything about her. Maybe we'll get lucky tonight and she'll grab a latte or get her nails done."

I don't have much hope of that. The shopping center is next to the freeway. She could've stopped there on her way to or from somewhere else. We could be on a wild goose chase. But it's time with Beau so I'll take it while I can.

He parks the car across the street in the parking lot of a closed U-Haul store and cuts the engine. It's dark where we're parked so it's easy to see the lit up shopping center. There's some action, the usual comings and goings. We're about a half hour earlier than the time stamp on Marie's photo. But that doesn't mean anything. That night could've been the only night she was here.

"Are you hungry?" he asks, reaching into the back seat. "I brought sandwiches." He hands me a plastic bag. "They're both the same. Turkey and cheese on sourdough."

"You cooked for me?"

"I made sandwiches."

"That's cooking in my book."

"Yeah well, don't get too excited."

"Do you cook?"

"No, but I'm trying to learn. What about you?"

"Pretty much everyday. Eating out is expensive and it's a habit. I have to vary my routine so no regular takeout and definitely no delivery." I take a bite of sandwich. "This is good. It's spicy."

"Chipotle mayo. Cora smears it on everything. Makes things taste less bland. I'm glad you like it."

"What's your favorite food?"

"Pizza. What's yours?"

"Chinese. Specifically Kung Pao chicken. I've gotten pretty good at cooking in a wok."

"Yeah? Maybe you can teach me how."

"I'd love to."

It's a worthless offer. This is a future thing that requires planning. Future and planning are two words I don't have much association with and Beau knows it. This whole conversation is make believe. We may as well be talking about moving in together or where we'll vacation next summer. We ride out the fantasy anyway. It's a very nice fantasy.

"You're really good at finding needles in Internet haystacks. Do you like it?" I ask.

"Surprisingly, yeah. I'm not good with people like Cora. I prefer the behind the scenes work where I don't have to make conversation or have people staring at me wondering where they know me from."

"Awkward."

"Very awkward."

"It'll get better. People will move on to the next Internet sensation and forget all about you."

"I hope you're right."

"Will you do me a favor?"

He glances unexpectedly at me. "Sure?"

"I need you to go somewhere with me and I want you to promise you won't reject it without giving it a try."

"Sounds dirty."

"It's not. The dirty part can come later...pun intended."

He barks out a laugh. "Well when you put it like that..."

Almost three hours later the shops are closing up without a Marie sighting. I knew this was a lost cause, but I keep my thoughts to myself. It takes Beau another fifteen minutes to call it a night. I remind him of the favor he promised me and give him directions on how to get there. I'm not sure what his reaction is going to be. If he's going to think this is stupid and try to blow it off or give it a try. I'm not even sure it will do him any good, but I feel like he needs this.

We pull into the parking lot of a cemetery. I can feel it in Beau the moment he realizes what this is all about. The air around him vibrates with anger and the weightier emotion of grief. He turns the car off and sits back in his seat. I bet he's regretting that promise he made me.

I get out of the car and walk through the gate. Behind me a car door slams and reluctant footsteps approach. I use the light of my phone to check the info I jotted down. Three more rows up on the left. I turn off the road onto the thick grass. It's so quiet here at night. In the distance a dog barks. A balloon bats against a tombstone pushed by the breeze that makes the trees whoosh above us. There's no other sound except the soft crunch of our footfalls. I stop at a grave with a simple mixed bouquet stuck into a buried vase.

Cassandra's grave.

Beau stops a few markers away. When I turn to him, he's looking off into the distance, his hands shoved deep in his pockets, his shoulders hunched and hard. His jaw works with all of the things he's trying hard not to say. He won't look at the grave or me. I walk forward past the headstone to a little bench under a tree some ways away. Beau doesn't follow. I sit so I'm looking away from him over the graveyard. Moonlight and silence makes the scene eerily serene. I close my eyes and hope Beau accepts my gift. It might be the only thing I can give him—peace.

17

BEAU

I know why Vera brought me here, what she's hoping to accomplish. I'm supposed to find closure. My eyes won't focus through the anger and I can barely breathe for the fisting in my chest. Cassandra lays buried feet from me. This is the closest I've been to her since that night I kissed her goodbye. I can't reconcile these two things. This finality doesn't exist in my mind. Logically I know she's dead, but until now the reality of it never really hit.

I make myself walk closer until I'm standing at her feet. Her headstone pronounces her a cherished daughter, sister, friend. She was more than that, and, at times, less. I'm not supposed to be pissed at her, but I am. She wasn't perfect. I wasn't perfect, but what we shared was in its way. Until she ruined it. I hadn't forgiven her when she died. We were trying to work things out. The sex was easy and a way we could try to reconnect. But even as I kissed her goodbye I doubted I could get over what she'd done.

I didn't tell her that. I was going to the next time I saw her. I couldn't get the thought of her and my best friend,

Dylan, out of my head. There are some things you just can't work past I guess.

Dylan had a thing for her the whole time Cassandra and I went out. He didn't think I knew about it, but I did. What was I supposed to do? Give her up to him? I shouldn't have been surprised he'd make a move the minute we broke up, but I was. Cassandra and I had a terrible fight over it. I said some things I can't ever take back. I regret that.

Dylan sat in the courtroom during my trial several times. I knew he was there, but I never acknowledged him. He even tried to visit me in prison a few times. I left his name on the visitor's list just to fuck with him. As soon as I saw him I turned around and walked right back out. I let him believe there was a chance I'd forgive him one of those times. There wasn't. It was stupid and childish, but it was the only payback I could accomplish from prison besides tossing his letters in the trash unopened. He finally got the message and stopped the letters and visits.

I hope the guilt ate up his gut every single day.

That's an ugly thought to have standing over the grave of the woman who put herself between us. Whether it was intentional or not the result was the same. I lost my best friend and then I lost the only woman I ever loved within months of each other.

And then I lost my freedom.

I kneel in the damp grass. The knees of my jeans are soaked in a matter of minutes, but I don't care. I want to touch her one more time. I want to tell her I'm sorry. There is only the hard, cold granite of her headstone to talk to and six feet of earth between us to touch. The grass is unexpectedly cold against my cheek and the wetness seeps into the front of my clothes all the way to my skin. The blades of the grass poke through from between my fingers as her hair might if I could touch her. I close my eyes and breathe in the scent of the earth. It's nothing like how she used to smell. I can't seem to recall her scent exactly, but I know if I were to smell it again I'd recognize it.

I blame her for dying.

If she hadn't died I wouldn't have gone to prison and lost six years of my life. I wouldn't be in the shit storm I'm in, trying to rebuild my life. That's some fucked up shit right there. I hate myself for feeling this way. It's so *wrong*, but I can't seem to make myself stop. I know her death wasn't her fault. I *know* it, but that doesn't stop me from blaming her and only adds to the rage.

So many of my memories of her are contaminated by anger and grief. Even the good ones. *Especially* the good ones. I can't seem separate them. They're all tainted by what came after. I'm sorry about that most of all. I'm failing her in that way. She deserves better than me. She deserves someone like Dylan who probably put those fucking flowers on her grave and visits her on a regular basis. She doesn't deserve me who had to be tricked into coming.

All of these thoughts and more pour out of me and into the earth beneath me. I'm leaving everything here because I won't ever come back. I won't jab a bunch of flowers into the vase next to Dylan's. I won't show up on her birthday or the anniversary of her death. I won't stand at the end of her grave, trying to remember what she sounded like or how she smelled.

I rise slowly and look for Vera. She still sits on a bench a few feet away with her back to me to give me privacy. I head back to the car alone. After a few moments I hear her behind me. We climb in the car and drive away. On the way back to her motel we don't speak. There's nothing to say. I wonder at her thoughts the way I wonder a lot of things about her—futilely.

She opens the door of her new room and closes and locks it behind us. Her hands shake as she unbuttons my shirt, her focus on the task. I stand still and let her strip me. I can't seem to find the strength to do it myself. She drops to her knees, unlaces my shoes, and slips them off. The socks come next, then the pants. She takes my hand and leads me to the bathroom where she turns on the shower. When it's hot she pushes me in and closes the curtain. I stand under the spray, letting it wash away the chill from the damp ground. It washes away other things too.

The curtain reopens and Vera steps in wearing a bra and panties. She pours shampoo into her hand and motions for me to lean down. Her hands are firm and unhurried as she washes my hair then the rest of me. The numbness eases with each stoke of the washcloth. By the time she nudges me under the spray to rinse I'm feeling almost like myself again.

She reaches for the knob to turn the water off, but I stop her. Wrapping my arms around her from behind, I hold on, my face buried in her shoulder. There's so much I can't say. Not because I'm ashamed, but because I simply don't have the words. If I were a poet or an artist I might be able to express myself in some tangible way. My hands begin to rove in the only way I know to show what I can't say. I cup her breasts in both hands, drawing a gasp from her. Her head drops back against my shoulder. I work the bra clasp and in seconds my hands are full of her bare flesh. My dick pulses. I need it now. Hard and fast.

I slide a hand down between her legs. Slipping one then two fingers inside her wet heat, I can feel how she wants me too. Her hips move against my hand. She reaches up and wraps her arms around my neck. The view down her body is magnificent. Kissing and biting her neck, I bring her to the brink of orgasm. I need to be inside her so bad I rip the fabric separating us. She turns in my arms and lift her so her back presses against the tile. Her legs grip my waist. She pulls me down for a kiss so desperate it steals my breath. I didn't imagine she could need me as badly as I need her right now.

She tears her mouth from mine. "Inside me. Now."

Gripping my dick, I find her entrance and flex my hips up and into her. The sensation is almost overwhelming. Something urgent and primal takes over. My thrusts are deep and punishing. She urges me on with her cries. The sound of the water is drowned out by the harsh slap of flesh on flesh. Her fingernails dig into my shoulders, setting something off inside me. I come at her with renewed focus. Coming is my only thought. I'm rough. Maybe too rough. She digs her heels into my back and bites my chest. I go off, slamming into her one last time. I come hard. My knees nearly buckle at the intensity of it.

She shoves her hand between her legs and rubs. She's almost there with me. I replace her hand with mine, bending down to take her nipple in my mouth. She grips the back of my head. Her fist pulls my hair. She jerks and comes on a loud moan. I push into her, using my pelvis to press against her clit. The sound she makes is somewhere between a cry and a groan.

Her head drops back against the tile and the look she gives me causes my stomach to dip like I'm on a roller-coaster. A strand of her hair drips water into her eyelashes. I smooth it away, tracing the edge of her face with my finger. It's such a delicate face in contrast to her personality. I don't know what to do with her in moments like this. There's so much to say, but the words don't form. She's more expressive when she's quiet than I am talking all day long. We haven't spoken since I pulled into the cemetery parking lot and yet it feels like we've talked nonstop.

I reluctantly pull out of her and help her find her feet. We're both a little shaky. I turn off the water and grab a towel. I dry her with the same care she washed me, wrapping it around her when I'm done. I give myself a quick dry and help her climb out of the tub. The bathroom is so steamy I can hardly see where the door is. We make our way into the bedroom and that's when I see it. A tattoo on her shoulder. It's the same tattoo Marie posted a drawing of on her Tumblr. I was too drunk to have seen it before or else she positioned her body so I wouldn't see it not even in the shower just now.

Something about it pokes at me.

She discards her towel and climbs in bed. I stop a few feet into the room, my memory snagging on Marie's first mention of the tattoo and Vera's extreme reaction. The thought of it made her physically ill. And then again when Marie posted a photo of the drawing. She went totally white, scaring the shit out of me again. What does the tattoo mean and why does Vera have it? It's more than just a way for that asshole Javier to mark the girls he's been with. It means something. Something bad.

"What's wrong?" Vera asks.

What does your tattoo mean? sits on the tip of my tongue, but I don't say it.

"Nothing," I answer instead, taking off my towel and climbing into bed.

"Are you sure? You had a look just now."

"It was seeing you naked."

"And that confuses you?"

"Sometimes."

I pull her in the way she likes—her back to my front. I can't see the tattoo from here. She's laying on it. Clever girl. I shouldn't think that it's on purpose. I shouldn't and yet I do. I want a better look at it, but if I ask to see it up close she might react the way she did at the office. I don't want to do anything to upset her. There are other ways I could find out about it. I have Marie's drawing and the Internet. It would be a simple Google image search. If I go looking for information behind her back, how will Vera react? Not good probably. We have an unspoken pact about not prying into each other's past lives.

I can't help it. It's driving me insane. I *have* to know.

"What does your tattoo mean?"

Her whole body goes bow tight. I'm not even sure she's breathing. The silence in the room reverberates in my ears. Other than the holes where her piercings were it's the only mark on her. That has to have meaning. I'm taking a chance here that we've come far enough for her to trust me with what might be her biggest secret yet. Bigger than learning she's not who she claims to be and learning her real name. I may have seriously fucked this up by not keeping my damn mouth shut.

She rolls onto her stomach, her face buried in her pillow. I can see the tattoo very clearly now. I trace around the heart shape. Up close I notice that what I thought was just an intricate design is really a series of numbers. No a date. And a number. The key is in the shape of the letter J. I get the J part is for Javier, but what do the numbers mean?

She turns her face toward me. That look from the diner is back. I now recognize it as the place in her head where she deals with things that hurt. It's defensive, protecting who she is as a person from what's about to happen. I hate it. I wish I'd never opened my mouth. Why did I have to fucking pry? Why did I choose causing her pain over avid curiosity? I want to take the question back, but it's too late.

"September twenty-nine is the day I became his. Sixteen is my preferred number. My *chosen* number. The order in which I *acquired*. It's a way for him to keep track of his inventory. Girls with this tattoo sell for the highest price."

I can't process what she's telling me. I know all the words, but they don't seem to fit in my brain.

She comes up on her forearms and leans in until our noses nearly touch. Her gaze is hot and challenging on mine. *Figure it out,* it dares, *don't make me say it.*

I can't get my jaw to work.

"He sold my virginity to a Taiwanese business man who had the highest bid." Her voice isn't hers. Neither is the expression on her face. "Men paid hundreds, sometimes thousands of dollars to *fuck* me."

My body burns with a fevered mixture of anger, fear, revulsion, and revenge. I bleed for her. I want to kill for her. Mostly I want to stuff the words back in her mouth and make them not exist or pull them all out of her so that she doesn't have to carry them around anymore.

"What number am I to *you*?"

Her question confuses me.

"How much am I worth to *you*?"

She's not making any sense.

I sit up and glance around the room. It feels like forever ago we were in the shower. How did we get here? When I look back at her she's watching me over her shoulder with the tattoo, taunting me with it. Her smile is far from polite. It's almost predatory. This is another test.

And there's no way to pass.

18

VERA

I've had men look at me like I was a prize or like I could solve all their problems. They've looked at me like I was a toy or a dream come true. They've looked at me with pity, lust, disgust, blame, and shame. They've looked at me like they owned me and like I was nothing.

But they've never looked at me the way Beau is looking at me right now.

"That's not fair to either one of us," he says. His voice is careful yet determined. There's an anger burning just under the surface and sincerity woven throughout it. "What we *are* is not what either of us *was*."

He rips the rug out from under me. He doesn't let me torture him or myself. He sees things in me I didn't know were there. He delivers hope on a silver platter. Where he gets it from I don't know. Like a magician he pulls it from thin air and presents it to me as though I have a right to take a portion of it.

What I am is not what I was. It's not what he is. We aren't who we were before. I like that idea. I want it to be true. I tell him that.

"I want that to be true."

"What else do you want?"

"I want to not have to prepare for the worst."

"What else?"

"I want my sister to be safe. I want to meet my brother and father. I want a family."

"Is that all?"

"I want to stop running. I just want to stand still. I'm tired of temporary. I'm tired of always having to watch my back. I'm tired of being afraid *all the time*."

"Are you afraid right now?"

"No. I should be." I touch his hand. He follows the movement with his gaze. "You don't scare me."

"Really? Cuz you scare the shit out of me."

Again he surprises me.

He laughs at my shocked expression. "Ahh, Vera. You have no idea what you do to me, do you?"

He does things to me too.

His slow blink is followed by an even slower smile. There's something innocent and shy about it as though he read my thoughts. He lies down on his side next to me, pillowing his head on his hands. I do the same and we stare at each other. So many thoughts run through my head. It's like a stampede. I can't grab a hold of one. They slip by one after the other.

I told him my secret. Well, one of them. The one that shames me and makes me less. He's not looking at me like I'm less. He will though. He won't understand all of the things I've done and why I did them. The closer we get the scarier it is that he'll ask and I'll tell because I don't know how to be any other way with him. Maybe because I know he won't go looking for the answer on his own I can't lie to him. Even if it means I'll loose him.

"Why do you keep it?" he asks gently. "The tattoo?"

"I've thought about tattooing over it, but it would still be there underneath. Same with having it removed. It will never really go away. Even if it miraculously vanished tomorrow what happened to me won't."

"There's more isn't there?"

I nod. *So much more.*

"Okay."

His simple acceptance makes me want to tell him the rest. The words tremble in the corners of my brain, afraid to come out. I could push them forward, but I'm a coward. And I'm selfish. I want him for however long I can have him. If I tell him now, that will be the end. Beau can and has accepted more about me than any other person would, but I know his limits. He'll see this final piece as a betrayal. So I'll keep my mouth shut and hold on to whatever time I can get with him.

I touch a finger to one of his tattoos. "What does this mean?"

"Nothing. It's some stupid shit I put on my body because I was angry and it made me look the rest of the convicts."

"What about this one?"

"Same thing. They're all the same."

"Prison tattoos. Very tough."

"The best defense is a good offense."

"Was it very bad for you?"

"It was hell. Every day." He says it so matter-of-factly, but the look in his eyes is far from dispassionate. "I didn't think I'd ever get out."

"Neither did I."

"And yet here we are."

"Yeah."

The silence that descends around us is full of what-ifs.

What if one of us had gotten out and the other hadn't? What if neither of us had gotten out? What if I'd chosen another agency? What if he wasn't there the day I came in? What if we stayed away from each other like we should have?

"Do you think there's some greater purpose for everything we've been through?" I ask. "Some point to it all?"

"If there is I haven't seen it. Sometimes bad shit just happens to good people."

"Yeah, that's pretty much what I think too." I roll onto my back and stare up at the stained ceiling. "For a long time I fantasized about being rescued. After a while I stopped thinking about the future. I stopped thinking about anything at all. I made a place in my head where I could escape to where no one could reach me. It wasn't perfect. It cracked and shook. Every time that happened I'd build it back stronger than it was before. After a while it became solid and impenetrable." Closing my eyes, I push back at the memories that swell up inside me. "I hate it there."

"I hate seeing you go there."

Rolling my head to the side, I find him watching me with a fierce frown. I shift to my side and massage the crease between his brows with my thumb. He shouldn't worry over me like this. It won't change anything. He catches my hand and kisses the inside of my wrist. It might be the most erotic thing a man has ever done to me. I rise up, forcing him to his back. He still holds my hand in his. My breasts press against his chest. I like the way my skin feels next to his. Bringing my leg over his, I straddle him. The sheet falls, exposing me. His thumb traces back and forth over the spot he kissed. The connection in our gazes is a touch that moves over every part of me.

I lied when I told him he didn't scare me. But it's a good kind of scary. It's the kind that makes me hope and want. We put our palms together, lacing our fingers. He tugs me down for a kiss. Our lips meet. It's a gentle, testing sort of kiss that quickly gets out of control. We unclasp our hands, the need to touch overwhelming. I thread my fingers through his hair. He runs his hands down my back, then up before banding his arms around me. There's a strength in him that I need. Like an open source of bravery I can tap into when my supply gets low.

I lift my head and look down at him, smoothing the hair back from his face. It's a good face, a handsome face. It's become as familiar to me as my own so I know when something isn't right with him like now. His brow is smooth, but there's trouble in his eyes.

"What's wrong?" I ask.

"Nothing."

"Don't bullshit me."

"It's not something wrong. It's something I've been thinking."

"And that is...?"

"This is going to be over as soon as we find your sister, isn't it?"

I don't answer. I don't make promises or conjure false hope. Instead I kiss him. We have now. That's going to have to be enough. He rolls us so he's on top. I like the weight and feel of him on top of me and the way he looks at me when we're like this. His touch is gentle, almost reverent. Everything slows. Discovering caresses. Long open mouthed kisses. I can't get enough of him. He slides into me and it's perfect. We rock together. This isn't the same frenzied coupling of before. It's deliberate. Each of us trying say what can't be said out loud.

I bring my legs up, trying to take him deeper. I want more of him. I want everything he's got, everything I don't deserve. In return I give him everything I've got. I don't have any other experiences to compare this to. It's all new. His thrusts become more insistent, more demanding. I'm right there with him. God he feels so good. He sucks my nipple into his mouth and I lose my mind, writhing beneath him. He makes a growling sound and lunges at me harder. It's his name I shout when I come. He buries his face in my neck and thrusts one last time, driving as deep as he can go.

His breath is hot against the side of my face, drying the tears that somehow leaked out of the corners of my eyes. I was an idiot to think this could just be a for-now thing or that I could walk away any time. It's complicated and messy and necessary. He smoothes away my tears with his thumbs, his gaze steady and understanding on mine. Every minute with him makes it harder and harder to be me. I wish I could be someone else for him. Someone who will stay. Someone who can offer more...more than just now.

19

BEAU

I'm in full search mode. I left Vera's room at the ass-crack of dawn to pry Cora out of bed so we could get to the office extra early this morning. After last night I've got a fire under my ass to get to Marie before that bastard marks her like he did Vera and sells her virginity to the highest bidder. I spent most of the morning learning what I can about sex trafficking. What a fucking nightmare. Who knew that shit went on right under everyone's noses? Third world countries sure, but not in the middle of the United fucking States. If I ever get my hands on that asshole they'll have a real reason to put me away this time.

I also got Cora to agree to put the newest agent at the office, Nolan Perry, at the shopping center Vera and I staked out last night. I'm hoping we'll get lucky there. We have almost no leads on this girl. Her Tumblr is the only link we have to her. I've been stalking it and her other social media accounts nonstop. Something's got to pop. It's got to. We're on an impossible time clock here with someone else moving the hands.

I lay awake next to Vera most of the night, my mind spinning. Finding Marie means possibly losing Vera. I only know a portion of her story. There's a big piece she's not sharing with me and she's not likely to give it up. I went through a thousand scenarios, trying to figure out what it could be, but came up with nothing. All I can do is move forward, keep looking.

Cora's glances at me are full of worry. It's driving me fucking nuts. I'd tell her I've got this, but the truth is I don't. I don't have a fucking handle on anything right now. I don't know how to explain any of this to her when I don't understand any of it myself. She doesn't get the sudden urgency and I can't tell her. Not in a way that makes sense. Not without betraying Vera. And I'd never do that.

I have too few clues to track down. Javier Abano is a fucking ghost. If that's even his real name. There's no record of his birth, ever having lived in the San Diego area, having a California driver's license or anything else real people do. The J in the tattoos is the only real clue I have to go on. It could stand for just about anything, but from what I've learned about him so far I know it's personal. He takes the time to select and groom his high-end girls. He takes pride in his stock, acquiring only the best, most desirable girls. He marks them with a fucking inventory bar code.

How do you find a guy who seems to fly under the radar of every police and government agency?

I do an image search using key words to describe Vera's tattoo. At first I get nothing. So I refine my search using new key words. It takes several tries and scrolling through pages of unhelpful images before I get a hit. One here, one there, one a little further down. I mark all of the sources and start with the first one. It's from Pinterest. I click on the image and find that it was re-pinned from another account. Following the re-pins back, I discover what I think might be the original account it was posted to. I bookmark the account and add it to the bookmark file labeled 'tattoo'. Going back to the original search, I click on the next link.

It's tedious work, but after a few hours I have some solid leads that include websites for tattoo artists and parlors, social media accounts, and blogs. Vera was number sixteen. According to the photo Marie posted, she'll be number fifty-three. If Marie's sudden social media black out is anything to go on, Javier learned to clamp down on his prospects' Internet usage. But he wasn't as careful early on. I found four tattoos with numbers lower than Vera's—two, seven, eleven, and fourteen. I figure he got better as he went a long. If there are going to be any clues about this asshole the early girls will likely be the ones to give them to me.

I try not to think about what happened and what is happening to these girls who are now women. I need to focus and think logically. Flying around in a blind rage, punching walls won't help them and it won't help me find Marie. But I can't help but think of Vera and what she went through. It's why we're looking for her sister. It's time to have a much more detailed conversation with Vera and ask her some difficult questions. As one of the early girls she might have useful information and not even realize it.

It's also time to share what's going on with Cora. I need help. There's no one I trust more in this world than Cora. Once she knows the whole story I know she'll fight as hard for Marie as she did for me. I have to tell Vera my plan. It's her story too. I send her a text, laying out some of the work I've done and asking her permission to confide in Cora. She doesn't respond right away like she usually does. I don't have to tell her time is kicking our ass and that we're working against an unknown countdown clock. She knows all of this. It was difficult for her to share her story with me. It's going to be torture to share it with Cora.

After twenty minutes of silence I get this text: I trust you.

Those three words pack a powerful punch. I might be the only person in the world she says them to. She's one of two people I can say them to. I text her back and tell her that I trust her too. She responds with a kiss emoji. I set my phone down to stop myself from keeping the conversation going. There's so much more to say, but I need to fill Cora in so we can get started sorting through the leads I found.

"I need your help," I say to Cora as I shut our office door.

I sit on the edge of her desk and tell her about everything—Javier, the tattoo, the girls, Marie's Tumblr posts, Vera. When I finish Cora sits back in her chair with an amazed sort of dazed expression. She doesn't speak for several long minutes. Finally she gets up from her chair and puts her arms around me. It takes me a sec to react. Not many people have touched me in the past six years so unexpected physical contact still takes me by surprise. If she notices, she doesn't let on.

She pulls back and grips me by the shoulders. "I'm so proud of you. Oh, don't look so surprised. You've done amazing work on this case."

"Thank you."

"I knew there had to be more going on here, but you were so secretive I was worried. And then the drinking and the affair... I didn't know what to do. I can't believe all of that is happening right here in San Diego."

"I've identified four other girls. I need your help to track down clues about this asshole. I want to know where he is and how he operates. I think the girls will tell us."

"Give me what you've got. I'll get on it right away."

I send Cora the info on eleven and fourteen and then start with number two—a girl named Barbara Moore. Barbara disappeared eight years ago from her foster home here in San Diego. She's described as troubled, having multiple run-ins with the law and bouncing around in the system. It's assumed she ran away and after the first couple of weeks she stops appearing in the news. A missing fifteen-year-old in foster care doesn't hold interest I guess.

Barbara posted a photo of her tattoo to Facebook shortly before her disappearance. Not a drawing like Marie's. An actual photograph. I extract the location of where the picture was taken and add notes to my file to follow up on later. Then I delve into the world of Barbara Moore, a pretty, blond, sophomore in high school, who likes the Foo Fighters, the Twilight saga, Starbucks, Pringles, and Southpark. There are quite a few posts about a mysterious man she met. She calls him Jay. This might be the first real clue as to what Javier's real name is. Or not. It's too early to tell.

Jay sweeps her off her feet. He's attentive, tells her she's beautiful, and spends time with her. He's more sophisticated than guys her age. He's interested in her and the things she's interested in. He even takes her to a Foo Fighter's concert. The dates of the posts get further and further apart the closer to her disappearance. I go back to the first few times she mentions 'Jay'.

She met him at the Starbucks near her high school. He struck up a conversation with her. Next thing she knew she missed her first period class so she just stayed and talked to him. He was a good listener. They exchange phone numbers. Texts and phone calls escalate to ditching school and staying out past curfew. The posts follow a similar pattern as Marie's. He isolates her, makes her fall in love with him, and controls her world. She's a virgin just like Marie is and Vera was. She talks about finally going all the way with 'Jay' and him wanting her to be as in love with him as he is with her. Exactly like Marie.

It makes me want to hurl.

Putting blue pins in a map on the wall, I keep track of the locations Barbara mentions meeting with 'Jay'. I add a white pin to the location where Marie took the photo of the tattoo drawing. Moving on to the next girl, I go through the same thing this time using green pins in the map. Cora adds yellow pins for number eleven and red for number fourteen. It takes us all day to map out an area that's approximately twenty by twenty-five miles—Javier's hunting ground.

Marie's pin is near the upper left corner so we're pretty sure he's still in the same area if not just outside. I create a separate search for girls age fourteen to eighteen who were in foster or group homes and went missing from the time Barbara disappeared until now—one hundred and eight in just over a ten-year period. Not all of them are Javier's victims, but there are just too damn many. Tomorrow we're going to divide the list and search each name individually.

This fucker has a pattern. I can see it. It's possible he has a source in child services who is helping him find and target these girls. They're all described the same way—troubled, incorrigible, violent, defiant, at risk behavior, failing in school, hard to place, and in some cases there's notes about drug or alcohol abuse. They all have parents who are either deceased or incarcerated and no older siblings or other relatives in their lives.

They're the perfect fucking victims. No one would look very far or long for them and there's no one to ask questions or care if they disappeared.

He also has a type and Marie breaks it. All four of the

girls we found who posted about the tattoo were white—two brunette, one redhead, and one blond. Vera is white, but her sister is half white and half black. They're also the only siblings he's targeted. None of the other girls had a sister who also vanished. Why is he breaking type with Marie? Why her? Could it because of Vera? Could it be a way to draw her back to him or to get back at her for breaking free of him?

I need a lot more information if I'm going to find Javier and I'm going to have to ask Vera some very difficult questions tonight. She's the only one of the girls we can actually talk to. She's not going to like it, but she might know more than she thinks she does. She might be the key to finding Marie and maybe the other girls as well. I text her and ask her to come to the office.

There's a knock on the office door. Savannah pokes her head in. Her gaze immediately goes to me. "Vera Swain is here to see you."

I just sent the text.

"Were you expecting her?" Cora asks.

"Send her in," I tell Savannah.

Savannah disappears.

I hold up my phone for Cora. "I just barely texted her and asked her to come. She hasn't even responded yet."

"I wonder what's up."

There's another knock and then Vera comes into the room. I stand. She closes the door after her and walks straight toward me, ignoring Cora. Her eyes are huge and her hands shake. I take them in mine and tug her toward me. She presses her face into my shirt. Holding her to me, I can feel how tightly strung she is. Over her head I catch Cora's crossed arms and raised brows.

"What's wrong?" I ask Vera.

She pulls back and looks up at me, her eyes pooling with tears. I've never seen her cry. Not like this. Shit. It's bad.

I take her face in my hands. "What is it?"

"She got the tattoo."

Behind her Cora gasps, her hand going to her mouth. She knows what this means. We're too late. I can't take my eyes off Vera. She cracks me in two. Tears stream down her cheeks and she looks at me like she's lost.

I can't accept that it's too late. It can't be. "We'll find her."

"He's going to start the auction."

"We'll find her," I repeat. "We will."

She shakes her head. "He's going to her isolate now. Take her somewhere. She's going to think it's romantic. He's prepping her." She covers her face with her hands. "So she won't fight the winner. She won't fight at all."

Cora slips out the door, leaving us alone. I don't know what to say to Vera so I just hold her. She doesn't break down. Her tears are silent, soaking the front of my shirt. They don't last long. She's not one to linger on useless emotion. She breaks out of my embrace and swipes at the last of her tears. Taking a deep, determined breath, she paces away and sheds what's left of her anguish. When she turns back to me, it's like the last few minutes didn't happen. If it weren't for the redness around her eyes and the wet spot on my shirt I'd think I imagined it.

"You wanted me to come down here," she prompts.

I try to put it as gently as possible. "We need to talk about what happened to you."

She nods, pulls a chair over to my desk, and sits down, waiting for me to recover my shit and get with the program.

I join her at my desk. "Is there anything you haven't told me that might help us find Marie? Maybe something that seems like nothing?"

"I've been going over and over everything. I was alone a lot of the time. When he moved me it was always at night and I was blindfolded so I couldn't see where I came from or where I was going."

"I found four girls who came before you. They all have the same tattoo with different numbers." I bring up the photos of the girls on my computer and point to each one in turn. "Barbara Moore, Kaley Riccio, Rosalyn Bauer, and Kiersten Paulie."

She taps Kiersten Paulie's photo. "I know this girl. She had a different name though. We were all given new names. Hers was Ariel like The Little Mermaid. Probably because of her red hair. We worked together a few times." She stares at the screen as she says this so I can't read her expression.

"Tell me about her."

"There's not much to tell. It's not like we sat around chatting and painting each other's nails. We fucked guys together." She rubs her forehead and lets out a sigh. "I'm sorry. That's not helping."

"Would you be more comfortable talking to Cora than me?"

"No." She tears her gaze from the screen. "Why? You don't want to hear about all the twisted shit I had to do?"

"There's nothing you could tell me that would change my opinion of you."

"Nothing?"

I shake my head.

She considers me for a moment no doubt trying to decide if I'm bullshitting her or not. I'm not. We both had to do some fucked up shit to survive.

"Keep going," she finally says. "Tell me what else you found."

I show her the info I've gathered so far about the other

girls and the map with all the pins on it. I tell her my theory about a possibility of a connection to child services. When I'm done she sits back in her seat. She looks weary, exhausted. I take her hand and run my thumb across her knuckles.

"We're going to find her," I vow, hoping I'm right.

20

VERA

"Somehow I believe you will," I tell Beau. If anyone can find Marie it's him. "You're too damned stubborn to allow anything else to happen."

He laughs and brings my hand to his lips to kiss the back. "If only I could've stubborned my way out of prison."

"If anyone could have it would've be you."

"Thanks." He stares down at our joined hands, his mood turning serious again. "I need to ask you more questions about your life before and during the time you met Javier."

I expected this. In an odd way I want it. I saw a counselor briefly just after I first escaped. Talking about it helped, but I couldn't give too many specifics. Even though I was living under a different name at the time it was still too great a risk. Javier has powerful allies. One of my regulars was an asshole cop who liked to brag as he fucked about all the power he had, what a big man he was. He was a fucking sadist coward who could only get off when I screamed in pain. There were more. Rumors about someone in the District Attorney's office, politicians, businessmen—powerful men—fucking underage girls.

That's why when I ran I had to run far and fast and change everything about me from my looks to my name to my habits.

"What do you want to know?" I ask Beau.

"Everything you can think of. Where you went to school, who you lived with, who your friends were, who your social worker was, that sort of thing."

"My social worker was Ramon Diaz. Before him I had Cindy Zimmerman. I don't remember who was before her. I got kicked out of high school for ditching so I went to a continuation school. I lived in a group home that sucked, but it was better than the one I was in before. I moved around so much I didn't have any friends except for Jordan. We got moved to the group home at the same time. He was the first guy I ever kissed. We got caught and they moved him to another home. I had to go to pregnancy prevention classes because I was suddenly 'at risk'.

"My mother was a whore so they were worried I was going to turn out like her. They were right. I turned out just like her."

"It wasn't your choice."

"No. But what's the difference? The result's the same. Do you feel less like an ex-con because you didn't actually commit the crime you went to prison for?"

"No."

"See? There's no difference."

"Wait a minute. You said something about pregnancy prevention classes."

"Yeah."

He grips his mouse and clicks around until he finds what he's looking for. "Barbara Moore took classes like that." He points to the screen. "She called them a joke since she was still a virgin. And here..." He does some more clicking, bringing up a blog. "Kaley Riccio's boyfriend got caught with his hand up her shirt and she had to go to classes. The same with Rosalyn Bauer and Kiersten Paulie. All of you took pregnancy prevention classes for 'at risk' girls. Where did you take your classes?"

"A room in the Family and Youth Center downtown. They even had a van that picked us up and took us there."

His hands are wizard hands on the computer keys. Screens pop up and down like jackrabbits. I can't keep up with what he's doing so I sit back and watch. A myriad of micro expressions flicker across his face. He's probably not even aware he's doing it; he's concentrating so hard.

"Do you remember the names of any of the girls you took the classes with?" he asks, not taking his eyes off the screen.

"A few."

He pushes a tablet toward me, still focused on the computer. "Write down their names for me."

I flip through pages of notes he's made on my sister's case, mesmerized. He's taken tiny, nothing bits of information and turned them into real leads and threads to follow. How he found those other girls...amazing. And the map on the wall. He's finding patterns, connecting dots. I only hope we get to Marie in time.

I think back to those stupid pregnancy prevention classes they made me take. If they only knew how pointless they'd end up being for me they might not have wasted their time. I wonder if they kept any of the other girls from getting pregnant. There were eight of us in the class I went to, but I only got friendly with two of them—Carrie Bennett and Sasha Dixon. The others kept to themselves mostly. Especially the twins. They didn't socialize with any of us. Tracy and Stacy Casey. I remember them because of their stupid names. Who makes their kids names rhyme?

I write down the four names and concentrate hard on coming up with more, but I can't remember. It was a long time ago. So much has happened since then. I thought my life sucked when I was taking those classes. I had no idea how much worse it could get.

"What was the name of the organization that put on the classes?" Beau asks.

"Christian Youth Ministries or something like that."

"Was it Youth Encounter Christian Ministry?"

"Yeah, that's the one. Why?"

He directs my attention to the computer. "Youth Encounter Christian Ministry helps foster and refugee young women see their potential, practice healthy behaviors, and prevent teen pregnancy by teaching life skills and giving the girls a sense of purpose."

"Yeah we sewed and did crafts and shit while they talked to us about making good life choices. Clearly it worked."

"Was this woman in charge when you were there?" He points at the photo of a woman with a lace, collared blouse, pearls, and tightly held back hair. "Is she who you emulated your new look after?"

She's exactly who I was trying to look like minus the long hair tied back into a tight bun. Emmaline Markham.

I nod. "She was the only woman who ever seemed to care about me. We talked a lot. She was the reason I started getting good grades and getting my shit together."

"Did she spend the same kind of time with the other girls in the class?"

"She interviewed each of us when we first started the classes, but I was the one she talked to the most. I don't know. We just sort of hit it off. She was really nice. She made me feel less like a freak for being in foster care. A couple times she took me home after class when I stayed behind to help her prepare the materials for class the next day."

He goes back to pounding the keyboard and clicking the mouse. There's a determined set to his mouth. He squints at the screen. Shakes his head. Does some more clicking and up pops a photo of one of the girls he showed me earlier with Emmaline.

"She got close to Rosalyn Bauer too," he says. "I found this photo on Rosalyn's Facebook page. I bet I could find a connection between Emmaline Markham and the other girls too. Emmaline took an interest in them, culled them from the group, and told Javier about them."

"No. She wouldn't do that."

"Her and the classes are only links I can find between you and the other girls who had the tattoo and disappeared. That's not a coincidence."

"She wouldn't do that."

"I know you don't want to believe it, but how else do you explain it?"

I open my mouth, expecting my brain to come up with something—*anything*—that will prove Emmaline's innocence, but nothing comes out. He's right. It is too big a coincidence to be a fluke. My mind spins with the realization that the time I spent with Emmaline was all a lie. All of those questions she asked, making me think she was *so* interested in me, that she *liked* me, that I was worthwhile to *someone* was all to steal my life from me and send me straight to hell. How could I have been so fucking gullible? I told her things I've never told anyone else. The only other person I've confided in to that extent is Beau.

He watches me work through it all, waiting patiently, never judging. No one was ever there for me the way he's there for me. No one ever got me the way he gets me. I don't know what he gets out of being with me, but I know it's no where near what I've gotten out of being with him.

"I'm so sorry," he says, squeezing my hand. "What she did was fucking cruel to you and the other girls."

"A part of me wants to keep denying it, but the other part just can't. The evidence is too overwhelming. God, I was such a fucking idiot. I thought she was my friend. I thought he was in love with me. How could I have been so stupid?"

"You were young and needed someone to love and believe in you and you had no one. You and the other girls were the perfect targets. Like shooting fish in a barrel. Those assholes took advantage of you. It's not your fault. They're pros. They knew what to say to get you and the others to believe them."

"Still. I don't know. I thought I knew it all when I was fourteen. I didn't know shit."

"None of us did. You're not supposed to. That's what the adults are for. To help us. Only the adults in your life failed you."

"An understatement."

"The thing that's been driving me bat shit crazy during all this is, why would Javier go after Marie? She doesn't fit with the type he seems to prefer. She's not white and she has a sibling—you—who might come looking for her. Emmaline didn't vet her. She breaks type. I can't see him taking a chance on her unless he had a damn good reason. I keep going back to—why her?"

"To get back at me for escaping? To replace me? Who the hell knows why?"

I do know why. He's hoping to draw me out. He doesn't want her. He wants me.

"Something about it just doesn't sit right." He goes back to working the keyboard.

I stand and pace away. I can't sit still. Beau is right. He's breaking type for a *very* specific reason. I was such an idiot to think I could find Marie and get away. I never should've come back here. I never should've told Javier about Marie. God, I was so, *so* stupid. I should disappear like I told Beau I might. Go back where it's safe, where no one will get hurt.

"You told Javier about Marie after you were together for a while, didn't you?" he asks. "Just before you got the tattoo."

"Yes."

"Did you tell Emmaline about her?"

"No."

"By then it was too late." He stands and comes toward me. "He was already prepping you. He probably didn't think a younger half sibling with a different last name could be much of a threat. He'd invested too much time to walk away."

I take a step backward then two. "What point are you making?"

"He went after Marie specifically with a goal in mind." He comes at me until I hit a bookshelf. "He's not the kind of asshole who would risk his whole operation for revenge. That's not what this is about." He leans in as I lean back. "What *is* it about, Vera?"

"I don't know what you mean."

"What made you run when you did? Why didn't you take off sooner? Why did you escape at all?"

"I had to." I put my hands on his chest and push at him. "I couldn't stand it anymore. I couldn't let one more stranger *fuck* me."

Shaking his head, he eases up, but doesn't back off. "That's not the real reason."

"Why do you care? What does it matter?"

"Because this has been about something else all along. Sure it's about finding your sister, but it's also about you." He cradles my face in his hands. "Tell me what it is that's got you so fucking terrified you're backing away from me like I'll hurt you."

I break out of his hold and step around him. Rubbing my arms, I move to the other side of the room. He doesn't follow. He just watches me with that patient Beau gaze that tears at my defenses.

"The one thing I really like about you besides the sex is that you don't ask a lot questions," I say. "Why change?"

"Because I've gotten more info on this case from girls on the Internet than I have from you and I'm starting to get fucking sick of it."

"I don't know anything else that will help find Marie. What does it matter *why* he's going after her? He's after her. That's all you need to know."

"I also need to know why we started this between us when you're going to bail any minute and I don't get to know why. I just get left behind. I'm sick of getting left behind. Cassandra fucking left me and now you're going to do it too. I know it has something to do with Javier and the reason you ran, changed your name, and your appearance. *Why*?"

"I *can't*. Please stop asking me."

"You're the only fucking person who gets me." He pounds his fist over his heart. Misery grinds his voice, making the edges rough. "That means something to me."

"You get me too. I know you do. Please try to understand. I'd give you more if I could. I'd give you fucking everything. But I can't give you this. Please. Let it go."

Growling, he shoves his hands in his hair and presses his palms against his eyes. I hate seeing him like this. I hate that

I brought him to this. I go to him and pull his arms down so I can see his face. Lacing my fingers with his, I try to get him to look at me. He's pissed at me, but that's not all he is. He's hurt. The anger and frustration I can handle. The thought that I cause him pain shames me. He's been nothing but good to me even when he had no reason to be.

I kiss him. He doesn't respond right away and then he wraps his arms around me still holding my hands in his and kisses me back. It's a conciliatory kiss. I won, but I don't feel like a winner.

I 've run a thousand scenarios through my mind about what Vera isn't telling me. I have a feeling they're not going to come anywhere near the actual truth. And if I keep pressing her she'll give something away without meaning to and I'll finally have a clue to chase. Other than her real name. I've been tempted so many times to search it. I know I'll find something if I do. The look on her face when I told her I found her is the only reason I haven't. Stark terror. That's the only way to describe it. I can't be the one to put that look on her face again.

So I give in. I won't search for the truth. I'll stop asking her why. I'll focus on the girls and finding Marie. The closer we get the closer I am to losing Vera. But I can't think about that. I sure as hell can't think about that when I'm kissing her. I can't think about much at all except kissing her more. She fits so perfectly against me. With her arms behind her, her breasts thrust forward. I fucking love her tits. I fucking love everything about her. I can't think straight for the thoughts she puts in my head. Like now when she's trying to be so sweet and distracting.

It's working. I am distracted. Or maybe I just want to be. I don't want to look in the dark corners of her life any more than she wants to shine a light on them. But the time might come when that's no longer an option and I'll have to press her and make her tell me. And it's looking more and more likely that will be sooner rather than later.

"Fine," I tell her, breaking the kiss. "You win."

"This isn't a contest."

"I know that. I won't keep pressuring you. Is that what you want to hear?"

"Thank you."

"Don't thank me. Let's find Marie and then we'll see where we are." I release her and go back to my chair before I end up bending her over Cora's desk. My will power is shit where she's concerned.

She follows me and sits back down in her chair. The sideways glances she keeps sneaking while I work are filled with regret. She's not any happier than I am about the line she's drawn. That's the only bright spot because it shows I'm not wrong about her. She's a good person in a fucked up situation. I know what that's like. I can't fault her for trying to protect herself even from me. It's hard to share the worst shit with the people you want to think the best of you. I get that. I get her.

The more I dig into the four other girls with the tattoo the more I'm convinced Emmaline is the key. Shortly after finishing their pregnancy prevention classes they all met Javier or Jay or Daddy or whatever it is they call him. They're swept off their feet, romanced, paid attention to. Then the tattoo, then they disappear. The pattern repeats with all the girls, including Vera, and with the exception of Emmaline not vetting Marie.

We need to talk to Emmaline. She could lead us straight

to Javier. This is where I need to bring Cora back in. She and the other investigators are much more skilled than me in interviewing people. I'd have a hard time being calm if I met her. What she did to Vera and the other girls is fucking sick. Who does shit like that?

I go get Cora to bring her up to date on the new information we found. Vera gives up her seat to Cora and wanders over to the map with all the pins. As I fill Cora in, I watch Vera study the map out of the corner of my eye. Cora asks me a question and I look away to answer her. It takes me a few minutes before I bring my attention back to Vera. When I do I see her pick up a pin. She stares at it for a moment, glances at the map, then back at the pin again before sticking it in the map.

"What's that pin for?" I ask.

She flinches at my question. At first I'm not sure if she's going to answer. She looks at the map again then back at me. "It's where I escaped from. The last house he kept me in. It's the only one I know the location of."

Cora and I get up from the desk and go to the map. Vera stuck the black-headed pin in almost the exact center of the area where all of the other pins are.

"What's the address?"

"11841 Plymouth Drive."

I plug the address into a real estate site that will tell me who owns the property. It was sold three years ago, right about the time Vera escaped. I check the record before that. Conrad Investments, Inc. was the previous owner. I switch windows and search the California Secretary of State's website for that corporate name. Bingo. I get a name of the agent for service of process and an address.

"Do the names Conrad Investments, Inc. or Chad Perez ring a bell?" I ask Vera.

"No. I knew very little about the people who kept me captive. They never used names. We called the head guy Sergeant and the others Sir or Private. If we needed a doctor we called him Doctor. We weren't people. We were property. I had very little interaction with the other girls. Even then we were brought together for a job and separated right after. The rooms were monitored so there was no way we could communicate with each other. I'm sorry I can't be more help."

"Don't be. That pin is another lead to follow." I go to LinkedIn and pull up Chad Perez's profile. "Come here," I tell Vera. "Does this guy look familiar?"

She leans over my shoulder. "No. Not at all."

"I'd be surprised if he did. I need to look more closely at what Conrad Investments, Inc. does. I have a feeling it's a shell corporation and we're going to have to dig a lot deeper to find out who really used that house. Cora—" I turn to my sister. "—we need to interview Emmaline and this Chad guy at Conrad. First thing tomorrow."

"I'll get right on it. I think it would be best if Mr. Nash tackled Emmaline. She's going to need the lighter touch of someone with more experience than me. I can take Nolan with me to talk to the guy at Conrad. Chances are this guy is just a pencil pusher and has no idea what went on in that house. I think I know just the angle to take with him." Cora puts her hand on mine over the mouse. "It's late. Why don't the two of you take off, get something to eat? You can work on this some more tomorrow."

I start to argue, but Cora gestures with her head toward Vera who is studying the map as though it's a viper preparing to strike. I know a little bit about the memories that pin represents. The deeper we get into this the more

Vera's had to share her past and it's starting to take its toll on her.

"Yeah. Okay. I didn't realize how late it was. Why don't we walk you to your car?"

Cora gathers her stuff while I save my searches and make a couple of notes for tomorrow. All the while Vera is quiet, keeping herself separate.

Cora lays her hand on Vera's arm. "I'll only tell the guys the necessary information to get the job done. What's been said in this room stays in this room."

"Thank you."

We all walk out to the parking lot. I make sure Cora gets in her car safely and watch as she drives off. It's the first time I make the assumption I'm going with Vera to her motel room. Does that make this a relationship? What does that make us? She doesn't comment as we climb in her car and she pulls out of the parking lot. Instead of turning left she turns right. The last time she took me someplace unexpected was to Cassandra's grave. I wonder what she has in mind this time.

We drive for a while and then it hits me that we're in the area on the map where all the pins are. I force myself to stare straight ahead and not have any reaction. I know where she's taking me. What I don't know is why. This is her trip, her point to make. I'm just going to have to ride it out with her and see where it takes us. She's quiet during the drive, but I know her mind isn't. I can practically hear the words scrambling in her brain. My pulse kicks up in response to hers as we turn onto Plymouth Drive. She makes a U-turn and parks across the street from the house where she was held captive.

I can't see her face, only a portion of her profile. Glancing past her, I stare at the house where her nightmare ended. It's ordinary, like the others on the street. A dark barks. A dad waters his lawn. A teenager washes his car in the driveway. A runner jogs by. Amongst all this normalcy a monster sold girls into sexual slavery. Didn't anyone wonder about the cars that came and went? How only men entered and exited the house? Didn't they notice *anything*? All it would've taken was one person, one nosey neighbor to save those girls, to save Vera.

My mouth fills with the bitter taste of frustration and anger, my whole body vibrates with it. I can only imagine what Vera's feeling. How many times did she hope to be rescued before she gave up? What did it take for her to finally free herself? How was she able to do it and the others weren't? Where did she go? The questions keep piling up, but I don't voice them. She brought me here for a reason and it wasn't to cure my curiosity.

"My room was upstairs. The window on the right," she says, pointing at the house. "It was boarded up with curtains over top so the men wouldn't notice. Sometimes it was hard to tell when it was night and when it was day. They made two rooms out of one to house more of us. I don't know who was in the other half. We never saw each other.

"I always knew when it was Monday. Those were the busiest days. Something about the weekend not working out for them maybe. I don't know. They all didn't come for a fuck. Some just wanted someone to talk to. I hated them the most. Stupid, right? But it's like, why the hell should I listen to your whiney ass? I'm locked up here forced to have sex with strangers and you want me to sympathize with you not getting a fucking promotion at work? Not one of them got the fucking irony of that. Not one. Stupid fucking bastards."

She takes a deep breath and lays her head back on the headrest, still staring at the house. "This is the second time

I've come back since I escaped. I was angrier the first time than I am this time. Isn't that strange? I feel more defiant this time. *You bent me but you didn't break me. I'm still standing. I'm free.* That's pretty much how I feel. I think you're partially responsible for that. For just being quiet while I say all kinds of stupid, rambling shit. It's a gift you have."

She holds her hand out to me, her attention still on the house. I take it in both of mine, pressing hers between them. If I could pull her memories from her and carry them for her for a while I would. She did that for me with Cassandra. The pain is still there and some of the anger, but it's not near what it once was. I hope I can do that for her.

"Sex isn't mechanical with you. I hope you know that. You've given me so many firsts you have no idea. Thank you for that too." She pulls her hand from mine and starts the car. "I'm done here. I don't ever want to come back."

I glance behind us at the house as we drive away. I'm going to have nightmares about it. About Vera and all of the other girls who were held inside. If I thought she was brave before I was wrong. She's a fucking superhero. I admire her more than anyone else I've ever met. She makes what I went through almost insignificant by comparison. She's a rock star. A goddess. She's fucking courageous. And she's mine...for a time.

22

VERA

I don't know why I took Beau to that house. It felt necessary I guess. That's probably the best way to put it. The only way to put it. Necessary. Like if I didn't take him there right then I was going to fly apart into a thousand little pieces. I can't give him the answers he wants, but I can give him all of the rest of me. The good, the bad and the seriously fucked up.

And there's a whole hell of a lot of seriously fucked up that's for sure.

I don't question why we work the way we do. We just do. We're symbiotic. I've never felt this way with a person before and I can't help but wonder if he and Cassandra were like this or if this is new for him too. I don't know anything about relationships. Maybe this is normal and everybody who has an affair feels the same way. I don't dare ask him though. I'm not jealous anymore, just curious. He might not like the question or read something else into it. Something permanent. Something I can't give him.

We go back to my motel room and order pizza. People

our age go out to the movies, parties, clubs, and friends' houses. Not us. We're more comfortable away from crowds. We don't want to see or be seen. We're not tied to social media. We don't binge watch TV shows. It hadn't really occurred to me until this moment how odd we must seem to other people. How totally out of place we are in society. We don't even talk unnecessarily to fill the void. There are no awkward silences. That's unusual too. Over the past few years I've watched the interactions people have with each other to try to get a sense of what's normal. I have no perspective on what's customary. I'm relearning how to be a person and not doing a very good job of it.

Beau never makes me feel that way though. It's one of the things I like best about him. There are *so many* things I like about him from the way he looks to how I feel when I'm with him.

He kicks off his shoes, lies down on the bed, stacking his hands under his head, and stares at the ceiling. His thinking pose. I lie down next to him and mimic him. Except I can't concentrate so I turn my head on the pillow to look at him only to find him watching me.

"What?" I ask.

"You're remarkable."

"No I'm not."

"You are."

"I think you're remarkable."

"Not hardly."

I shift to my side, pillowing my head on my bent arm. "How did you keep track of time in prison?"

This time he copies my pose. "Counted the days."

"Like with slashes on the wall or something?"

"No, in my head. I kept a running total."

"You never forgot or lost track?"

"No. Not even once."

"I lost track," I say. "A lot. I think it was not knowing night from day. There was no routine either. The days just kind of blended together. Plus I lost chunks of time fucking. I'd zone out then all of a sudden it was dinner or breakfast. There are no clocks in my head. I think maybe it was better that way. Made time go by faster. When I escaped I found out how many years I'd been held—almost four."

"Two thousand, two hundred and seventy one days for me."

"You still remember the number of days? How long is that?"

"A little over six years."

"Damn. I'm sorry."

"I'm sorry too."

I laugh at how ridiculous we are. "It's kind of dumb we're apologizing to each other, isn't it?"

"A few people told me they were sorry for what happened to me. How many people told you?"

"You're the only one."

"Then it's not so dumb, is it?"

"Maybe not."

"I could kill him for what he did to you."

"Please don't." I put a hand on his arm. "I couldn't stand it if you spent another minute in prison. Especially if it was because of me."

"I hate what he and Emmaline did to you."

"Killing them wouldn't make what I went through disappear. Please. Promise me you won't do anything stupid."

"I do a lot of stupid shit."

I shake him by the arm. "You know what I mean. Stop

being stubborn. Promise me you won't do anything to get yourself locked up again. It's not worth it. *I'm* not worth it. Please."

He moves closer. "Don't you know I'd do anything for you? Haven't I already proven you're more than worth it?" His gaze drops to my mouth.

"When you look at me like that I start to believe all kinds of things." He goes for a kiss, but I stop him with a finger to his lips. "Promise me."

He licks my finger.

"Beau," I warn.

His gaze turns wicked. He takes my finger in his mouth and sucks. Shit. That fucking goes straight to my pussy. I try to pull my hand away, but he grips my wrist and holds it. Sliding my finger in and out of his mouth, he licks and sucks. There's no doubt where he wants to put his mouth next. A knock at the door breaks the moment. Saved by the pizza delivery guy. He releases me and I go to the bathroom for a little cool down while he answers the door.

When I come out he's got our dinner spread out on the little table. I sit across from him and pick up a slice of pepperoni.

"You didn't promise," I say.

"I know I didn't."

"Are you fucking kidding me?"

"Fine." He tosses down his slice of pizza. "I promise. Happy?"

"Yes. Actually. I am."

"It's not like I have plans to commit murder. I just don't know how I'll react if I ever see them. I really fucking hate what they did to you. I don't think you fully get how much."

"I wouldn't make you promise if I didn't."

He picks up his pizza and takes an angry bite, glaring at me over the top.

"If it's any consolation, after dinner I'll let you put that tongue to use anywhere you want."

His brows rise. "Anywhere?"

"Anywhere."

23

BEAU

I wake up before Vera does and watch her sleep. She accuses me of snoring, but she makes this little wheezing sound that's actually kind of cute. I won't tell her about it. She'd only deny it. The sheet slipped down, revealing both her breasts. Her nipples are hard and puckered. I should pull the sheet up. She's clearly cold. Except the view is so nice with her arms over her head, making her tits rise. If I had a camera or was an artist I'd capture her just like this with her face soft and relaxed, the morning sun bathing her in a warm glow.

One of her legs is bent out to the side, spreading her open. I have the urge to accept that offer and climb between her legs. She's the sexiest woman I've ever seen. Being with her, making her scream in ecstasy is the greatest fucking experience of my life. She talked about experiencing firsts with me. I've had a few firsts with her too. She probably wouldn't believe me if I told her. She seems to think she couldn't match let alone exceed anything that's ever happened to me. There's really no comparison.

She stirs, rolling on her side away from me. The new

view is pretty fucking great too. This time I don't resist and put my arms around her, tucking her into me. She's warm and smells like sex. My already hard dick gets harder. She wiggles her backside against it, making me groan. She's awake and fucking torturing me. I cup a breast in one hand and slide the other between her legs. Rolling her nipple, I slip a finger through her slickness. She's wet and about to get a lot wetter. I thrust two, then three fingers into her. Her hips flex in time with my strokes. She's faking sleep, letting me do all the work. I don't mind. I sink my teeth into her neck in gentle bites I know drive her crazy. The gasp that escapes her lips makes my dick weep.

Her legs part and it's all the invitation I need. Gripping my dick, I maneuver until I'm right at her entrance. She reaches back and rakes her fingers into my hair. It fucking drives me wild when she does that. I thrust deep into her and her fingers tighten in my hair. I'm a fucking wild man, gripping her hip and hitting hard. God damn she feels so fucking good. I'm gonna come too soon so I strum her clit to get her there before me. The whimpers she makes drive me insane. I sink my teeth into her neck and she cries out. I lunge one last time, digging my fingers into her thigh to get as far into her as I can.

Jesus. God. Fuck. Fuck. Fuuuuuck.

My heart is going to jump out of my chest. I rotate my hips into her, wanting to stay buried as deep as possible. She feels so damn good. Soft. Hot. Her fingers massage where she practically ripped my hair out. I don't care. That was fucking amazing. I kiss her behind her ear and feel her smile.

"Good morning," I say.

"It certainly is. Do I have a mark on my neck?"

I lean up to see. "A little bit, but it looks like it'll go away."

She holds her hand up with strands of my hair between her fingers. I laugh. It was so worth it.

"I'm going to slowly make you bald."

I catch her hand and slip my fingers between hers. "As long as you like bald men I don't care."

She pulls my arm around her. "I like you any way I can get you."

"I like you too."

She looks at the clock beside the bed and groans. "You're going to be late to work if we don't get up."

"No round two?"

"Not today."

The world creeps in, a slithering reality that totally shits all over my post sex high. I wish I could keep her in this room forever, happy and safe. I want more mornings like this with her. I want *all* my mornings to be with her.

I pull out of her slowly. She makes an *uhn* noise. I know exactly how she feels. I hate being separated from her too. She rolls and gives me a kiss, then gets up to head to the bathroom. Her hips sway seductively. Just before she turns to go in the bathroom she gives me a naughty look over her shoulder like she knew I'd be watching and closes the door. I flip onto my back and stare up at the ceiling. I'm fucking gone over her. That look did it. I'm done.

My phone vibrates next to the empty pizza box. I grab it and look at the display. Cora.

"Hello?"

"Do you need me to swing by and pick you up?"

"No, but could you grab me a clean shirt and some socks and bring them to the office?"

"What about underwear?"

"Don't own any."

"Eww. More than I wanted to know. Maybe you should take some of your things to keep over there." She doesn't sound happy about trying to be happy for me.

I glance at the bathroom door at the sound of the shower being turned on. "I don't think we're there yet." But I sure as hell want to be.

"I have some news. We got a hit last night. Nolan spied our girl with an older man at that shopping center, coming out of the Starbucks. I'll text you the photos. He followed them for a while in his car, but they spotted him and then lost him when they ran a red. That asshole now has a face."

All of the air locks in my lungs. I want to see and yet I don't. This is it. The beginning of the end with Vera.

"Beau?"

"Don't send them. We'll look at them when we get to the office. Don't mention that you already told me about them."

She doesn't say anything for a minute. Then, "Tell me the sex hasn't fucked you in the head."

"It's fucked me in the head and pretty much everywhere else."

"God damn it."

"If it's any consolation I'm about to get my teeth kicked in."

"It's not. That's actually worse. Why are you telling me this shit?"

"You fucking *asked*."

"Forget I asked. Just get to the office as soon as you can."

"Fine. Bye."

"Bye."

I jab at the End button and barely resist chucking my phone at the wall. Instead I set it down and head for the bathroom to try to talk Vera into round two.

24

VERA

Something's up. Beau's been acting weird since he climbed in the shower with me, got down on his knees, and went to town on me as if it was the last time he was ever going to get to eat me out. Then he bent me over and relentlessly pounded into me, making me come so hard that if he hadn't been holding me I would've fallen on my face in the tub. He keeps touching me and glancing at me. I haven't been out of his sight once since the shower. I want to ask what happened, but I have a feeling I'm about to find out whether I want to or not.

We get out of the car at the agency and he's immediately at my side with his arm around me, holding me tight against him like he's my bodyguard and we're under a sniper attack. I come to a stop a couple feet from the door. I have to know what I'm walking into here.

"What?" Beau asks.

"Before we go in I need to know what I'm up against."

"What are you talking about?"

"What happened between the time I left you in bed and when you joined me in the shower?"

"I don't know what you mean."

"The fuck you do. What happened?"

He glances at the office door then back at me and sighs. "Cora called."

"And?"

"Javier showed up at that shopping center with Marie. Or at least we assume that's who she was with. We need you to confirm. Nolan took photos."

All of the air leaves my body on a soft *oh*.

I haven't seen his face since he slit Cherry's throat right in front of me as a warning and then punished me.

"Cherry didn't keep her mouth shut," he sneered, still holding her black hair in his fist as she clamped her hands to her neck, the blood gushing between her fingers as she gasped her last breath. "Now she can't talk at all."

His laugh echoed in the bare room. I can still hear it in my head. He made me sleep in the room with her body that night, her sightless eyes shining in the darkness, the combined stench of blood and shit gagging me. In the morning he came and got me and took me to his office. Obediently I got undressed and went to my knees in front of him. He sat back as I unbuckled his belt and unzipped his pants. I sucked him off as I was trained to do. As all the girls were trained to do when he brought us in there. All the while he caressed my face, telling me he loved me. When I was done and had re-buckle his belt, he made me bend over his desk naked. He unbuckled his belt again and beat me with it, holding me down with a hand on my back while I screamed in agony and he struck me over and over.

When he finished he yanked me up by the hair. "You've always been one of my favorites, but I'll cut you like I did Cherry if you try the shit she did. Got it?"

"Y-y-yes, sir."

"Vera?" Beau jostles me out of my memories. "Hey. You're okay."

I shake my head, looking around. Suddenly he's everywhere. I can feel him. He'll come at me out of nowhere with his hooked knife and his horrible laugh.

"I have to go."

I start for my car. I've got to run, get out of here before he finds me. He'll make me pay for outsmarting him and escaping. He'll want to shut my mouth the way he did Cherry's only he'll make me suffer, make me suck him off like that last time before he beat me. Maybe he'll let his guys have a go at me first. He did that when Cinnamon tried to escape. They rotated her between them for three days before she was put back into service. I don't know what all they did to her, but she was never right after that.

Beau grips me by the arm and pulls me back against him. "What about Marie? You came here to find her. He's got her. You can't just leave and let him have her."

His words freeze me and I stop trying to struggle to get out of his hold. I can't bear for Javier to turn her into what he turned me into. I don't ever want to see her eyes go blank. She deserves a normal life. It's my fault he knew about her in the first place. If I hadn't told him about her she wouldn't be about to be sold to the highest bidder. She has no idea her innocence is about to be stolen. She has no idea her life is no longer hers. She has no idea that the man she thinks she loves is a monster.

"Let's go inside," Beau pleads. "See what Cora has to say. We're close. Closer than we've ever been to getting her back. Come on."

I let him tow me into the office. Savannah does a double take at the sight of us together, her brows disappearing into her bangs. Cora's at her desk when we walk in, talking to a man I've never seen before. I pause in the doorway.

"It's okay. That's Nolan. He's one of the investigators. He's the one who staked out the shopping center and got photos of Marie last night. Come on." Beau nudges me forward.

"Nolan Perry." Nolan offers his hand to me. He's about Beau's age with brown hair and brown eyes. He looks nice, but then I've met a lot of men who looked harmless and turned out to be anything but. I don't take his hand and he drops it, looking a little nervous.

Cora gives Beau a look I don't understand.

He shrugs at her. "She asked."

"So I'm guessing you're all filled in," Cora says to me. "We uploaded the photos to my computer. Come have a look." She clicks the mouse, then she and Nolan back away from the computer.

I edge toward the desk, the bagel I had earlier threatening to come up. I haven't seen his face since the morning he beat me. All eyes are on me. I can feel them staring, judging. Beau is at my back. He puts a hand on my shoulder in silent support. Wrapping my arms around me, I force myself to look. The shot is blurry. Taken at night, it has a grainy quality to it, but I can clearly make them out. Javier has his arm across Marie's shoulders. She's smiling up at him, so honest in her devotion. I can see myself in her and in the way she sees only him.

He's a little older, grayer. I don't know what I saw in him. The man I'm looking at now feels like a stranger yet I know everything about him. How he likes his steak. His favorite color. The way he takes his coffee. His love for crossword puzzles. The kind of cologne he wears.

The look on his face when he kills.

Beau squeezes my shoulder. "Is that him?"

I nod. I can't get any words to cross the back of my throat.

"Fucker," Beau spits out.

"It was pretty slick the way he gave me the slip," Nolan says. "I thought I might catch up to him so I cut over a block then back, but he was gone. Just vanished. I did manage to get his license plate though. We can run it."

"We need to be careful," Cora tells him. "This guy hasn't operated the way he has for as long as he has without some help high up. We can't risk running the usual checks on him. He's sure to have his records flagged to let anyone know they're being accessed. Thank you for your help, Nolan. I'll let you know if we need anything else."

"Sure," Nolan nods toward me. "It was nice meeting you."

"Thanks, Nolan," Beau says.

No one speaks until the door closes behind Nolan.

"Mr. Nash is meeting with Emmaline Markham at ten." Cora says. "Chad Perez is out of the office today so I made an appointment with him for tomorrow. The more I think about it the more I'm convinced talking to him might be a waste of time. He's probably just a worker bee and doesn't have a clue what went on in that house. And if he does, he's not likely to tell us the truth about it. But I'll give it my best shot."

"What angle are you taking with him?"

Their conversation goes on without me. I can't stop staring at the slideshow of photos. It's like a movie playing my worst nightmare over and over. Marie and Javier coming out of Starbucks. Javier putting his arm around her. Her looking up at him. Him leaning into the car to kiss her.

Wait.

Why is he out with her? Why isn't he isolating her?

I drag the chair under me, open up the Internet browser, and pull up Marie's Tumblr account. She posted again after getting the tattoo. Something about a fun night out with 'Daddy'. Last night.

"What is it?" Beau asks.

I get my phone out of my pocket and bring up her Instagram account. She posted a pic of the tattoo. Same with her Twitter. All of a sudden her social media is flooded with the image. He wants me to know. He's got her and he wants me to know it. He wants me to come get her. He knew I'd look for Marie. He's taunting me, trying to draw me out.

"How close did Nolan get to them?" I ask Cora.

"Close enough to get his license plate."

"And close enough for *him* to get Nolan's plate. He's going to know Nolan works here. It won't be hard for him to find out." I stand so abruptly the chair flies back and hits Beau. "I can't be here." My hand automatically goes to the gun strapped to my thigh in reassurance.

"Oh, shit," Beau says under his breath.

"You think he's going to come after you?" Cora asks.

"I know he is."

"Why?" She looks at Beau. "What am I missing here?"

He shakes his head.

"No. Not this time," she tells him, propping her hands on her hips. "Somebody needs to tell me what the hell is going on." She turns to me. "Why would he come after you? It's not just because you escaped, is it?"

"No. And that's all I can tell you. I have to go." I pull what's left of my ready cash from the pocket in my bra. It's close to two grand. I peel of two hundreds and stuff them back in my pocket, dropping the rest of the bills on the desk. "Please keep searching for Marie. He's not going to sell her the way he did me, but that doesn't mean she's not still in danger. If this isn't enough money I'll send you more when I get to a place that's safe." I sling my bag over my shoulder and head for the door.

"Wait," Cora yells.

But I don't wait. I open the door and look down the hall. There's a back door at the other end. I head for it. I can't get my car from the front of the building. I'm going to have to find another mode of transportation. I'm already thinking ahead about changing my look, my name, my motel room, *my everything*. I reach for the handle, but a big hand slaps flat on the door above my head.

Beau's arm slips around my waist and drags me hard against him. He puts his mouth to my ear. "Oh, no you don't. You're not leaving without me."

25

BEAU

I s she motherfucking kidding me? If she thinks I'm just going to let her walk out and into who the fuck knows what, then she doesn't know me at all.

"Don't do this," she says.

"You're not alone anymore. Don't you get it?"

"I can't drag you into this. You have no idea what I'm up against."

"I have a damn good idea what that fucking asshole is capable of."

"Please don't make me hurt you."

"The only way you could do that is if you walk out that door without me."

She sags in my embrace, her head bent.

"We can help you," I say. "We can protect you."

"I don't see how *you* can when the police couldn't."

"What do you mean?"

She doesn't answer.

"Vera. Talk to me."

"I can't stay here. It's not safe. He'll be watching the office. He probably already has photos of us coming in here.

He knows what I look like now. He knows what you look like and—thanks to your overprotective streak—what you are to me. You're going to be a target now too."

"That's an argument for us to stick together not separate."

"Why do you have to be so damn stubborn *and* smart?" She tips her head back on my chest. "Fine. Come with me. But that means leaving your cell phone, Cora, your job, *everything* behind. Are you sure you want to do that? Do you even understand what that means?"

I hesitate. I'm not an idiot. Leave everything and everyone behind. I've been toying with the idea ever since I got out, but now that it can be a reality I'm not sure if I can do it. I'd be hurting Cora. I'd be throwing away an incredible opportunity doing work I actually like *and* am good at. I'd lose any chance at reconnecting with my parents.

On the other hand I'd get to be with Vera.

"What's going on?"

I release Vera and turn toward Cora. She's got her hands on her hips. Her gaze bounces between Vera and me, then sticks on me. I pull my cell phone out of my pocket and look at it. Cora follows the movement. I can see the moment she realizes what I mean to do. She glares at Vera, her eyes hot and angry.

I hold my phone out to Cora. "I'm going with her."

"Why?"

"She needs me."

"And I don't?"

"You have Leo now."

"That doesn't mean I don't need you anymore. Don't go."

"I'm sorry." I take her hand and put my phone in it, curling her fingers around it. "I'll contact you when I can."

"What about your job? What about mom and dad and

the life you're building here?"

"I barely have the beginnings of a life here. It's not enough. I can start over somewhere new where I'm not recognized and stared at." I reach back and take Vera's hand. "I have more with Vera than without her."

"What exactly do you have with her? A life on the run? Do you even know why she's running? I bet she hasn't told you the real reason, has she?" She leans around me to glare at Vera. "Go on. Tell him the truth *Gwendolyn*."

Vera gasps, covering her mouth with her hands.

"Shit." I spy Nolan and Savannah behind Cora, hovering just around the corner. "Not here." I jerk my head toward the office.

Vera doesn't want to go back in there. It takes some convincing, but I finally talk her into it.

Once we're inside with the door closed I round on Cora. "How did you find out?"

"I was suspicious of her from the start, remember? When you started spending time with her I got worried. So I checked the search history on your computer. You knew she wasn't who she said she was from the start, but didn't tell me. What did she say to get you to keep it quiet? Is that when the sex started? God. You're just like every other guy. Jerked around by your dick."

"It was nothing like that. You don't know the whole story."

"I know more than you do."

"What are you talking about?"

"A simple Google search. That's all it took to find out everything I needed to know about Gwendolyn Marie Johnston."

"No. Please don't tell him," Vera begs. "Please. He doesn't deserve that. Don't do that to him."

"Me?" Cora asks. "I'm not the one fucking him and lying to him."

"We don't *fuck*," Vera spits out. "*Fucking* is having your virginity sold to the highest bidder and being tied down so he can collect his prize. *Fucking* is not knowing the name of the guy sticking his cock wherever the fuck he wants because he paid to get off on you. *Fucking* is being forced to your knees, to your stomach or to all fours to fulfill whatever fucked up request some sick fuck has. *Fucking* is paying your room and board in blowjobs whenever and wherever the Master wants. What Beau and I do isn't *fucking*."

"Am I supposed to feel *sorry* for you?"

"Knock it off!" I put my arms out, separating them. "Both of you."

"If you don't tell him," Cora challenges Vera. "I will."

"No. You won't," I tell Cora.

"I don't want to come between you and your sister." Vera pulls her hand from mine. "I should go."

"Goodbye," Cora says.

"Hold on a minute. Both of you." God. I can't think with the two of them going at it like this. I let out a frustrated breath. "I can't leave things like this between us," I tell Cora. "I know I don't know the whole story, but neither do you."

Cora crosses her arms. "I know enough."

"I'm going with her. Don't leave things like this between us."

"I'm not the one doing this to us. She is. I love you but you're all kinds of stupid right now because of her. You need to hear the truth, Beau. Once you do if you decide you still want to go with her I won't stand in your way."

I look to Vera. Her eyes are wide and round on Cora, her chest heaving. She looks like cornered animal facing off a predator, trembling in the corner. I glance back at Cora, silently begging me to stay. This is an impossible situation. If I choose one, I lose the other. I don't know what to do.

"I escaped instead of testifying and an innocent man went to prison," Vera blurts out.

I whip my head her direction. "*What?*"

"Sam French. He's still in prison," Cora says. "The Freedom Project is looking for her. So is the FBI. They need her to corroborate his and another missing witness's story. She's also wanted in another crime. Have I gotten anything wrong?" she asks Vera.

"No."

"How could..." I can't wrap my head around it. She knows my story. She *knows* it. How could she be a part of putting an innocent man in prison? How could she look me in the eye, fucking sympathize with me, when she did the same damn thing to another person?

"I don't expect you to understand—"

"Understand? Of course I fucking don't *understand*. How *could* you?"

"Are you still going with her?" Cora ask-sneers.

"I can't... I can't fucking *think*. Just shut up. Both of you. God damn it!"

"I'm sorry." Vera turns for the door.

I grab her by the arm. Hard. And pull her to me. "You're not fucking going anywhere."

She tries to twist out of my grip. "Let me go. I'm not safe here. I'm not safe anywhere."

"I really don't fucking care right now. You're not leaving that man in prison."

"You don't understand."

"You're damn right I don't. How can you fucking live with yourself and what you've done?"

"That missing witness isn't missing. She's *dead*."

"**I**s this more of your *lies*?" Cora's face is full of hate for me. "You'll say and do *anything*, won't you?"

"Wait a minute," Beau tells Cora with a hand out. He turns to me. "Is this true?"

I nod.

"How do you know she's dead? You said *she* right?"

It may as well come out now. All of it. Beau already hates me. If I have any chance at all I have to come clean.

"Cherry," I start. "Her name was Cherry. Or at least that's what she was called. I don't know her real name. Javier slit her throat right in front of me." I shudder at the memory, a chill racing up my spine. "We were supposed to testify that we saw Sam French, the man who was wrongfully convicted, kill a city councilman's his wife in their home. It was meant to look like a home invasion.

"There was a party, drinking, drugs. Cherry and I were hired for the party. We only left Hell House—that's what we called where we were kept—on special occasions for *very* special clients under guard. Sam was one of the guards. Javier always went with us. He has very strict rules about parties. Anyone who isn't on the guest list doesn't get in. The councilman's wife came in through the garage, slipping past Sam. She was supposed to be at a spa for the weekend and came home early. She freaked out when she walked in on Cherry and me with her husband.

"Javier shot the wife. He got Sam to help him make it look like a home invasion. Sam didn't know—none of us knew—Javier planned to pin it on Sam. It was payback for being so careless. Cherry and I were supposed to say we were with the councilman at his election office helping with fliers. We were his alibi.

"You have to understand. This was a very *special* councilman. Whatever Javier wanted this guy got passed. He was a perverted fuck." I close my eyes on the memories of that night and what I had to do. "Didn't give a shit about his wife either. I think he was glad she was dead, like Javier did him a favor.

"Cherry got cold feet and told the cops the truth. Javier found out. He killed her for going against him and as a lesson to me. He...punished me. Severely. In advance, so I didn't get the same idea Cherry did. When he held me down I took something. He doesn't know I have this..." I pull a thumb drive from the pocket in my bra.

"What is it?" Beau asks.

"How he keeps his books. His clients. The money. The girls. Everything. I pulled it out of his laptop and palmed it. I couldn't work that night because of the welts."

Cora winces. She's been quietly judging the whole time I've been talking. Up until now I don't think she believed me. She finally might be.

"So I had the night off," I continue. "If I didn't get out right then I knew I'd never get out. He'd discover I had the thumb drive and that would be it. I'd end up like Cherry. I waited until the guard outside my room stopped one of the girls to get him off, then I pried the wood off my window with a piece of the bed frame and climbed out."

"You jumped out a second story window?" Beau asks in disbelief.

"I lowered myself as far as I could go, yes. I got lucky. There was a bush under the window."

"Where did you go?" This from Cora.

"I couldn't go to the police so I went to a fire station and hid. When they went out on a call I took what I could use—some cash, clothes, a car—"

"The other crimes," Cora chimes in. I don't hate her for trying to protect her brother even though she destroyed any chance I might have had with Beau.

"I drove as far as I could," I continue. "Ditched the car. Got on a bus. I just kept going as fast and as far as I could. I changed everything I could to stay hidden. I only came back for Marie. But I was too late. He already had her."

"Why did you take the thumb drive?" Beau asks. "What were you planning to do with it?"

"Revenge maybe? To prove I could hurt him a fraction as much as he hurt me? I don't know. After a while I came to see it as insurance. I had something over him I could use to negotiate with if I had to. I really don't know. There was no plan. It was there. I knew what it was. I took it...while he beat me. It was me trying to be defiant I guess. How dumb. God. I was *so* dumb."

I laugh at how ridiculous I was back then. How ridiculous I am now. This whole thing is just so stupid. I don't know what I was thinking then and I don't know what to think now. I wrap my arms around myself and lose it, laughing like a fucking lunatic. Cora stares. Beau takes a step toward me, but I shake my head at him to stay away. I can't be touched right now. I can't restrain of myself. Everything is spinning out of control. All of my careful planning, every well thought out move, how I kept myself separate, alone, all of it was for nothing.

It's all out now. Every ugly thing I did. How desperate and sad I am. How totally and completely *stupid* I've been about everything. How after all the things I've been through I still held onto hope. Hope of a better life. Hope to be person of worth. Hope to find someone like Beau and the sheer, ridiculous, comical hope that I could hold onto him, that what I've done, who I've been could just be ignored or forgotten. That's what's so god damn funny to me now. I believed it! I tried to pretend I didn't. I ignored the part of me that wanted and honestly believed I could have normal things, a normal life.

But it was there all the while. That seed of hope. I should've killed it a long time ago. It's disintegrating now, eating at me up from the inside, spreading like poison through me. It fucking hurts. I drop to my knees. Then all fours. I'm dying. I'm on my face on the floor. Beau and Vera crouch beside me, but I can't hear them. The other voices are too loud. All of the things they said to me, those men. All of the ugly vile things they did to me. I can feel them touching me, pulling at me. They all want a piece of me. They take and take and take till nothing's left but an empty shell. I'm nothing. This is what they made me.

Nothing.

27

BEAU

"Should we get her to a hospital?" Cora asks.

I don't know what the fuck to do. Vera is scaring the shit out of me. She's always been so strong. She says things so bluntly, so matter-of-factly that I don't look past her candid words to what she might be burying deep down underneath. I forget how young she is, how young she *was* when all of that shit happened to her. I don't know how she survived this long.

"Go," I tell Cora.

She gives me a worried look as she stands, then leaves the room, closing the door behind her.

Vera lies on her side away from me, crumpled into a ball. The sounds she makes. The keening. The shaking. I put a hand on her shoulder. She shrinks away as though my touch burns. I don't know where she is, but she's not here. She's gone to that place in her head. It's not the comforting, blank place it once was. There's no strength for her to draw from anymore. I don't know what to say or do for her. I've never felt so helpless in my whole life. The only thing to compare would be my first few weeks in prison. I try to think of what would've helped me back then, what someone could've done for me.

Nothing.

Not a damn thing. There was nothing anyone could've said or done that would've brought me back from that dark place. I know where she is and what's waiting for her there. I lie down next to her where I can see her face. Not too close. Just so she knows I'm here. My fingers are barely an inch from where hers claw the carpet. Squeezing my eyes closed, I pray for the first time in more than six years. I request for peace for Vera. I demand justice for her and for Cherry and for all of the other girls. I plead for the strength to look past what she's done and the understanding to accept it. I appeal to whatever higher power to make me a better man and ask for forgiveness for myself and for Vera.

I beg for her pain to be taken away and for that fucker to suffer twice as much as she has.

When I open my eyes, Vera's staring at me, but she's not seeing me. Her whimpers rip at me. She's a wounded child in a woman's body. I want to touch her, hold her, but I'm not sure that's safe for her. All I can do is be with her. A tear drips off her nose into the carpet. Another follows slower than the others. And another even slower until they stop altogether. Her body jerks, her lower lip getting sucked in with each hitching breath. The light flickers behind her eyes. She's coming back.

"Vera," I whisper. "I'm here. Hey. I'm here."

Her wet lashes flutter and then her gaze connects with mine. I put my pinkie finger on hers. She doesn't flinch away. I ease my hand over hers until I can grip it and hold on. She walked me back from the brink and now it's my turn to do it for her. I don't think about how ridiculous we must look lying on the floor side-by-side, holding hands. We've had so many moments like this. It's part of who we are...who we were. Where we go from here I don't know. I can't promise her the things I might have promised her before.

I understand why she did what she did.

A part of me thinks that I might have made the same choice she did. But I can't put aside what happened to me to follow that any further than entertaining the possibility. She knew that all along. How horrifying that must have been for her. All this time. All we've been through. All the while she knew it would end like this. Goddamn but she's stronger than I ever gave her credit for. She could've walked away any time. She could've rejected me when I came after her, needing her and not knowing why. But she didn't. She took me in and healed me.

I'd bleed for her, but I can't be with her. That's a hard fucking thing to acknowledge.

I suck in a rough breath. This is a death we're mourning together. I don't know where we go from here, but we go there separately. I'll help her any way I can. My mission for her isn't over. It won't be until Marie is safe and that fucker is either dead or behind bars. Preferably dead. Prison's too good for him.

She pulls her hand from mine and rolls to her back, scrubbing her hands over her face. I don't need to ask if she's okay. She will be. That's the one thing I'll always be sure of about her. We'll both be okay, but we'll never be the same. I'll never meet another person like her. I'll never have the same connection with anyone else or know the same level of calm that I have when I'm with her.

I sit up when she does, mirroring her movements until we're both standing. She smooths her skirt down, going through the motions of putting herself back together again. She's very good at that. She's had to be.

When she's done she faces me with her chin up. "I'll do whatever it takes to get Marie back. If that means staying then that's what I'll do. What's our next step?"

"We need Cora."

"Whatever it takes."

"Are you sure?"

"No. I haven't been sure in forever."

"We'll do our best to protect you."

"I know you'll try. Why don't you go get Cora?"

She's not any more confident than I am that we can pull this off. But we've gotten this far. I can't see how we can give up now. I'm glad she's not giving up either. I want to touch her. Out of habit maybe or maybe I just need that physical reassurance. But I don't. Instead I got out into the hall to find Cora.

She's not in the reception area so I go to the conference room and find her talking to Mr. Nash. He doesn't spend as much time in the office as he used to since Cora came to work here so I don't see him often.

When he spots me, hovering just outside the door, he waves me in. "I've been hearing good things about your work."

"Thank you."

"Cora and I have been discussing the case you're working on."

My gaze shifts to Cora. I know she wouldn't say anything to Mr. Nash about Vera and me, but still. I know she's mad. And worried.

"My visit with Emmaline Markham didn't go as smoothly as I'd hoped. I think I might have inadvertently tipped her off. She was suspicious as all get out. I don't think she bought my reporter doing a story on her program angle so I put Jerry on her. He's the best surveillance guy we've got.

Former Special Ops. If you see Jerry it's because he wants to be seen. I'm hoping she's going to lead us to our girl. Now, about our client..." He motions for me to sit at the table. "Cora's filled me in on her situation."

I work to keep my face impassive as I take a seat across from him and Cora.

"I may have a way to help her, but she might not like it," Mr. Nash says. "I have a friend in the FBI who would be very interested in what she has to say about this sex trafficking ring. It could mean federal protection. Possibly a new life, a new identity. She'd have to leave everyone and everything behind and start over, including her sister. She'd have to testify in Sam French's hearing and the case against the asshole who trafficked her. It would mean months of isolation followed by being set up in a new city with a new identity. Most people don't get what that means."

"She would," I answer. She's already done it once. She could do it again.

He studies me for a moment. "You couldn't go with her," he says quietly.

I glare at Cora. How could she fucking tell him?

"Your sister didn't betray you. You betrayed yourself." He holds up a hand. "I don't want to know about it. I'm not happy about it, but I understand how these things can happen." He glances at Cora. "I watched my son go through the same thing with your sister."

"I'm sorry."

"Like I said. I understand. Why don't you have Vera come in here so we can talk about our next steps?"

I go back to the office half expecting it to be empty when I walk in. Vera sits in my office chair, her hands folded over her bag in her lap. She looks up when I walk in. There's a resigned set to her jaw. She did something to her face, some make up or something. She's always pretty, but to me, in this moment, she's breathtaking. The back of my eyes sting and my throat feels like I tried to swallow a bite that wouldn't go down. I want to say something to her, something meaningful and memorable. My mind is blank. Even if I could think of what to say I'm not sure I could actually say it.

"You say the most when you don't speak," she tells me as though reading my thoughts. "You have a very expressive face if you know how to read it." She stands. "If I don't get the chance to tell you, I want you to know that you're the most remarkable person I've ever met."

"Thank you."

She draws her bag over her shoulder. "Well?"

"Mr. Nash wants to see you in the conference room."

"Okay."

As she walks past me, I whisper, "I'll never forget you."

Her steps falter, but she keeps moving. I follow her down the hall and close the door behind us. I wait for her to take her seat and then choose a chair two down from hers. I can't be next to her right now. Just being in the same room is damn near killing me.

Cora makes the introductions, her gaze flickering to me then away. I'm not sure yet how I feel about how she forced Vera to tell me the truth. I honestly didn't want to know. I guess somewhere deep down inside I knew it would end Vera and me. Even those few times I tried to pressure her into telling me I didn't really have my heart in it. I'll deal with Cora and what she did later. Right now I'm anxious to see how Vera takes what Mr. Nash has to say. What would I do in her place? Take the deal. Easy answer for me, but not so easy for Vera. She doesn't have any faith that the police or even the FBI can protect her. I have to admit after learning what that fucker's capable of I have my doubts too.

Mr. Nash extends the offer he told me about to Vera—to talk to his FBI friend. He lays it all out for her, including the real possibility she might not walk away from the crimes she committed when she stole that car and property. He makes no promises.

"I'll see about talking to your friend when Marie is safe."

"What about your safety?" I ask.

She makes a noise that's half laugh half scoff. "I'm not safe. I'll never be safe. I'm already dead."

28

VERA

M r. Nash is a nice man—I've gotten good at telling good men from sadistic sons of bitches —but he's naïve. As soon as I talk to his friend I'm dead.

The thing about being a high-end prostitute is that you service high-end clients. I've fucked some of the most powerful men in the state and some very influential, visiting dignitaries, including an FBI agent or three. Unless Mr. Nash's friend has an extremely high level of authority he can't keep my identity completely secret from the entire FBI. Javier will know—probably within a day or two—that I intend to bury him. The one thing Javier cannot stand is betrayal. I've already betrayed him, but if I take it to the next level he won't care about making the kill himself. He'll get whoever he can to do it.

This is the decision I made in that hallway when I told Beau the truth—suicide.

I can tell by the looks on their faces none of them get what I'm saying. Even after everything Beau's been through he, his sister, and Mr. Nash still believe that good will always prevail. It doesn't. Sometimes evil wins and there's nothing you can do about it.

"My friend in the FBI can protect you," Mr. Nash says.

"How high up is your friend?"

"He's a Special Agent."

"Is that higher or lower than an Assistant Special Agent in Charge?"

"Lower I believe."

I shake my head. "He can't help me."

"At least talk to him," Beau pleads.

"It is lower," Cora confirms, looking at her phone. "At the field office level the only position higher than an Assistant SAC is the Special Agent in Charge."

"Why can't he help you?" Mr. Nash asks.

"Because I fucked an Assistant SAC. Hell, he might not even be an assistant any more. The way he talked like he was such a big man—and they love to fucking talk—he could've been promoted since then. His credit card info is going to be on the thumb drive. As soon as he sees it I'm done." I lean across the table at Cora and Mr. Nash. "You can't help me."

"I trust my friend."

"I don't trust anyone except Beau. Not you. Not Cora. Not your FBI friend. No one."

"Let me talk to him, see what he can work out."

"How is that going to help Marie?"

"It'll help you *and* Marie."

"Don't you get it?" I pound on the table. "We'll both be dead as soon as you open your mouth."

"Do you remember his name?" Cora asks

"No. We weren't exactly at a garden party, you know."

"Would you recognize him if you saw him again?"

"I remember *all* of their faces."

She turns her phone toward me. "Is this him?"

It's the splash page for the local field office. Under the heading *San Diego Leadership* is a photo of a man I don't recognize listed as the Special Agent in Charge.

"No."

She hands her phone to Mr. Nash. "Can your friend get us in with him?"

"I should probably make sure I haven't fucked your friend first," I tell Mr. Nash.

He flushes at my crude language, then pulls out his phone and taps the screen. He shows it to me. "This is my friend."

"I don't know him," I say.

Mr. Nash tries to disguise his heavy exhale of relief by smoothing down his comb over. "Will you meet with him? He's going to need something to take to his boss."

I'm still not convinced this is a good idea. "Just because I didn't fuck him or his boss doesn't mean any of Javier's other girls didn't. I'll meet with him, but not here and not at his office."

"I'll see what I can arrange." Mr. Nash gets up from the table and leaves me with Cora and Beau.

"I'm sorry," Cora says. "I was trying to protect my brother."

"I know. So was I."

"In a weird way I can see that now. I hope things work out for you."

"They won't. But thanks." I have to look away from her face because all I see is pity.

"Can I talk to you outside?" Cora asks Beau.

"I'll be back in a minute, okay?"

"It's not like I'm not going anywhere."

He frowns at me before following Cora into the hall.

They close the door so I can't hear what they say. A spider hangs in a web in a corner of the room. I had one as a pet in the first room Javier put me in. I talked to it like it was it was that spider from the children's book about a pig. Stupid to think about now, but I was so lonely. The loneliness wasn't the worst part it was the best. I've gotten to where I prefer to be alone. The isolation Mr. Nash talked about? Heaven. It's weird because I used to love the noise and energy of crowds. The only person I can spend infinite amounts of time with is Beau.

Beau comes into the room and sits across the table from me. We're awkward now. I should've run while he was in here talking to Mr. Nash. It crossed my mind. It crossed Beau's too because he looked surprised to see me when he came back into the office. The way he looked at me then. No other man will ever look at me like that. I didn't think it was possible be looked at like that. He avoids my gaze now, already separating himself from me. It's protective, I know, but it still hurts. He can't forgive me. I didn't expect him to. He wants to. That should be of some consolation to me, but it's not because it's tearing him in two.

"Mr. Nash will make sure you're protected," he says.

I make a noncommittal noise that he can interpret any way he likes.

"He's on the phone with his FBI friend right now."

"If you have work or something to do you should go do it. You don't have to sit here with me."

"I know."

This is the first time our silence has been uncomfortable. He has something to say, but he's not sure if he should say it. I'm not sure if he should either. The silence stretches so thin I can hear it like the vibration of a plucked string, reverberating in the air around us. One of us is going to break it, but neither of us wants to be the one to do it.

I lay my head on the table and close my eyes so I don't have to look at him. Why is he here? I don't need a babysitter.

"It's not like I'm going to run," I mumble.

"You would've already done it if you were."

I want him to leave me alone. I need to get used to being without him. It's shocking to me how quickly I adapted to him being around all the time, invading my space. The void of that feels bigger with him near. Isn't that stupid? I miss him more when he's right next to me than when he's not in the room.

"I wish you'd leave," I tell him, not really meaning it. "Just go away."

"I can't."

I raise my head. "Why not?"

"I don't know."

"Is it to get back at me? Do you hate me that much now?"

"I don't hate you at all. The exact opposite."

"Then why are you punishing me?"

My choice of words surprises him. "Does it feel like that to you?"

I nod.

"Because being without you hurts more when I'm not with you."

"It's easier for me when you're not right here where I can see you, but can't touch you."

"What am I supposed to do?" The change in him is swift, catching me off guard. "How *could* you?" There's six years worth of agony and pent up rage in his voice. His hands form tight fists that shake. "How could you let that man go to prison when you could've prevented it?"

"I *told* you why."

"I know what you told me, but I still can't reconcile what you did with who you are and what you've been through. You of all people should know what it's like to be held against your will, to not know if you'll ever get out, to wonder *if* you'll ever get out. And knowing me, hearing what I went through. How can you live with what you did?"

"You want to know why I don't care about what happened to Sam? Because Sam liked the little girls. The eleven and twelve year olds. I was too old for him at fourteen. So no, I don't give three shits about what happened to Sam. I hope he's getting butt-fucked everyday. I hope he gets forced to his knees to suck cock like he forced Kitty and Bunny to suck his. I was glad when Javier pinned that murder on Sam. And I was pissed at Cherry for trying to screw it up with her crisis of conscious. If it wasn't for her stupidity she wouldn't be dead, I wouldn't have been beaten and stolen the thumb drive, I wouldn't have gone on the run, and I wouldn't be here with you now."

He shakes his head. "You're not making any sense. Some of those things are good things."

"That turned out bad. Stealing the thumb drive signed my death warrant. Going on the run is the reason Javier has Marie. I'm here with you, but not with you. You tell me how any of that's good."

He opens his mouth, then closes it. Slow blinks. Tries again, "But you'd still be with Javier if none of that happened."

He doesn't understand and I'm done trying to explain it. I lay my head back down. "Just go away."

"Vera." He says my name softly, with care, as though it's a fragile thing.

"*Please.*"

The quiet, dull snick of the door closing echoes through my whole body. I've said a lot of goodbyes in my life, but I never *felt* them. All I can see, touch, taste, smell, and hear is this one. I am nothing but goodbye.

29

BEAU

I stand outside the conference room door like a fucking guard because I can't be away from Vera and I can't be with her. I'm thoroughly and completely fucked in every way.

Her world has incomprehensible rules that change constantly. Just when I think I understand how it works she throws in a twist that turns everything around, inside out, and backwards. She's a fucking survivalist, navigating shifting terrain. Kill or be killed. I understand something of that mentality from prison. The fucked up shit that went down in there... Another place with fucked up rules and fucked up people who don't give a fuck.

I understand why she did what she did. I really do. I just can't get past it. Maybe there's something fundamentally wrong with me. Some defect that only lets me see things in black and white, right and wrong. Yes, that fucker should be locked up. He's a fucking sick bastard. But he should be locked up for the sick ass crimes he committed not the one he didn't because that means that the real killer, Javier, still walks free. It also means the councilman skates on having sex with underage girls and helping to cover up his wife's murder. A shit ton of wrongs don't make a shit ton of rights.

I wish I could see it the way Vera does. She used what little power she had to affect a small change for girls who were younger than her, but she never really *changed* their situation. Javier going to prison for murder...that would've affected a fucking *truckload* of change. I'm naïve. I know. Even after everything I've been through I fucking hold on to justice prevailing even though justice bent me over and fucked me in the ass.

And I'm hurting her with it. She called it a punishment. *Fucking hell.* What is *wrong* with me? Why can't I get past it? Why can't I shrug it off and take the win where I can get it like Vera? We're alike in so many ways except this central one. It's not fair. It's not fucking fair.

Cora finds me at my lowest, most pathetic, standing outside Vera's door. Her face creases with worry.

"Am I wrong here?" I ask her. "Sam French is a kid-fucking bastard yet I can't justify him going to prison for a murder he didn't commit."

She starts at this new information. "He's a *what*?"

"Vera says he liked the little girls. She was glad to put him away. But me? I don't fucking know. How can I not fucking *know*?"

She glances at the closed door. "I can't... She *said* that?"

"Saving those girls from one sick fuck didn't save them from all of the other sick fucks who paid to rape them. I'm expecting too much here, aren't I? Tell me I am."

"You are. You fucking are. And you're not. I didn't think. I didn't imagine. Where she comes from is not right. The way she talks about it... Beau, she's my age. I keep going over in my head the things she said. I didn't believe them at first. She says them like she's relaying something she heard from someone else. Like they didn't happen to *her*. That's fucking messed up. *She's* messed up. How could she not be?"

"See, that's the thing. She is and she isn't. Sometimes she's the most sane, most logical person I've ever met. Not sometimes, *most* of the time. I can't explain it right. Uugghh." I thunk the back of my head against the wall in frustration. "There's so much more to her than what she shows. I don't have words for what she's done for me. I *owe* her."

"That's not all you feel about her, is it?"

"No." I can't help being depressed about that.

"You care about her."

"Jesus. You *care* about passing a test. You *care* about being late for work. You *care* about your favorite TV show. What the fuck is *care*?"

"Oh, Beau." She sounds both miserable and glad. "What are you going to do?"

"Nothing. Not a fucking thing."

"Well, that's stupid."

"Excuse me?"

She taps my forehead. "Figure it out asshole." Then walks away. Just *walks* away. Like I'm supposed to understand what she means.

"What the fuck?" I mutter.

I stand at the door until my legs get tired and I slide down the wall to sit on the floor. Savannah's passed me three times, giving me odd looks. Cora came out of her office, looked down the hall at me, shook her head, and went into the file room. She repeated the process on the way back to her office. I know I'm fucking pitiful. I brace my arms on my knees and rest my forehead on my hands. I'm waiting for something. A miracle maybe. I don't know. There's nothing to do. We're at a place where we've gathered all of the information we can and now we're hoping it's enough for the authorities to want to take over. Wait. Wait. Wait. I was never good at it as a kid and I suck at it even more as an adult. Prison was one giant fucking wait.

The conference room opens and Vera comes out. She jerks to a stop when she sees me. "What are you doing?"

"Waiting."

"For what?"

"Anything."

"Where's the bathroom?"

"Around the corner on the other side of reception. There's a hall. I'll show you."

"The office isn't that big. I can find it."

I get to my feet.

"What? You think I'm going to dive for the door as soon as your back's turned?"

"Just come on." I lead the way and wave her toward the ladies' room.

When she comes out she rolls her eyes at me, then goes back into the conference room and closes the door. I take up my position outside again.

Mr. Nash finds me there almost an hour later. He shakes his head at how pathetic I am. "Get up, son. Let's go tell Vera the good news and the not so good news."

When we enter the room Vera is asleep in her chair, her head tipped to one side, her hair falling over half of her face. My heart takes a hard knock at the memory of the last time I saw her sleep and how different things were between us then. Mr. Nash gently wakes her. When she first sees me there's pure joy on her face for half a second before her memory wipes it away. What I wouldn't give to get it back.

"I spoke to my friend. He wants to meet with you. He spoke to his boss about your conditions. They want you to come down to their office. They're promising federal protection if your story checks out. They can bring you through a side entrance and take you straight to the SAC's office. My friend is on his way to pick you up right now. I want you to know that they're taking you very seriously. My friend didn't give me any details but they've been aware of various sex trafficking rings in and around the San Diego area, including the one you were drawn into. If it's the same guy they're looking at you could be invaluable to their investigation."

"Do I have to go alone?" Vera asks.

"Beau and I will follow behind you." Mr. Nash looks at me for confirmation and I nod. "Technically you're going to be in federal custody. We won't be able to go into the interrogation room with you. But we'll be waiting just outside."

"So basically once your friend comes and picks me up in his car they can do whatever they want to me. Charge me for stealing that car, prostitution, whatever they want, whatever I cop to during the interrogation. Yippee. I love being at the mercy of strange men. It always works out so well for me."

Mr. Nash clears his throat. "I also called a friend of mine who's an attorney to meet us at the federal building. She'll be with you in that room. It's the best I could do."

Vera lets out a breath and sits back in her seat. "Thank you."

"You're welcome. They're going to want the thumb drive and anything you can tell them about the organization and the murder of the councilman's wife, including the crimes committed against you."

"'The crimes committed against me.' That's the most polite way I've ever heard it put."

"Cora and I have some things we're putting together for you. The work Beau did was stellar. It builds an excellent picture that backs up everything you've said. The more of that we can gather the better." Mr. Nash rises and checks his watch. "He should be here in about twenty minutes." He closes the door after him, leaving Vera and me alone.

"If you give me your motel room key and I pack up your stuff for you," I offer.

She pulls the key card out of her bra and slides it across the table. That trick of hers catches me off guard every time. The only other time I've ever seen anyone use their clothing to store things was in prison.

"You should probably give me your guns and other weapons."

She pulls pepper spray, brass knuckles, and a taser from her bag and drops them on the table. She stands, propping a foot on a chair, and slides her skirt up. She unhooks her thigh holster and drops it on the table. Lifting her blouse, she removes the knives tucked in her waist. The blouse goes higher still, exposing the cups of her bra, so she can unclip the holster between her breasts. I try real hard not to stare and totally fail. Next comes the gun at the small of her back, then the switchblade from her panties. Last is the knife strapped to the inside of her thigh. I'm sweating by the time she finishes.

She stares longingly at her little pile of weaponry. Even naked she always had a knife or gun within reach, strategically placed and easy for her to get to. It's going to be hard for her to give up the ability to defend herself. Crossing her arms, she looks to me for direction.

"Are you hungry or thirsty?"

She sits down. "No."

"Is there anything else I can do for you?"

"No."

Her walls are back up. I'm shut out. Just like when I first

met her. She's looking at me like I'm an annoyance, a mosquito she wants to flick off. And yet I see it. That spark, that tiny little flame for me she can't turn off anymore than I can turn off mine for her. I hold on to it. I have a feeling I'm going to need the hope it represents. And so will she.

30

VERA

I'm taken to a room with a table and some chairs. It looks sort of like the conference room at the agency except a lot nicer. The chairs are beefy leather and glide like the floor is buttered. The table is a thick, shiny slab of wood. There's a bunch of flags in corners. The only ones I recognize are the California and American flags. There's a TV hung up high in one corner and a white board spans the width of one wall. The blind-covered window looks out on a hall. The slats are open enough that I can see people walk past. Most of them don't look in, but occasionally one or two will. I look for any familiar faces.

I've been told we're waiting for my attorney. The one Mr. Nash set me up with. Mr. Nash's FBI friend, Special Agent Carter, sits at one end of the table babysitting me. He's not so bad. At least he didn't cuff me and make me ride in the backseat of his car. Beau and Mr. Nash are waiting for me in the reception area. They weren't allowed to come back with me. I'm relieved about that.

Agent Carter gets a phone call. There's not much talking on his end, nothing to give away what the call could be about. When he ends it he tells me that my attorney will be here shortly. Sure enough a petite, black woman in a fire engine red suit with matching shoes, lips, and nails enters the room. She breathes confidence the way fish breath water. Agent Carter gets to his feet. They whisper to each other and then the agent leaves, closing the door behind him.

"You must be Gwendolyn," she says, holding her hand out to me.

I haven't been called that name in so long it takes me a few moments to respond. I take her hand and she gives it a couple of brief pumps.

"I'm Shayna Reese. You can call me Shay." She tosses her briefcase on the table like she doesn't give a fuck if she dents it and takes the seat next to me.

"Nice to meet you."

She opens her case and pulls out a couple of files. "Ed gave me copies of his files for my records and copies for me to give the FBI. I'm fairly up to speed on what's happening here." Stacking her hands on the files, she turns to me. "But I want to hear it from you."

"What do you want to know?"

"Everything. The condensed version. The Feebs are hungry to get in here and grill you."

I give her what she wants. She asks a bunch of questions for clarification. All the while she takes notes. She smells like a fashion magazine. When I was about twelve I'd go to the pharmacy down the street from my foster home and rub the scent strips from the magazines on my wrists, dreaming of the day when I could buy perfume that smelled like that—expensive, beautiful, desirable. The kind of scent that would make men want me the way the male models in the ads seemed to want the females. That was when I used to dream of such stupid things. Huh. I hadn't thought about doing that in a long, long while. It feels like forever ago.

Shay takes out her laptop and fires it up. She holds her palm out. "The thumb drive."

I hesitate. Not because I don't trust her, but because this is the final step off the cliff. I'm really doing this. I'm really putting Javier's nuts in a vice. I'm really becoming witness number one at his trial. I'm really giving up control of my life for the foreseeable future, maybe forever. I'm really giving up Beau. That last realization strikes a blow. My chest hitches and I can't feel my hands as I reach into my bra and give the thumb drive to Shay.

It's done.

She plugs it into her USB drive and clicks the file open. I know what's on it. I pretty much have it memorized. It looks like jibberish at first until you know what to look for. Then it's like ripping the curtains wide open on the fucked up world of underage sex trafficking.

He has us listed by the names he gave us—Cherry, Bunny, Kitty, Angel, Cinnamon, Porsche, Mercedes, Lexus, Diamond, Pearl, Crystal, Jasmine, Misty, Bambi, Brandi, Desiree, Scarlet, Ariel, Lola, Candi, Rain, Chanel, Lucky, Amber, Ginger, Jade, Star, Paris, Dallas, Tawny, Roxy, Coco, Trixie, Fantasy, Heavenly...and Eden—the name he gave me. Thirty-six girls from ten to seventeen years old. Older than that and you got downgraded to truck stops and strip bars.

There's a price list per act from blowjobs to anal to threesomes to BDSM. The more perverted the higher the price. The younger the girl the higher the price. The riskier the behavior the higher the price. Bareback cost extra and guys had to show they'd been tested to get on the special list. One positive AIDS test and both the guy and the girl were out. If I have anything to be grateful to Javier for it's that rule.

I walk Shay through every bit of it right down to the bank account numbers and password codes. Those are likely useless now. He would've changed everything once he realized that the thumb drive and I were gone. But the credit card numbers—how his clients paid—those can be easily traced back to their owners. The clients can provide the money half of the equation and where it all goes. They can give up the houses where the girls are kept. I tell Shay everything...including the one thing I couldn't tell Beau.

When I'm done she sits back in her seat with tears in her eyes. "I'm sorry," she whispers.

"Don't, okay? I don't need that from you or anybody else. What I need is Marie back safe and sound. And I need Javier to not get tipped off by that fucker right there," I say, pointing out the window.

Shay follows the line of my finger to where two men in suits stand in the hall talking.

"The one on the right snorts and grunts like a pig when he fucks. Sweats like one too. About eight thrusts in and he's done. Comes like a fucking freight train though, blowing and puffing. Plain old missionary for him. Always under the covers, which didn't help the sweating. Being under him was like being in an acid rain storm in the goddamn rainforest. Didn't give a fuck if I got off or not."

As I'm talking Shay gets up and discreetly closes the blinds, blocking the men from looking in the room.

"Some of them did though." I say. "You'd be surprised how much fucking effort they tried to put into it too. Mostly I faked it so they'd just *stop* because come on, really? You're paying for underage sex and you want to try to make it about *me*? Who the *fuck* are you kidding?"

She sits back down next to me. I can see she's trying real hard to keep it together, but she's shattered. Her hands and lower lip shake. She blinks back the tears I told her I didn't want. I have to look away from her while she tries to collect herself. I slide one of the files Mr. Nash gave her off the stack. She lets me. Beau's neat handwriting stares back at me and suddenly I'm struggling just as hard as Shay to get my shit together. I push the file away and stand to pace the room.

To give myself something to do I pick up one of the markers in the tray of the white board and start drawing. I draw the layout of both of the houses I was kept in, including where Javier's office was. I list the names of the assholes who guarded us as best as I can remember. Some of them are nicknames the guys gave each other, but I write them down anyway. I draw the layout of the councilman's house and mark an X on the spot where his wife died. I give up every last piece of information inside me, including the name of the artist who inked my tattoo.

When I'm done I drop the marker in the tray and turn around. Shay is on her feet, her eyes wide. She motions for me to step to one side so she can snap pics with her phone.

She tucks her phone in her bag and then moves toward me. Before I know what she means to do I'm enveloped in a hug so fierce all of the air is forced out of my lungs. I self-consciously hug her back. I'm not good at this stuff. She pulls back and smooths the hair out of my eyes. This close I can see she's older than I thought she was. Maybe my mom's age if my mom hadn't died with a needle in her arm.

"We're going to burn that mother*fucker*," she says, shocking me with her language. "You and me. We're going to take him down and all those assholes in this building and anywhere else in the world who ever laid a hand on you.

You stand behind me from now on, got that? I'm between you and whatever comes at you. You're mine now and I'm glad to have you." Her gaze sweeps over the white board. "Yes indeed. We're going to burn that motherfucker to the *ground*."

She squeezes my arms, her eyes dry, her grin as big as her face. "Are you ready to turn the FBI on its ass?"

31

BEAU

"What's taking so long?" I ask Mr. Nash.

We've been here for hours. No one's telling us anything. We haven't seen Vera since Agent Carter took her by the elbow and pulled her through the door I've been staring at ever since. I'm on my eighth cup of black coffee and jittering like I ate twelve bags of coke dusted Skittles.

Mr. Nash doesn't say anything, just calmly flips through a magazine that he's looked at twice before.

"Do you think they'll let us see her when they're done?"

"Maybe."

"Can you check with your friend again? See where they're at?"

"Probably the same place they were the last time I checked with him—in interrogation. This could take—"

"Hours. I know. You said that." I finish off my coffee and debate getting another.

"Sit down, son."

"I can't." I crumple the cup and toss it in the trash. "Too much coffee."

"Then why don't we take a walk? Carter will call me if anything develops."

"Yeah. Okay. You're sure?"

He stands and claps me on the shoulder. "I'm sure. Come on."

He tells the lady at the desk that we'll be back and we head out into the night. There's nothing surrounding the nondescript federal government building housing the offices of the FBI. No other office buildings or strip mall. Across the street is the 805 Freeway. The dull, incessant drone of traffic blends with the sound of crickets and the odd chirping bird. We stroll around the complex in silence. This isn't helping me calm down, but it gives me something to do other than drink coffee and stare at the door that won't open.

On our third lap Mr. Nash starts to tell the story of when he first met Cora. I've heard Cora's account and some of Leo's, but Mr. Nash's is by far the most interesting. I feel like I'm getting the true version of events. He talks about how fierce Cora was in trying to talk him into taking on my case. How determined she was that he help her.

"It wasn't like she gave me a choice," he laughs. "She wasn't going to leave until I gave in. There she was with her box of files and determination, delivering the most impassioned speech I've ever heard. And then Leo stepped up and volunteered himself to help her. Until then that kid practically got hives any time someone even mentioned investigative work. She not only moved me with her speech, she moved my stubborn mountain of a son. I knew right then that she would change his life and mine.

"My point is, sometimes people come into your life unexpectedly, unwantedly and jerk the rug out from under you. Your world's changed forever. Helping Maurice Battle win his freedom after thirty-nine years was incredible. Helping you win your freedom back...life altering. Because of Cora I don't see the world the way I saw it before she walked into my office, demanding we help her. After spending a few hours with Vera, listening to *her* story, my world has shifted again. People...*men* hurt and used that girl in reprehensible ways and yet she found a way to not only hold onto her humanity but to thrive and not let what happened to her change who she is as a person deep down. She has scars, she doesn't trust, she stares down men, daring them to try something, anything. She strikes a brave face because she *is* brave.

"Look, I know you're struggling with the choices she made. *She's* struggling with them. We all are. But she made the only choice she could. And she used it to try to help somebody else. I know you care about her. You're practically desperate with it. I remember feeling that way about my wife once upon a time. It's an incredible feeling that only comes around once, maybe twice. Even if you can't get past what she's done and be with her, can you at least find a way to forgive her so she can forgive herself? Because if you don't she'll keep torturing herself over it. She'll close herself off forever. She's far too young to spend her the rest of her life alone."

His last word echoes through the vacant walkway between the buildings.

Alone.

There's a difference between being alone and being lonely. My years in prison taught me that. I was never *lonely*. There were always people around. I could interact or not interact. But, regardless if I was in a crowd or by myself I was always *alone*. I suddenly realize that my anxiety since I found out what Vera did is that old feeling of being alone.

Mr. Nash's words about Vera closing herself off and torturing herself are also about me and the fucked up shit in my head.

Vera gave me forgiveness when I couldn't forgive myself. She took me to Cassandra's grave and helped me find the absolution I wasn't able to find on my own. Vera forgave me in Cassandra's place for the anger I carried around since the murder. That was a tremendous gift. It was my turn to do the same for her and I fucked it up. I couldn't see past my self-righteousness and personal experiences. Vera didn't have to understand my anger in order to release me from it.

My steps are heavy with these realizations. Vera is inside that building right now putting herself through hell for her sister and all of those other girls. She took that thumb drive and hid, knowing the price she might have to pay someday. She came back to San Diego to find her sister—putting her life at risk—and save Marie from the same fucker who put her though hell.

She let me in her motel room that first night and all the other nights I came looking for something I somehow instinctively knew only she could give me. She got drunk with me, made love with me, forgave me, cared about me, and laughed with me. She gave me the straight shit and never once lied to me even when it meant she might lose me.

And I couldn't give her the only thing she ever asked in return.

Not only that I tortured her with it, following her around like a lost fucking puppy, wanting her to fix what was broken inside me when it was me who broke it. I don't know what's going to happen tonight or tomorrow or the day after that. I don't know if Vera will want to see me or if I'll get the chance to see her, but I feel like I need to say something to her, something that will somehow free us both.

We're on our fifth lap when Mr. Nash gets a text. "They're moving her."

"What does that mean? Can we see her?"

He picks up his steps and I follow suit. "I don't know. Carter didn't say. Let's get back in there and find out."

32

VERA

The suits aren't very happy with me. I called out three of their fellow agents—two from this office and one from the Orange County field office—who like to fuck under age girls, including the pig from the hallway. They now have to investigate their own along with assholes from other law enforcement agencies and every-day-Joe child fuckers.

At first they doubted my story, but as Shay laid it out for them piece by piece she put together a picture they couldn't look away from. By the time they finished grilling me up one side and down the other they were finally convinced I'm telling the truth. I didn't waver once and repeated myself twelve different ways until they finally moved on to the next question and then the next. Shay called for a food and bath-room break halfway through. Shay and a female agent, who practically stuck her head under the stall door to make sure I was only peeing, escorted me to the bathroom.

I managed bites of sandwich between questions. And there was a shit ton of questions. If I didn't know the answer I just told them I didn't know, which seemed to please Shay.

I told them everything I could, holding nothing back. It got ugly and graphic in some places as I explained a couple of sex acts neither one of them had ever heard of before. By the time I finished Agent Carter, his boss—Special Agent in Charge Charles Fung—and Shay looked a little green, but wore it stoically. Who would make up the depraved shit I told them?

Carter and Fung retreat to a corner of the room and carry on a very heated, whispered discussion. Shay pulls me into the opposite corner and we have our own secret conversation.

"They're trying to figure out what to do with you and where to keep you so you're safe and the agents involved don't tip off Javier that you're in custody and talking," Shay says. "This is good. It means we're in a good position to get the charges against you dropped. If there are ever extenuating circumstances this is it. Agents buying children for sex." She shakes her head. "Disgusting."

"What are they going to do with me?"

"I think we're about to find out."

Fung approaches. "I think you'll agree that we have some very special circumstances here. I'm going to arrange for the U.S. Marshals to take you into protective custody outside the county. You'll remain with them during the investigation and trial. If there is one."

"What protections does my client have if there is no trial?" Shay asks.

"The evidence she provided is very compelling. The only way I can see there not being a trial is if there's a plea bargain, which is out of our hands and up to the Department of Justice. Our job is to investigate and to make sure you're safe," Fung says to me. "I promise you'll be safe."

"How long will it be before I'm out of protective

custody?"

"That I don't know. Could be months. Could be years. Depending. There'd likely be a permanent relocation and a new identity eventually."

I motion for Shay to follow me back to our corner. When we're alone I ask, "Will I get to say goodbye?"

"To the young man waiting for you out in reception?"

"He's still here?"

"He and Ed both. They've been waiting for a chance to see you."

"Can you arrange it?"

She gives a firm nod and goes to talk to Carter and Fung. A few moments later she returns. "You'll get a few minutes. They're bringing them back here."

I stare pensively at the door. Beau and I didn't leave things the way I wanted to leave them. I'm not sure how he's going to react when he sees me. I'm not even sure what to say to him. *Goodbye* seems too pedestrian. *Thank you* is not enough. *Nice knowing you* is incomplete.

I'll never forget you.

As close as that is it's not close enough.

I'll always care about you.

Better.

There will never be anyone else for me.

Exactly right.

But I can't say it out loud. Saying it out loud is so final. Like I'll never ever see him again. Which, I won't. The realization is a heavy blanket settling over me. This is a forever goodbye. The kind you say and then think on later how you should've said this or done that, but you can't go back.

He comes into the room and I'm hit with a wave of misery. His gaze searches the room for me, finding me huddled in the corner. He scoops me up in a sweet embrace, tucking his face in my neck, as he likes to do. I'm going to miss this. I'm going to miss so many things about him—the smell of him, the feel of him, the way he looks at me, even his snoring. I don't know how I'm going to sleep without him.

"They're putting me in protective custody," I tell him, my voice wavering.

His arms tighten around me in response. He knows what this means. I fist the back of his shirt, bringing him closer. I always knew my time with him would be short I just didn't know how short or that it would be so hard to let go.

He kisses my neck. "I'm sorry." Cradling my face in his hands, he kisses my cheeks, my nose, my eyes, my lips. "I'm so, so sorry." He drops more kisses between words. "I'm such a fucking idiot. Please forgive me. I didn't mean that stupid shit I said."

"Yes, you did."

He stops to look at me. "Okay I did, but I didn't *mean* it mean it. I just had to work through all the crap I've been through to see what you did in a new way." He puts his forehead to mine. "I'm sorry. I know you're a good person who's been through deeper shit than I'll ever know. I'm so sorry."

"Okay. Okay." I push him back, laughing. "Enough."

"Are you all right?" He glances around the room behind him only to find it empty. "Did everything go the way Mr. Nash said it might?"

"Pretty much exactly like he said it would. I like my lawyer. She's awesome. Please thank Mr. Nash for getting her for me."

"How long do we have?"

"I don't know. They didn't say. I wasn't even sure they'd let me see you."

He holds me to him. "I wasn't sure they'd allow it either."

"You're really okay with everything?"

"Yeah. I am."

"Thank you. That means a lot to me. I couldn't go away with you still hating me. I mean, I would've. It just would've been a lot harder dealing with that and everything else too. So thank you."

We lapse into one of our silences, holding onto each other. I close my eyes and breathe in the scent of him as he massages my scalp and we rock back and forth. I've had to say a lot of goodbyes in my life. None has ever been as hard as this one. There's so much to say and yet anything we say won't be enough. I can feel him grappling with it too. He kisses the top of my head. I nuzzle against his chest.

"You once asked me what I wanted," I say, looking up into his beautiful face.

"Yeah."

"I want you."

"I want you too."

He kisses me and I can feel how very much he wants me. It's more than the physical, which is an ache that won't go away. It's something deeper and harder to define. It's inside us and in the air around us. I have a feeling it's something that won't fade with time and distance. I will always think about him and I will always want him.

He lifts his head, tracing his thumb along my lower lip. "What am I going to do without you?"

"I was going to ask *you* that."

"There's no chance...?" He growls and shakes his head. "I know there isn't. I just... I wish I could visit you."

"I know. Me too. I'll be okay."

"Really? Cuz I'm not sure I will be."

"I was lying. I won't be, but I'll manage. Go." I push him away from me. "Meet someone new." I step back until we're separated. "Have a family. Get a dog. Buy a house. Have a good life."

He looks lost with his arms out open for me. My vision blurs. I fight to keep the tears back and from diving back into his embrace. It's over. We're over.

His arms fall to his sides. "I don't want to do any of that."

"You should. You deserve to be happy."

"So do you. Are you going to find someone else? Have a family?"

Biting my lip, I shake my head. There's no point in any of that for me. No one else is going to want me.

"You should go," I tell him, my voice hoarse.

He looks at the door, then back at me and does that slow blink thing. I don't know what he's thinking or what he's going to do. I want him to leave, but I need him to stay. The tension strings tight, bringing me to the balls of my feet.

"Only family can go with you," he says slowly. "I looked it up." Of course he did. He *would*. "We're not family. But we could be."

My heart practically stops in my chest. Everything slows. There's an incessant buzzing in my ears. I have to force myself to take a breath so I can stop this line of thinking before it gets out of control.

"No," I say, everything in me rejecting the hope. "We can't. We can't ever be a family."

He takes a step toward me, his face breaking into a grin. "We *could*."

"*No*. Stop saying that."

"Vera. Think about it."

"You idiot I have thought about it!"

He takes another step, making me take one back. If it's possible his smile gets even bigger. "You've always been so much smarter than me." He advances again.

I put a hand up to stop him. "No, Beau. We can't do this. You don't know everything about me."

"I know everything I need and want to know." He takes my hand in his and drops to one knee. "Vera—"

I yank my hand from his and back away, needing some distance and perspective. "Don't. *Please* don't."

"Marry me."

"No."

He gets to his feet. "Why not?"

"What about Cora?"

"She'll understand."

"You won't ever get to see her again."

"I know." The way he says it makes me realize he's thought about this. Actually *thought* it all the way through.

"What about your parents?"

"Cora will explain it to them."

"You want to leave that for her to do?"

"What is this really about?"

I wave him back. "Don't ask questions you don't really want the answers to."

"What's that supposed to mean?"

"I can't give you what you want."

"You're not already married are you?"

"No."

He props his hands on his hips. "Then what's the problem? Don't you want to marry me?"

"Yes," I say on a sob. "I want to fucking marry you more than anything."

"Ah, Vera, come here." He holds his arms out to me. "Whatever it is we'll fix it."

"It *can't* be fixed that's the problem."

I forget to move back when he moves forward. This time

he catches me, wrapping his arms around me. "Tell me what it is. I bet it's not as bad as you think."

The words leave me in a rush. "I can't ever get pregnant."

I'm too miserable and afraid to gauge his reaction past how utterly still he goes. His arms stop moving up and down my back. He might even have stopped breathing. I can practically hear him thinking, weighing things between us all over again. I want to believe it won't matter to him and I know him well enough to know that he'll think that initially. And then the reality of it will set in. It's funny how you never thought about wanting something until there's absolutely no possibility of ever having it. Then you want it more than *anything*. He's going to say it doesn't matter and I'll try to believe him because I want to. Resentment will build over the years. Little things here and there, piling up until there's a wall between us we can't see over. I need to stop him from trying to conjure up any hope.

"It's irreversible," I say, pulling away. "We were all sterilized. After he sold our virginity he took us to a doctor who gave us a morning after pill just in case and then he implanted these things in our fallopian tubes. I went to a doctor a few years ago who confirmed it. I can't get pregnant. Remember me telling you not to worry about it that night we got drunk? This is why. And this is why I can't marry you. We can't ever be a family. I can't give you what you want."

"How the fuck do you know what I want?"

"Don't be ridiculous."

"I'm not being ridiculous. You are."

"Don't tell me you never thought about having children."

His no answer is answer enough.

"That's what I thought." I put my palm on his cheek. "Thank you for your sweet proposal. But the answer's no."

33

BEAU

"Vera, don't." I catch her wrist. "Don't do this. Please. We can work it out. In vitro, adoption or that dog you talked about. We have options."

God. How could she not know that I don't give a shit about this. Not really. It's such a minor thing compared to everything else we've been through and all the shit that's still to come. As long as we have each other that's all that matters.

"I thought about all of the options," she says. "I even looked into them a little bit. I have to believe there's a reason things worked out the way they did. That maybe I'm not meant to be a parent."

"That's bullshit. You can be anything you want to be."

"But Beau, I can't be the person who takes you away from your family *and* keeps you from fulfilling your dreams. Don't you see that?"

"But you can be the person who takes *you* away from me. God, Vera." This is the first time in a long time that I've needed to hit something. "Listen to yourself. I'm fighting for us here and all you're doing is throwing excuses at me."

"They're not excuses they're reasons and very valid ones. I don't want you to ever wake up one day and resent me."

"If you make wake up tomorrow without you I *will* resent you."

"You don't mean that. You can't mean that."

"I got down on my knee and asked you to marry me. What do you think?"

"I want to believe it. You don't know how much."

"Do I need to do it again?" I drop to one knee, still holding onto her hand. She doesn't pull away this time. I tug her toward me until she's right up against me and put my hands on her waist. I have to crane my neck to see her beautiful face. "Vera, Gwendolyn, whoever you are, whoever you want to be, *will you marry me?*"

The door behind her opens. Her attorney, Mr. Nash, and Agent Carter jam together in the doorway at the sight of Vera and me. If Vera notices she shows no sign of it. Her gaze roams my face. I don't know what she's looking for but I hope to God she finds whatever she needs to answer me with a yes. Her lashes flutter, blinking away tears, and she puts a hand over her mouth. She's so alive for me in this moment, so vital and necessary. I draw her a little closer. I won't beg. If she tells me no again, I'll have to take it and walk away forever.

But I don't think it's going to be a no. I think she's going to say yes. She *wants* to say yes. It's that too-impossible-to-believe feeling you get when something you've wanted suddenly becomes something you can *have*. I know exactly how she feels. So many emotions cross over her face. I see the moment when she decides for certain, no going back.

"Yes," she sobs behind her hand, nodding. "I'll marry you."

I get to my feet and pick her up in a hug, swinging her

around as applause breaks out in the doorway. She wraps her legs around my waist and catches my face for a kiss. If we didn't have an audience I'd want to take things further. I set her down and we turn to face the crowd in the doorway.

"I see you made the most of your time," Mr. Nash says. "Are you sure about what this means?"

I glance at Vera. "*Very* sure."

She smiles up at me. "Me too."

"We'll have to arrange—" Whispering in his ear, another agent interrupts Agent Carter. Carter pushes Mr. Nash and Vera's lawyer into the room. "Lock the door. Don't move from this room until I come back for you." He closes the door after him.

"What's going on?" the lawyer asks.

"Something's happened," Mr. Nash says, turning the lock on the door. "From the little I overheard it's something about a breech in security."

Vera's brows draw together with concern. I squeeze her hand, trying to be of some comfort. I can't help worrying myself. All I want is for her to be safe and happy. I pull out a chair and sit, drawing her down onto my lap where I can put my arms around her. I need her near me. Vera introduces me to her lawyer, Shay, as the other two join us at the table. We sit in silence for over an hour before Agent Carter knocks on the door and Mr. Nash lets him in. Carter's gaze goes immediately to Vera.

She stiffens in my embrace. "What is it?"

"There's no easy way to put this," he starts.

"It's Marie, isn't it?"

"A young woman's body was dumped in the driveway of the building near the parking gate."

Vera sucks in a sharp breath. I tighten my arms around her.

"We believe it's your sister Marie," Carter continues. "I'm going to need you to look at a couple of photos. I've cropped them as best I can, but I want you to be prepared. There's a lot of blood."

Her body's stiff and tense against mine, her fingers digging into my forearms. I close my eyes and silently chant, *please don't let it be Marie*. Vera can't take any more blows. She's already been through so much, too much.

"Can I look at them?" I ask. "I know what Marie looks like."

"I need the next of kin to identify her. I'm sorry." Agent Carter taps his phone then turns it toward us. "Is this your sister?"

The shot is tight, from the chin up. Marie's eyes are open, staring at nothing. The blood on her face and in her hair is wet and shiny...fresh. Her mouth hangs open mid scream. The noise Vera makes causes all of the hair on the back of my neck to rise. She struggles against my hold, but I don't dare let her go. She beats at my arms. Her legs kick mine. I hold onto her tighter. It feels like she's breaking from the inside out, that if I let her go she'd fly apart into a million little pieces.

Shay and Mr. Nash come to look at the photo. Shay's hand goes to her mouth. Mr. Nash's lips presses into a grim line. I gather Vera to me as tightly as I can, cradling her in my lap. Turning her face into my chest, she fists my shirt and sobs. I failed her. I didn't save Marie.

"I'm sorry." I tell her over and over.

Agent Carter pockets his phone. "I'm sorry for your loss. We're going over the surveillance we have of what happened. The men wore dark masks and clothing. The car didn't have any plates. They pulled her out of the car and killed her, leaving her body where it would be easily found. It appears she was sexually assaulted."

"Let me guess," Vera says, tears streaming, her voice unexpectedly strong. "Her throat was cut."

"Yes."

"He likes the kind of knives with a hook at the end that curves back the opposite direction. It has a heavy black handle with a notched grip for his fingers. He held her by the hair and did it in one slow swipe. Right to left because he's left handed. She's a message for me just like Cherry was."

"We don't have those details. We'll know more after the autopsy."

"He's coming for me."

"He can't get to you," I tell her, looking to Agent Carter for confirmation.

"You're safe with us," he affirms. "We need to move you as soon as possible. The two agents you identified aren't in the building and won't be back until tomorrow morning. We need to keep them on as though nothing's changed until we finish our investigation of them." He turns to me. "You're going with her I take it."

"Yes."

"We're leaving in twenty minutes. We'll need your clothing sizes and a list of the minimal things you'll need to get you by for a few weeks. You won't get to say goodbye to anyone or contact them in anyway. I'm going to need both of your cell phones."

"I don't have mine," I say. "I gave it to my sister."

Vera slides hers across the table.

"Will my client be able to contact me if she needs me?" Shay asks.

"We'll arrange for it."

"What do you want me to tell your sister?" Mr. Nash asks me.

"Tell her that I finally figured it out. She'll know what that means."

34

VERA

I can't get the image of Marie's face out of my head. It overlaps with Cherry's. Both of them died because of me. Two sets of sightless eyes staring at me, blaming me. I started this journey to save Marie and ended up being the reason she's dead. There's no place in my head I can go to escape that fact. Killing her and dumping her body on the FBI's doorstep is a big giant fuck you to the Feds and a message to me that they can't protect me. No one can. He's coming for me. He knows where I am and he'll take down anyone who stands between him and me.

I know him too well. This is personal. I was more than one of his favorites. I was, for a while, his mistress. I had it better than the other girls during that time. He didn't rent me out, keeping me for his personal amusement. I had a big bedroom with it's own bathroom, access to movies, a personal trainer, hairstylist, and pretty lingerie. He brought me gifts and fucked me for hours, but never spent the night in my bed. He didn't let the other men touch me. My piercings were his idea. They were his stamp on me, an outward sign of his total dominance.

That's when I started spending time with him in his office while he worked. While I sat at his feet or rubbed his shoulders I quietly learned how he ran his business. He underestimated me and my ability to memorize anything and everything. I knew the combination to his safe, the passwords to his computer, bank account, and the thumb drive I stole. He had no idea. In my sick, twisted mind I made myself out to be his partner. I had dreams of us getting married and running the business together. He had other ideas.

I don't know what changed, but one day he stopped coming to my room. He stopped calling me to his office. Three days went by without me seeing him. On day four I was put back into rotation with the other girls. I never knew why.

I got to keep the room, but all of the other perks were gone. I cried for him, actually *cried*. He came to see me a week later and I pleaded with him to take me back. I thought I loved him. He made me think the pathetic attention he gave me was true affection. Or maybe I wanted to believe it was. He fucked with my head so many times I lost track of everything, including myself.

He laughed while I begged. After that the only time I saw him was when he called me to his office for punishment or to go out on a special assignment like the one with the councilman. It wasn't Cherry's death that lit the fuse of my escape. It was doing that job with her and finding out she was pierced exactly the same way I was. I knew then that *she* was the one who replaced me. Her being put back into rotation meant that she had also been replaced. Until that time I held out the hope that he'd want me back someday. It wasn't revenge that drove me to leave him and take the thumb drive it was jealousy.

Stupid. I was so stupid to waste any emotion on that bastard. Even now I can't bring myself to hate him. He's already taken so much from me he's not going to get any more.

Beau and I were shuttled through an underground passage in the FBI building to another building about a half mile away. It felt like we walked forever, taking unmarked, seemingly random turns until we went up a set of stairs and came out into another office building. A car took us to an apartment building somewhere. I don't know where because we were blindfolded and made to wear headphones so that we couldn't hear anything. The only thing that got me through it was Beau's arm around me and the feel of his big, solid body next to mine.

I still can't believe he asked me to marry him. Is this even happening? Everything that's happened since being in FBI custody seems so surreal. I'm struggling to play catch up. Just when I adapt to the latest turn of events and think I might finally have a grasp on things something else happens and my world spins out of control. I feel a bit like a tennis ball being batted back and forth.

We're in this apartment with a US Marshall babysitter and another outside and all I can think about is who is going to plan Marie's funeral? Who's going to attend it? Who's going to choose the flowers and stand over her grave mourning her? I'm her only family. When I agreed to talk to the FBI I thought Marie would eventually be with me. I pictured us getting to know each other and being a family. I never imagined Javier would kill her. I should've. I should've seen this coming. Even if I did could I have done anything about it?

Beau tells me it's not my fault. I think he really believes it. His natural optimism is both a blessing and an annoyance. He wants to see the best in me even when he has to dig down deep to find it. Even when the hole fills back in with all of my bullshit he just keeps digging and digging. I fear one day he'll get tired and give up to sit back and watch the hole fill until you can't even see a dent where it once was. There is no good in me. There is only survival.

I'm tired.

Not the sleepy kind of weary. Soul-deep exhaustion. The kind that makes you stop flailing and splashing. Where you give up and just let the water take you under, watching resigned as the surface gets further and further away and the dark depth welcomes you. You stop thinking. You stop feeling. You stop *being*.

I roll my head to the side in the strange bed, in the strange room and watch Beau sleep. He lies on his stomach his face turned toward me. One of his arms wraps around my middle. He's the buoy keeping me afloat. Just when I think I'll drift away on the sea of *fuck* that is my life he's there, offering his hand to me. He should've let me go. That should've been goodbye in the FBI conference room. It never should've been an offer to spend forever with me. He's throwing away his life on me.

Why? echoes like a bass drum in my head, a constant, relentless boom that shook me out of a deep sleep. I fail him on every level. Except for maybe the sex. But we can't live on sex and denial. At some point the one will stop covering for the other and then they'll both stop working. We'll be forced to face the fact that what feels like a connection is really just a temporary escape.

He pulls me toward him, turning so that I'm tucked into him the way we fit best—back to front. He's got my back even in sleep. What do *I* do for *him*?

"You're thinking too loud," he mumbles. "I can't sleep."

"Sorry."

"Anything I can help you with?"

"No."

"What kind of ring would you like?"

"Ring?"

"Engagement ring."

"I don't need a ring."

"Bullshit." He kisses my shoulder. "Every girl needs a ring."

"Who am I going to show it to?"

He's temporarily baffled by my question. "I'm getting you a ring as soon as I can."

"Who's going to come to our wedding? What names should we use for the wedding registry? Who's going to stand up for us? How are you going to pay for this ring I *have* to have? Who's going to pay for the wedding?"

"Wait a minute." He rolls me to my back so he can see me. "Is this what's got your wheels spinning in the middle of the night?"

"Well…yes."

"I should've known. Stop worrying. It'll all work out."

"Nothing ever works out for us. Haven't you noticed?"

"Some things've worked out."

"Like what? Look where we are. Look what we're doing. Look at *why* we're here. I wouldn't call this *working out for us.*"

I stumped him again. "It's temporary. Come on. What kind of dress do you want?"

"You can't be serious."

"I'm not saying we'll get married tomorrow. We'll do it when we can the way we can. In the meantime, tell me about your dream wedding."

"I don't have a dream wedding."

"Please. Every girl dreams about her wedding. There wouldn't be all those shows on TV about them if they didn't."

"When would I have dreamed of a white wedding? When my virginity was sold? When I was on my back with my legs in the air while some fat, married businessman sweated over me? When I—"

"Okay. I get it. Could you at least give me some kind of hint about the ring? Diamonds or colored stones?"

"This is pointless."

"Gold or platinum?"

"You're being ridiculous."

"A round stone or another shape like a rectangle or a heart or a square?"

I sigh. "You're relentless."

"New or vintage?"

"I don't care."

"See." He bites my earlobe and makes me shiver. "I got an answer. If it was up to me and you gave me no clues— which, I might point out, you haven't—I'd buy you a vintage ring. Something with some history to it. Not too big because you have small hands. A diamond with maybe some smaller ones on the sides. A flat setting so it didn't stick up and get stuck on everything. White gold because no one can tell the difference between it and platinum. You'd complain I spent too much unnecessarily if I got you platinum. Something simple, yet elegant. Maybe with some swirls to it like your handwriting. Am I close?"

It's exactly perfect what he's described. This time I'm the one who doesn't know what to say.

"Ah-ha!" he crows. "Do I know you or what?"

"You *might* know me."

"Let me try the dress. Although this one's harder because you don't dress like you." He goes silent for a moment and I find myself hanging on to what he could possibly say next. "Not white. Not beige. That in between color. No lace. It makes you itch."

I look up at him startled.

"You dig at your neck every time you wear one of those flimsy blouses with a lace collar," he explains. "No satin. Too shiny. Silk, like pale butter. Loose, not too tight fitting, but with lots of cleavage because I can't get enough of your tits."

To prove it he palms one. I laugh.

"Just below your knee for modesty. With sleeves," he continues. "But it's a trick because you don't wear a damn thing under it to drive me crazy and because you like the way the fabric feels against your bare skin."

He steals my breath. I can picture it and the way it looks and feels and the way he stares at me in it, like he can't wait to rip it off me.

"Roses," he whispers against my skin as he crawls on top of me, dropping kisses down my body between words. "You'll carry roses...because they're old fashioned...and simple. We'll get married outside...in a garden...at sunset. We won't need anybody there...we have all we need right... here." He licks my navel and my legs fall open wider to him.

I reach down, sifting my fingers in his hair the way he likes. He licks my clit with the flat of his tongue and has to grip my thighs to keep me on the bed. He's aces at oral. I didn't think I'd like it. He's my first. I'd done just about everything sexually before him except this. *Fuck me* he's good. The US Marshal in the next room must think he's killing me in here. He does this thing where he hooks two fingers up inside me and thrusts. My hips come off the bed. I howl his name.

He chuckles, rubbing the back of his hand over his mouth. "Bet you can't wait to marry me now."

35

BEAU

Later when it's quiet and she's tucked up against me the way she likes, it hits me what all that shit was about the wedding. I haven't done my job. I haven't told her how I feel about her. I'm shit at the touchy feeling stuff. That was always a complaint of Cassandra's. I clearly haven't learned anything since then. Vera deserves to know that my world hasn't been the same since she walked into it. That I spend almost every waking second thinking about her and reliving moments with her. That when she's not with me I *feel* it, absently looking around like I misplaced something and not remembering what the hell it was.

I've heard lots of talk about soul mates and *the one*, but I never really knew what that shit meant. I'm still not sure I do. Those terms are inadequate for what I feel for Vera. I suppose they're close. And if I had to choose a label *the one* would be closest because I can't imagine ever feeling like this again and I never felt it before. Not in the same way that's for sure. I try not to make comparisons, but it's like driving a car. If you've only ever driven a Mercedes and then you suddenly get handed the keys to a Porsche you're going to automatically compare the similarities and the differences. And it will be the differences that stand out the most.

So it is with the only two women I've ever slept with and loved.

My mom always used to say that relationships always work out better when the man loves the woman a little bit more. That was certainly true of my parents' relationship. And I'm pretty damn sure it's true of Vera and me. That's okay if what my mom said is true. Although it's hard to make that assertion with the way things are between my parents now.

Even though I wore her out pretty good, Vera still isn't sleeping. I wish I could fix things for her. Losing Marie was a blow I'm not sure she can come all the way back from. She hasn't been the same since Carter showed her that photo. Always before she'd eventually bounce back. Not this time and it scares the fuck out of me. I know a little something about grief and guilt and how the two wrap around you and squeeze until you can't feel anything else. They eat at you until that's *all you are*. I could tell her a thousand times in a thousand ways that it's not her fault, but she's never going to believe me.

I didn't believe Cora or Vera when they told me the same thing. It wasn't until I was able to work through the grief that I was finally able to let it go.

"We should have a memorial service for Marie," I tell her quietly.

"Who's going to come?"

"You and me."

"There's no point."

"Of course there's a point."

"Who's going to choose her casket and headstone? Who's going to put flowers on her grave? Who's going to visit it on holidays and her birthday?" Her voice gets a little louder with each question. Now we're getting to the bottom of what's been keeping her up.

"We'll talk to the agents and see if they can help us with her arrangements. If we choose cremation we can take her with us wherever we go. Then when we're settled we can do something permanent for her and you can visit her whenever you want."

She's quiet so long I wonder if she might have fallen asleep. Or she's plotting my death.

"You're always way ahead of me," she grumbles. "It's annoying."

I snuggle in deeper next to her. "But not as annoying as my snoring."

"Definitely not."

"I love you."

There's nothing from her for quite a while and I start to get the feeling that I'm way ahead of her on this too. That's okay. She'll get there. Eventually. Hopefully.

"No one's ever said that to me and actually meant it." There's shame in her tone as if it's *her* fault no one's ever loved her before.

"Well, *I'm* saying it. *I love you.* You don't have to say it back. Just try to get used to it. Okay?"

"I'm not sure if I will."

"Then I'll just have to keep saying it."

"What if I can't ever say it back?"

"Then you don't say it." I'm not worried about this. I don't need the words to know how she feels about me. It's in everything she does and thinks and says. She just needs to figure that out like I had to figure it out.

"You don't have to say it if I don't say it."

"Oh, but I do," I say, tickling her. "I love you. I love you. I love you. I love you."

She squirms around, giggling and trying to push me away. It's the freest and easiest I've ever seen her in too long. The silliness and laughter gives way to a very serious kiss. She's quiet after, stroking my face. I'd give anything to know what she's thinking. Maybe she's working on that I love you. Then again maybe not. She's got more than my twinge of insecurity to deal with right now.

"I think maybe I do love you," she says, thinking out loud.

"Please don't humor me. And don't you dare say it during sex. I'll never believe it."

"I *definitely* love you during sex."

"See, now that's just wrong."

"I'm serious," she goes on. "I think I love you."

"Jesus. Why are you torturing me? Next you're going to tell me you *think* I make you come."

"Oh, no. There is no *think* on that one. You *definitely* do."

"Love is like an orgasm. You either come or you don't. Once you have an orgasm you know for sure when you don't. There is no kind-of-sort-of-maybe in climaxing."

"That's beautiful. You should write poetry." She makes a motion like she's writing in the air. "Love is like an orgasm... Barreling toward a chasm... It's so very taxing... When you're climaxing... Once you come... You know you're done... Love is like an orgasm."

I groan. "That's awful."

"I'm going to find a way to put it in our vows."

I tighten my hold on her. "*God* I love you."

36

VERA

"I'm never going to get to meet my dad and brother am I?" I ask Beau out of the blue.

We've been cooped up in this apartment for almost two weeks. There's nothing to do. We can't take a walk. We can't make phone calls. We can't use the computer or watch TV. The only thing we can do is have lots and lots of sex, which we've been doing pretty much nonstop night and day. The Marshals assigned to watch over us have gotten to where they don't even roll their eyes anymore when Beau picks me up and takes me to the bedroom. I'm pretty sure we're on our way to setting some kind of world record.

"Probably not," he answers my question grimly.

He doesn't like it when I point out all of the negatives of our situation. This is pretty much when he tosses me over his shoulder, throws me on the bed, and makes me scream his name. He'd be doing that right now if we hadn't just collapsed on the bed after some pretty strenuous doggy style sex.

"I wonder what they look like," I say. "I don't look very

much like my mom. At least from what I can remember. I lost the pictures I had. There was one of her and me, one of her alone and one of her and me and Marie taken right before child services took us away. I wonder if he has any photos of my mom. Like from their wedding."

He doesn't answer. This is one of those conversations I have one sided while he broods over how to fix it for me. There's no fixing my family. Half of them are dead and the other half are lost to me.

"I wonder if I look like my brother," I continue. "Like how you and Cora look so much alike."

"You think we look alike?"

"Oh, yeah. Totally. Your personalities are similar too. I wonder—"

A commotion from the living room makes me halt midsentence. Beau and I exchange looks, then we bolt out of bed and start throwing our clothes on. Something's wrong. The voices are agitated and growing louder. Beau up ends the table in the corner, rips two legs off, and hands one to me. They're not very big, but they'll do some damage if we have to.

Beau jams what's left of the table under the doorknob. There's no lock so this is the only barrier against us and whoever's out there. Beau goes to the side of the door that opens and signals me to go the other. If they have guns we don't have much of a chance, which is why I motion for Beau to crouch down low. We at least have the element of surprise and the possibility of knocking their legs out from under them and maybe the gun from their hands if they should get past our barricade.

Someone knocks on the door. "Beau! Gwendolyn!"

"Carter," Beau whispers.

"I thought he wasn't supposed to know we're here," I whisper back.

"Come on out," Carter says. "I have some good news for you."

"Do we trust him?" Beau asks.

I shake my head. "He's not using my right name."

Beau motions with his head toward the window. "Just a minute!" he answers Carter.

This isn't right. Something is very wrong here. I go to the window and look out a crack in the blinds. We're two stories up so I have a good view of the street. One of Javier's men waits by a car. He's here. He's come for me. I shake my head like crazy for Beau not to open the door. My heart is hammering double time. He's come for his revenge. I tighten my grip on the table leg. Sweat drips in slick line down my back.

The doorknob turns, but the table keeps the door from opening.

Someone pounds on the door. "Eeeeden. It's meee," Javier taunts. "Let me in precious. I've missed yooouu."

That voice crawls out of my worst nightmares. He's talked me into and out of so many things with that voice.

Beau swings his gaze away from me and toward the door. He knows who's on the other side and now he knows my *other* name. My past and my future stand on either side of the door. Javier will kill Beau. What he does with me after that I don't care. There won't be anything left of me to matter.

Something solid hits the door, shaking the whole wall. There's no way out. There's only Javier coming in. The door is slammed again. This time the table makes a terrible noise. Beau hunkers down next to the door, balancing on the balls of his feet. I take up my position on the other side. He squeezes my arm briefly as I pass. The door is hit again and again. The table gives way and a guy in black breaks through the door. Debris flies at me. I'm hit with chucks of wood and knocked to the floor.

The guy turns toward Beau gun drawn. I whack him in the back of the knees and he goes down, howling in pain. His head hits the bedframe with a sickening *thunk*. His gun clatters against the wood floor and disappears under the bed. Beau rears up, going for the guy. He doesn't see Javier coming in through the door, but I do. I leap between them. My back explodes in pain. I fall...

37

BEAU

Javier swings the gun toward Vera on the floor. I charge, catching him around the waist, and push him back through the door. We hit the ground with me on top. He strikes me in the head hard enough that my vision darkens. I reach out blindly, wrapping my hand around metal. We grapple for the gun. Behind me another fight breaks out. All I can think about is Vera. This asshole's strong, but I'm stronger. I straddle him, gaining the upper hand, and twist his hands toward his face.

Vera's moan from the other room is all the boost I need. Pushing hard, I jam the gun under his chin. For a split second I see the terror he inflicted on so many innocents reflected in his black eyes, then BOOM. The top of his head blows off, splattering the wall behind him. I twist the gun from his hand and go back for Vera. The guy Vera hit is down, his head bleeding. Carter leans over Vera. She's sprawled on her stomach. There's a black mark on the back of her shirt. Blood oozes out around her.

I aim the gun at Carter. "Get the fuck away from her!"

He puts his palms up and backs away from Vera. "She needs an ambulance."

"Call one!"

He reaches into his coat pocket. I pull the trigger before I know what I mean to do. Carter spins back, the gun he pulled drops with him. I look around. The Marshall is on the ground next the couch. I didn't see him before. I need a fucking phone. Digging in Carter's pockets, I find his, but it's fucking password protected. I toss it and search the other guy. His lights up. I punch in 9-1-1 and go to Vera. She's out. It's bad. It's *so* fucking bad.

"9-1-1 what's your emergency?"

"She's shot. I need an ambulance."

"Sir, where are you?"

I glance around the apartment. "I don't fucking know!"

"Can you find an address?"

"I can't leave her."

"Sir, I can't help her if I don't know where you are. Can you help me?"

I stagger to my feet and out the front door. A guy is coming up the stairs.

I point my gun at him. "Not another fucking step."

He puts his hands up.

"Where the fuck are we?"

"*No hablo Ingles.*"

I search below, looking for something I can give the dispatcher. A small crowd of neighbors gathers. They shrink back when they see the gun in my hand. The guy on the stairs goes for the back of his waistband. I fire. He tumbles down the stairs. The neighbors scream and scatter.

"Sir!" the dispatcher demands. "Where are you?"

"I don't fucking know. He was going for his gun. I had to shoot him."

There's some mumbling on the other line.

"Can't you fucking trace my call?"

"We're trying to find you."

Sirens scream, but they sound too far away. There's a number on the door, but it's only the apartment number. I don't know what the fuck street we're on or even what city we're in. I go back into the apartment, looking for something —some mail, a flier, anything—that will tell me where the fuck we are. There's no landline. No fucking papers or notepads. Nothing.

Vera moans. I go to her. I'm shaking so fucking bad. There's so much goddamned blood.

"Help her!" I scream into the phone. "Please. Somebody help her."

"I need your location, sir."

I drop the phone on the bed. So fucking useless. I lie down next to Vera. Her eyes are barely open, but I know she sees me. I take her hand. The sirens get louder and louder until it sounds like they're in the next room.

"I love you," I tell her. "You're going to be okay. He's dead. He can't ever hurt you again. I love you." I keep repeating it over and over.

Her eyelids close, but there's a faint smile around her lips. I know she hears me. She can't fucking die. She can't. There's noise in the living room.

I start to get up to get her help.

"Freeze," someone shouts. "Don't move. Drop the weapon."

I toss the gun away from me. "Please. You have to help her. She needs an ambulance."

"Hands behind your head. Don't move. Don't *fucking* move."

I do as I'm told. I don't want to leave Vera. Three of them

pile on top of me and cuff me. They're rough, but I take it. They haul me up by my arms.

"Please. Help her. Don't let her die," I tell them as they're hauling me out. "Vera! I love you!"

Outside the crowd is back. A woman, talking to an officer, points at me coming down the stairs. At the bottom we have to navigate around the guy I shot. All I can think about is Vera. I beg and beg for an ambulance for her, but none come. They can't just let her die. I can't lose her. I can't lose her.

They shove me into the back of a car and take off. I don't give a fuck where they take me or what they do to me. All I care about is Vera.

They keep me cuffed and bring me into an interrogation room, dumping me in a chair. I lean back, resting my head on the wall and close my eyes. All I can see is the small smile on Vera's lips. I hold on to that image.

A detective comes in and introduces himself. I don't tell him shit. I've been here before. I tell them I want my lawyer. When they ask for a name I give them Shayla Reese's name. She's the only one who can help me. She knows why we were in that apartment and who Javier is. She knows Vera's story. I ask for updates on Vera, but no one's telling me shit. They think I shot her. I can't stop shaking. I killed people. I blew Javier's fucking brains out. I'm not sorry about it, but I'm not coping too well with it either. I shot three people, including an FBI agent. I'm going down this time.

I can't be still. Banging my head on the wall, I try to get the image of Vera lying in a pool of blood out of my head. If she dies I don't care what they do to me. They can toss me back in prison until I fucking rot. I don't care. I'm dead if she's dead. No one's telling me anything. They just stare at me. They know who I am. They know I escaped prison once. They don't want me to escape again. I see the contempt in their eyes.

It's hours or days, who can fucking tell, before the door finally opens and Shay walks in. I bolt up straight in my chair. She's my link to the outside and Vera. There's a grim set to her mouth. Her gaze doesn't quite meet mine.

"How's Vera?"

She waits until the detective closes the door to speak. "She's in surgery. That's all I know right now. You, however, are in some serious trouble. What the hell happened in that apartment?"

I give her all the details I can remember. When I'm done I ask the other question I've been anxious for the answer to.

"Are they all dead?"

"The Marshall, Javier Abano, Agent Carter, and the guy you shot on the stairs are. The other guy they found in the bedroom with Vera is in grave condition. They don't expect him to survive his head wound."

I lower my head. "Fuck." I'm not sorry Javier's dead, but I don't feel good about it. I killed three people today. I don't know how to reconcile it. That's not who I am. That's not who I want to be. Fuck. Fuck. Fuck.

"You did what you had to do to save yourself and Vera."

"But still…"

"I know." She pats me on the shoulder. "I know. I'm sorry."

"What the hell went wrong with Agent Carter?"

"I don't know. Ed's beside himself. He trusted Carter. The cops are still trying to sort it out with the Feds. Only Carter and the Special Agent in Charge knew about your situation. With Carter dead it's up to the SAC to work it out for us. I'm doing my best to try to be in the loop, but no one's talking to me. This is such a clusterfuck for the marshals *and* the FBI. They each lost a man and the FBI doesn't want to admit that their agent was corrupt and compromised your situation. They're trying to pin some of it on you. They won't get to though. I won't let them. But you might be in here for a while until it all gets sorted out."

"I wish I could see her." I'm having a hard time focusing on what Shay's saying. I honestly don't give a fuck about me except that as long as I'm in here I can't be with Vera.

She pats my shoulder. "I know you do. Let's talk to these detectives and work on getting you out of here so you can do that. Are you up for it?"

"Whatever it takes."

"Let me see if I can't get them to uncuff you while we're at it."

"Thanks."

She goes out into the hall. I'm trying real hard to hang on and not lose my shit. That would only make my situation worse. I can't believe I'm in cuffs, sitting in a police station, being accused of murder. Again. I'm not at all comforted by the fact that I actually did the crime this time. I'm not proud of what I did. I'm fucking torn up. I can't stop replaying what happened, wondering if I could've done *something* different. If I should've been on the other side of the door instead of Vera. Then I could've been the one to take the bullet instead of her. Then what? I would've been down and Javier could've taken Vera. I keep running the what if's through my head, trying to sort out how it could've gone down different, but I don't see how.

Damn, Vera. Why did she have to jump in front of me? She *thinks* she loves me. If taking a bullet for someone isn't love I don't know what is.

38

VERA

I'm alive.

Barely.

At least it feels that way.

Everything fucking hurts.

I try to open my eyes, but I'm too damn tired.

SOMEONE'S next to my bed, holding my hand. I can't turn my head to see who it is. I still can't open my eyes. Maybe I'm not alive. Maybe this is death. I want to move, but can't manage to make the effort. I want to ask whoever it is about Beau because I know it's not him with me. Where is he? The last thing I remember is his face next to mine so I know he's okay. Or he was.

Goddam I'm tired.

THIS TIME I manage to open my eyes. It's dark. I'm alone. Where's Beau? He should be here. He'd be here if he could be. Maybe he didn't make it and I only imagined it. I try to call out for him, but my throat's been cut with razor blades. My cry comes out as an undecipherable groan.

My body's heavy. So damn heavy.

I try to call out again for someone. Anyone. I have to know he's okay. He would never leave me alone like this. Something must've happened. Where is he? *Where is he?*

I can't coordinate my arms. There's supposed to be a call button. I need to talk to someone. I need to know what happened. My head is dead weight on my shoulders. All of my efforts only serve to wear me out and don't get me anywhere. My lids droop. I can't keep them open. I'm slipping...

THE PERSON'S BACK, stroking my hand and whispering to me. I'm finally able to move my head. It flops to one side. I blink at Cora sitting next to me. She's smiling. I croak out incoherent gibberish that makes me cough. She hurries for a cup on the tray in front over my bed and puts the straw to my lips. I suck. Sweet, sweet water. Didn't realize how dry my mouth was until this moment. I drink too fast and choke. It fucking HURTS. She takes the cup away and grabs a tissue to wipe the water dribbling out of my mouth.

I close my eyes, waiting for the pain to get the fuck back. It finally subsides.

"Beau," I barely rasp out.

She smiles, but it doesn't go all the way to her eyes. "He's okay. He constantly asks me about you. He'll be glad to know your first word was his name. He's been worried about you."

"Where?"

"He's okay," she repeats. "I owe you for saving my brother."

"Where?" I say more forcibly.

"He's in jail. There's been some issue with what happened. There's a cop outside dying to get in here and talk to you. Are you up for it?"

"Jail?" I can't keep the panic from my voice. What the fuck is he doing in jail?

"It's a mix up." She glances toward the door. "The cop's back," she whispers. "You don't have to talk to him if you're not up to it."

"No. Want to."

"She's awake," a male voice says.

Cora puts the straw to my lips so I can have another drink. "Her throat is really rough and she's having a hard time speaking. Let me check with her nurse."

"No," I say. "I can talk."

The man comes to stand at my bedside. "I'm Detective Johansson. We need to ask you a few questions about what happened to you."

"We?"

"My partner's talking to your doctor. She'll be right in. I'm going to need you to step out into the hall," he tells Cora.

"Are you sure you're up for this?" she asks me.

"I'm okay."

"I'll be right outside if you need me." She squeezes my hand. "We're family now." She gives the detective a dirty look that he doesn't see as she leaves.

I bite my lip to keep from chuckling. You always know what Cora thinks of you.

As soon as she's gone the detective starts in. "There's some confusion about your name."

I stare blankly at him. I'm not so doped up that I don't know assuming someone else's identity isn't illegal.

"Are you going to answer my question?"

"You didn't ask a question."

"Why did you assume the identity of a dead girl?"

"Javier Abano wanted me dead."

"Why?"

"I took a thumb drive that had information about how he abducted young girls and sold them for sex."

"You were one of his victims?"

"Yes."

"Who shot you?"

"Javier Abano."

"You're sure about that."

"As sure as you're standing here."

"What happened?"

"Javier somehow found out where Beau and I were being held by the US Marshals and the FBI. He broke in and tried to shoot Beau. I stepped in front of him and Javier shot me instead."

I tell him everything I can remember until I passed out. He takes me through it again and again, going over why we were in that apartment in the first place. His partner appears part way through and asks some questions of her own. I'm so tired my words slur, but I keep going because what I have to say could free Beau. They ask me if I need a rest and if I want them to come back later at least three times maybe more. I tell them no every time. I can't hold my head up anymore and I'm still talking with my eyes closed when a nurse comes in. She tries to put a halt to it. I have to work at raising my head to prove I can keep going.

The nurse doesn't buy it and shoos everyone out. He checks my vitals. I'm so tired, but I want to talk to Cora. I ask the nurse about her, but he tells me she left. I want to know about Beau. He's what I'm thinking about when I drift off.

I WAKE UP three more times alone. It's day. It's night. It's still night. Or maybe the next night. I don't know what fucking day it is or how long I've been here. They tell me I'm healing well as they poke and prod at me. I finally get to eat some Jell-O and it tastes like heavenly green slime. But I can swallow it so that's a plus.

The next time I wake up Cora's back.

"Where's Beau?"

She looks up past me. I roll my head and there he is. I try to reach for him. He takes my hand. Tears stream down my face. *Finally.* Finally I get to see for myself he's okay. He lowers his head to my hand. When he lifts it his eyes are damp. I touch his beautiful face, trying to reassure myself he's real that he's really here.

"I love you," I blurt out.

He gets the biggest grin on his face. "I know. Took you long enough to figure it out."

THANK YOU FOR READING ATONE! The next book in the RECOVERED INNOCENCE series is RECLAIM.

➤CLICK HERE TO READ RECLAIM

If you enjoyed VINDICATE, please consider leaving a review on your favorite book site. Reviews help readers find books!

➤ATONE (RECOVERED INNOCENCE novel)

➤GOODREADS

Join my VIP Facebook group Babes with Books for exclusive sneak peeks at my upcoming books & other, members only, perks:

➤www.facebook.com/groups/BabesWithBooksReaderGroup

Sign up to receive my newsletter for new release alerts, exclusive bonus content, and giveaways!

➤**www.bethyarnall.com/newsletter**

Turn the page to read an excerpt from **RECLAIM** now!

EXCERPT FROM RECLAIM

Nolan

I'm kind of a fuck up. It's not something I aspire to. It just sort of happens. The effort's there. It's the execution that's lacking. I'm not a total loser. I have a few things going for me. I'm told I'm good looking, but my appearance hasn't delivered a single date for months. I've never had a steady girlfriend. I went to school —a good school—and got a college degree, but that didn't translate into a job in my chosen field. I bought the winning lottery ticket once and lost it. I don't play the lottery anymore. The company that manufactured my first new car went out of business less than a year after I bought it.

I joke a lot about having bad luck and being cursed. That's not what it is. I'm just one of those people who have to work harder than anyone else. Nothing comes easy to me. I get what I'm after...eventually. Usually on the third or forth try. Never the first. I envy people who coast through life thinking about wanting something and then BAM. They have it. My best friend Dominic is like that. He thought about settling down and getting married. A week later he met his wife. They talked about having children. She was pregnant within a month.

I don't get people like that.

If it weren't for my obstinate determination I wouldn't have achieved a single thing in my life. Stubborn to a fault. That's how my friends and family describe me.

At least I learn from my lessons. My friend Mike is one of those guys who keeps doing the same thing over and over, lamenting all the while about how he can never catch a break. You gotta make your own breaks. At least those of us who don't get things handed to them. I'm always looking out for the next thing, the next whatever it's going to be that'll take me where I want to go. However circuitous the route. No straight lines to anything for me. Nope. The road to all of my achievements has been twisty and windy, filled with flooded potholes. Every once in a while something will fly out in front of me, forcing me change course to avoid it.

It's those unexpected detours that have lead to the most interesting things in my life. Take my new job at Nash Security and Investigations. Totally not what I saw myself doing when they handed me my college diploma for my degree in criminal justice. I was going to be a police officer. Or maybe a sheriff. Okay, a small part of me kinda hoped the FBI would recruit me right out of college. That didn't happen. Also it turns out that I'm not cut out to be a cop. A little more than halfway through the entrance application I had the sudden, overwhelming realization that I didn't want to go into law enforcement.

After that revelation—another something leaping across my road, making me jerk the wheel to avoid it—I found myself on an unfamiliar street, fenced in by unfamiliar surroundings, driving along at a snail's pace. That was the year I wandered aimlessly through job after job, looking for

The Thing. *My* Thing. Who and what I was meant to be. And then I came across the story of how this PI firm, Nash Securities and Investigations, had helped to clear a man named Beau Hollis who was wrongly convicted for the rape and murder of his ex-girlfriend. That sounded like a really cool job. I mean, freeing someone after years in prison. Giving them their life back. That's a fucking incredible thing.

I wanted to be a part of *that*.

It was the first time I ever had that feeling about anything. I sure as shit didn't have it about selling cars or driving a delivery truck or in customer service for an electronics company. Even the free pizza I got to eat doing deliveries for an Italian restaurant didn't give me the sensation of being imminently *useful*. Contributing to society. Doing good. Making wrong things right. That's what I want to do.

Expect as usual I managed to screw things up the first chance I got.

Backing up.

I got the job at the agency that I wanted to work for, Nash Security and Investigations, nailing the interview. That never happens to me. I should've known it was too good to be true. Like I said, nothing's ever been handed to me. Definitely not something as big and as sought after as this job was for me. The very first assignment they give me on my own I screwed up. Like huge, major, no-going-back-from-this, lives-in-danger kind of fuck up. It should've been a cakewalk. Watch this retail center. See if this guy shows up. Follow him. See where he goes. Simple, right?

Not for me.

I got close enough to get his license plate. I followed him, thinking I was cool and important, then the guy lost me. One minute he was there then the next POOF. Gone.

When I got back to the office to give my boss, Cora Hollis, the car and tag info the client, Vera Swain, pointed out that if I got close enough to get the guy's plate then I was close enough for him to get *my* plate. And son of a bitch if he hadn't. That's how the asshole found Vera—through me. Finding her resulted in the bastard killing her sister and nearly killing Vera and Cora's brother Beau, the guy who'd just gotten his life back after spending years in prison.

All of that shit was on me. Why Cora didn't fire me on the spot I have no idea. Hell, *I* would've fired me. A young girl died because of me. I almost got Beau and Vera killed. All because I can't get anything right the first time out. This was one case where the effort and the thought didn't count. *I tried* didn't mean shit. *I'm sorry* wasn't enough. *I didn't mean to* was useless.

Cora insisted there was nothing to forgive. An honest mistake, she called it. Could've happened to anyone, she said. You'll do better next time, she placated. Would I though? Second and third tries were iffy for me. Nearly as dicey as the first time. And that first time was a giant cluster-fuck of epic proportions. I know it'll get better from here on out, but that's not much consolation. Like a category five hurricane downgrading to a three or a four. Still a major disaster. There will be damage, it's just a matter of how much and who it will effect.

I show up at the office and keep my head down. I do as I'm told the way I'm told. I try to absorb as much as I can from Jerry one of the old-timers whose unenviable job it is to show me the ropes. I hope the guy has good life insurance. I joked about that once with him. He didn't laugh.

Cora hasn't been in the office much the past few weeks. She visits Vera in the hospital pretty regular. So does Beau. Now that he's out of jail after being accused of shooting

Vera. That guy's luck is as shit as mine. No. Shittier. *Way* shittier. I've never been in jail for anything let alone being accused of hurting the woman I love...twice. That's some powerfully bad karma he's carrying around. When I think about all he's been through I can't feel too sorry for myself. If I don't think about how he wouldn't have gone to jail that second time because of me and how Vera wouldn't have gotten shot and how her sister wouldn't be dead.

Yeah. I try not to think about that. I do my job. I put in my best effort. I pray it'll be enough. Maybe one of these days it will be. I'm not sure why I'm here except that because Cora's not around a lot there's a ton of work that needs to get done. I owe her that at least. Whatever she asks I do. Take out the trash—it's out. Run a few copies—they're done. Pick up lunch—I get the order *exactly* right. All I have to offer is my best effort. What happens after that is a complete and utter mystery. Could be good. Could be bad. Who knows? It's me we're talking about.

I'm running a computer search for client—a job Beau held for a while before the shooting—when Cora walks in, muttering over the open file in her hands. She's really pretty, like make you drop your sandwich and stare like an idiot kind of pretty. She doesn't even know it. That makes her sexier. Even if she weren't my boss she'd be way off limits to me. She's dating the son of the owner of the agency. I don't even exist to her on any level except employee. That's okay though. I'd screw that up too. She's not the kind of person you mess around with casually. She's an all-in kind of woman. The kind you marry and never cheat on. Her boyfriend is a lucky son of bitch and he knows it.

"You almost done with that search?" she asks me.

All I get is the top of her blue and black streaked head. I can't help but stare at her when she's not looking. Leaning back a little in my chair, I crane my neck to check out her legs in the skirt she's wearing. Nice. High heels look good on her, making her legs longer somehow. It's one of those tricks only women know that make a man forget his name and apparently the question they've just been asked.

"Nolan?"

Shit. My gaze snaps up to hers. Busted. "Ah, yeah. Just about."

"Good. I have something here I want you to take a look at."

My mind spins her innocent words into something lurid. I give myself a stern lecture about workplace decorum and about not horning in on another guy's woman. That's not cool. That's not who I am or who I want to be. I just wish my boss were a little less hot.

"Oh, yeah?" I ask.

She slides the folder she's holding in front of me and leans in with a hand on my desk. "The Freedom Project sent these cases over for our review. Every year we choose one and work it pro bono. I wish we could work on them all." She sighs. "I see Beau in every face and it's hard to say no. I need an objective opinion."

She separates the three pages, spreading them across my desk. Her arm brushes mine briefly and I instinctively flinch away. If she notices it doesn't show in her face. All of her focus is on the papers in front of her. There's a crease between her brows and her bottom lip is pinched between her teeth. This is important to her. Even if I didn't know her brother's story I'd know it in the look on her face and how she touches the black and white mug shots of the three incarcerated people staring back at her.

"What do you want me to do?" I ask.

"Read the case summary and the notes from the

Freedom Project's staff. We need to choose one and I just can't decide. It feels like I'm handing down a sentence to other two if I don't select them."

And she thinks I won't get the same feeling? I glance up at her.

"We're not," she amends. "Their cases will get handled by another PI firm, but it won't be us, you know?"

"Yeah, I think I get it. That makes me feel better about choosing." That's a lie. I'm lousy at making decisions. She should already know this about me.

"Have a look and let me know what you think. I need to get back to them by the end of the day."

"Sure thing."

She leaves her scent behind and the lingering sense of doom that I'll make the wrong choice. God, really? She's leaving this up to me? Someone's life's in my hands, the hands of a fuck up. Does she have *any* idea what she's doing?

I pick up the first sheaf of paper. Bruce Swanson was convicted of the brutal murder of his parents, Doug and Nancy Swanson. As the only child he stood to inherit his parents' vast estate, which entailed a personal fortune of close to eleven million dollars, a company worth twice that, and various real estate properties worth millions more. The conviction hinged on hinkey DNA evidence and a questionable witness—a cousin who inherited everything when Bruce went away. As an only child I'm tempted to choose poor Bruce who should be sitting on fat stacks instead of a thin prison mattress.

I force myself to put the paper down and pick up the next one. D'Shawnte Devon was convicted of attempted murder for the drive by shooting of a rival gang member based on faulty eyewitness testimony. Three people—who also happen to be members of his gang and thus deemed unreliable—said that D'Shawnte was at a bar-b-que at the time of the shooting. There was nothing to tie him physically to the crime and although the eyewitnesses later recanted, D'Shawnte remains in prison for a crime he didn't commit.

That one sucks. D'Shawnte reminds me of me and my bad luck. I'm starting to see what Cora was saying about not being able to choose. You only have to have a smidgeon of empathy to want to do something that could change these people's world.

The third page has a photo of a woman. A *young* woman. Nineteen. Dang. She looks younger. Like maybe fifteen. Carla Ruiz is an undocumented immigrant in prison for the murder of her son. Even though the coroner declared the boy's death an accident the district attorney filed murder charges and won. There's a note about a witness that wasn't called by the defense who could've corroborated the coroner's report. She was convicted for a crime that wasn't even a crime. That's harsh. She lost her son then her freedom. I wonder what will happen to her if she's freed. Will she be forced to go back to Mexico or will she get to stay in the U.S.?

I set her sheet next to the other two, my gaze bouncing from one to the other then the other. Who to pick? Eeny meeny miny mo? Roshambo? Put their names in a cup and draw one?

Cora's depending on me to make a decision based on something real not something arbitrary. I'll probably have to justify my decision. It would be pretty tough to defend rock, paper, scissors.

I look at their faces. They're all young. Under thirty when they went inside. They're older than that now.

D'Shawte is in his forties. Bruce is thirty-six and Carla is nearly thirty. I should pick D'Shawnte. He's been in the longest. But Bruce reminds me of myself except for the rich parents. Carla lost her son. That's a horrible thing. Uuuugh. I just don't know.

I set the pages aside and try to go back to the computer searches I was doing. But my gaze strays. With I sigh I tear up little pieces of paper, write their names on them, and shake the folded scraps in my hands. I hope this is the right thing to do. I close my eyes and choose. Carla. I'm disappointed and yet not. I take her page out and look at it again.

"Well?" Cora stands in the doorway ankles and arms crossed. "Were you able to pick one?"

As subtle as I can I scoop up the little pieces of paper and ball them in my hand. I can't let her know how I couldn't come to a decision. That I let fate randomly decide. I don't know why I did it. Fate has never been anything but a bitch to me.

I hold up the page. "Carla Ruiz."

She unfolds herself and comes toward me. She takes the sheet and nods. "This one got to me too. What made you choose her?"

I *knew* it. "She lost twice—her son and her freedom. That's too much for anyone let alone someone so young."

"Yeah. I thought the same thing." There's a look in her eyes that I don't like seeing. Sadness. She's too pretty to be sad. "Beau was a year younger than her when he went to prison."

"That must've been awful."

She nods, her focus on Carla's photo.

"How's Vera doing?" I have to ask. Then I hold my breath, waiting for the answer.

Her bright blue gaze slides from the paper to me and it's

a warm wave crashing over me, making my breath catch. It's the same blue as the streaks in her hair. Startling. Mesmerizing. Totally off limits.

She smiles. "She's coming home today. That's why Beau isn't here. He's getting her settled in."

"That's good. I'm glad." So, so glad. It's like someone just lifted a stadium off my shoulders.

"Thanks for taking up the slack." She motions with the paper. "And for helping me choose."

"Sure. Any time."

She starts to turn away, then comes back. "We're still a little short around here. You've been so great about working over time and filling in I hate to ask..."

"Whatever you need."

"Since you helped me pick the case I'd like you to take lead on it. I'll help. It's not like I'd be leaving you on your own. It's just that the work you've been doing has been really great and I'd like you to start heading up a few cases. Jerry's been making noises about retiring and with Mr. Nash in semi retirement already we really need another lead investigator around here. You've more than shown you can handle it. This could be a training case. Leads make more money and you'd get out of the office more. What do you say?"

I open my mouth to speak—because she clearly expects a response—but nothing comes out except a squeak. A horrible, embarrassing squeak. I cough to cover it up. She caught me totally off guard. Her eyes are hopeful and before I form the thought I'm nodding my head. *What am I doing? Make it stop.*

"Sure," I say, completing the humiliation. My brain is having a meltdown. While it burns the rest of me goes on automatic, responding totally separately from my brain. I can almost smell the smoke that is surely bellowing out my ears.

"Oh, *thank you*." Cora says. Her smile fans the flames. Sirens go off in my head. "I'll set up the appointment for us to meet with the Freedom Project staff attorney," she continues, totally unaware of the mass casualties in my skull. "You're going to do great. Just great." She backs away toward the door. "I'm looking forward to working with you."

Before I can stop her she's gone.

What have I done?

ALSO BY BETH YARNALL

Dangerous Lines

Lost

Saved

Fake

Real

Urge

Rare

Betray

Recovered Innocence

Vindicate

Atone

Reclaim

The Misadventures of Maggie Mae

Wake Up, Maggie

You're Mine, Maggie

Find Me, Maggie

Azalea March Mysteries

Killing It In Vegas

Beth Writing as Betty Paper

Crazy On You

Captive

Tinsel

Piano Lessons

BETH'S BOOKS FOR WRITERS

Crafting Unputdownable Fiction series

Going Deep Into Deep Point of View

Making Description Work Hard For You

Some Like It Hot: Writing Sex and Romance

ABOUT THE AUTHOR

USA Today best selling author and Rita® finalist, Beth Yarnall, writes mysteries, romantic suspense, and the occasional hilarious tweet. She lives in Southern California with her husband, two sons, and their rescue dogs where she is hard at work on her next novel. For more information about Beth and her novels please visit her website- www.beth-yarnall.com

facebook.com/bethyarnallauthor

amazon.com/author/bethyarnall

bookbub.com/authors/beth-yarnall

www.ingramcontent.com/pod-product-compliance
Lightning Source LLC
Chambersburg PA
CBHW020244180626
46810CB00006B/2352